BRASS LEANED FORWARD A LITTLE. "RITA BENNETT WAS HOW OLD?"

"Late fifties. But she looked younger."

"Did she look twenty?"

Black's mouth dropped open, but no words came out.

"The woman in the casket," Grissom said, "was at least thirty years younger than the woman whose name was on the headstone. Any ideas?"

"There's no way . . . " Black's eyes flashed in sudden alarm. "And you think I . . . we . . . had something to do with this . . . this switching of bodies?"

Brass said, "We're making no accusations, Mr. Black."

"We're just gathering evidence," Grissom said.

"What evidence do you *have?*"

"A body in a coffin. The coffin belongs to Rita Bennett. The body doesn't."

"Who the hell was in the coffin?"

"We don't know yet; we're working on identifying her now. You also have to agree it would be very hard to switch the bodies after the vault was sealed and the grave was filled in."

Grasping at straws, Black said, "But not impossible."

"The grave hadn't been disturbed," Grissom said, "and the vault was still sealed tight when we did the exhumation. . . . The evidence indicates the switch was made *before* the vault was sealed."

Original novels by Max Allan Collins in the CSI series:

CSI: Crime Scene Investigation
Double Dealer
Sin City
Cold Burn
Body of Evidence
Grave Matters

CSI: Miami
Florida Getaway
Heat Wave

CSI:

CRIME SCENE INVESTIGATION ™

GRAVE MATTERS
a novel

Max Allan Collins

Based on the hit CBS series
"CSI: Crime Scene Investigation"
Produced by CBS Productions, a
business unit of CBS Broadcasting Inc.
and Alliance Atlantis Productions Inc.
Executive Producers: Jerry Bruckheimer,
Carol Mendelsohn, Anthony E. Zuiker, Ann Donahue,
Danny Cannon, Jonathan Littman
Co-Executive Producers:
Cynthia Chvatal & William Petersen
Series created by: Anthony E. Zuiker

POCKET
BOOKS

London · New York · Sydney · Toronto

An *Original* Publication of POCKET BOOKS

Published by
POCKET BOOKS, a division of Simon & Schuster UK Ltd.
Africa House, 64–78 Kingsway, London WC2B 6AH
POCKET BOOKS www.simonsays.co.uk

ISBN: 0-7434-9575-6

First Pocket Books printing October 2004

10 9 8 7 6 5 4

Cover design by Patrick Kang

Printed and bound in Great Britain

A CIP catalogue record for this book is available from the British Library

For Skip Willits—
who knows that art matters.

I would like to acknowledge my assistant on this work, forensics researcher/co-plotter, **Matthew V. Clemens.**
Further acknowledgments appear at the conclusion of this novel.

M.A.C.

"I never guess. It is a shocking habit."

    —*The Sign of Four*, ARTHUR CONAN DOYLE

"Very few of us are what we seem."

    —*Partners in Crime*, AGATHA CHRISTIE

1

AUGUST HEAT PUMMELED LAS VEGAS, the nighttime temperature hovering just over 100 degrees, driving the natives inside the air-conditioned sanctity of their homes. Out on Las Vegas Boulevard, in front of Treasure Island, electronically controlled sprayers over the sidewalks cool-misted the crowd as they watched pirates killing each other . . . though where mist stopped and the sweat started, who could say?

Downtown, on Fremont Street, even as the evening light show flashed overhead like gaudy lightning, many of the usual gawkers ducked into the coolness of casinos lining the pedestrian mall. Hearing Sinatra sing about luck being a lady, craning your head back to watch giant tumbling electric dice, wasn't nearly so much fun when salty pools of perspiration settled in and around your eyes.

In the desert around the city, even the animals were hunkering down, seeking the coolest spots Mother Nature could provide. Coyotes lay silent, too parched to howl, and the snakes sought refuge under rocks, away from the scorching desert air, slithering into coiled solitude as if finally accepting guilt for the Garden of Eden.

During the day, when the heat did its worst, the temperature rising to over 110 degrees, tourists still milled around the Strip, shuffling with the dutiful doggedness of the vacationer ("We *paid* for this fun package, and by God . . .") from one attraction to the next, all of them bleeding sweat, each weary traveler trudging along shell-shocked, wondering how they aimed for an oasis and wound up instead in the Ninth Circle of Hell. The endless parade—this Bataan Death March outfitted in garish T-shirts, Bermuda shorts, and dark socks with sandals—took each step as if absorbing a punch.

Stuck in traffic, watching the sorry spectacle, Captain Jim Brass could relate, even though his Ford Taurus's air conditioner was cranked to the max. *It's not the heat,* he thought, *it's the humanity.* The coolness of the car's interior did nothing to relieve the sensation that he was being pummeled with each throb of a massive headache that had settled behind his eyes like a house guest that had no intention of leaving, though the party was long since over.

He hadn't even taken off his sportcoat, a sharp brown number that with his gold-patterned tie reflected an improved fashion sense that admittedly had taken him years past his divorce to cultivate. A compact man with short brown hair and a melancholy mien that belied an inner alertness, Jim Brass fought hard against cynicism, and mostly won. But what Brass had not seen in his almost twenty-five years on the

Las Vegas Police Department, he was not anxious to.

As usual, the summer heat had brought out the crazies—local and imported. Here it was, not even the fifteenth of August, and already the city was pushing double-digit homicides for the month. LVPD had averaged investigating just over a dozen homicides per month for the last two years—a staggering number for a department short of bodies, at least the right kind of bodies—and now the heat seemed to be driving that number off the graph.

Brass worried that the hotter this oven of a desert got, the sooner the city might boil over. . . .

And, of course, the politics of Brass's job were as unrelenting as the blinding sun.

There was, as the saying went, a new sheriff in town . . . who was bringing down some heat of his own. Former Sheriff Brian Mobley, had—after a failed mayoral bid—resigned; Mobley had never been anybody's favorite administrator, and few mourned his passing. But Sheriff Rory Atwater, while possessing better people skills than his predecessor, was no pushover. Atwater wanted the spate of killings stopped, and—Brass had already learned, in the new sheriff's first few months on the job—what Rory Atwater wanted, Rory Atwater generally got.

Both sheriffs were good, honest cops; but each was, in his way, a career politician, which only reflected the reality of the waters both lawmen had to swim in. The difference was: Mobley had always seemed like a high-school bully trying to behave himself while running for class president; Atwater, on the other hand, was smoother, more polished, and there were those in the department who considered the new boss a barracuda in a tailored suit.

Sighing to himself, stuck behind an SUV at a light, Brass pondered the latest absurdity: Atwater's meetings and memos had made it clear the sheriff expected these murders (and probably the damned heat wave as well) to stop simply because the man *wanted* them to . . . as if he could *will* homicide to take its own Vegas vacation. And it was up to Brass and the rest of the LVPD to turn the sheriff's desire into reality . . . with the results expected sooner, not later.

The snarled line of cars pulled forward another yard and Brass eased ahead, his eyes flicking toward the switch for the flashers. He was tempted, but he wouldn't break the rules and, besides, what the hell good would it do? Even if the cars ahead were willing to move out of the way, they couldn't.

Another twenty minutes passed before Brass finally slipped the Taurus into a parking place and hustled from the car into HQ, the broiling temperature popping beads of sweat out on his forehead, despite the short walk into the building. Sidestepping the metal detector, Brass nodded to the uniformed officer guarding the entrance and resisted the urge to mop his brow with his sleeve; the fabric wouldn't like it. Metal detectors had become SOP for many government buildings after 9/11, and Vegas had been no different from hundreds of other American cities in jumping on the security bandwagon.

The officer at the door was a post-9/11 occurrence as well. City Hall's atrium lobby was large and saw a great deal of foot traffic during any given day. Today was typical, with pedestrians seemingly everywhere and Brass having to duck in and out of the crowd as he made his way toward the elevator.

He had just squeezed in, touched the button for the correct floor, and was watching the doors slide shut when a suit-coated arm broke through and stopped them. Amid frowns and sighs from the half-dozen other people in the car—irritation was high on a hot day like this—Sheriff Rory Atwater strode into the elevator and gave them all a quick once-over and smile, as if this were a meeting he'd convened. Then he nodded and turned to face front.

The sheriff—in a double-breasted gray suit, white shirt with a red and blue patterned tie—showed no sign whatever that he had spent even a second in the blast furnace outside. The man's wide gray eyes matched his suit and his light brown hair, slowly turning silver, was close-cropped and as neatly trimmed as his thick mustache. The effect was dignified and gave weight to his self-possession, serving to make him appear older than his forty-five years.

"Well, this saves me a phone call," Atwater said cheerfully, tossing a grin toward the detective who found himself at the sheriff's side.

Brass managed to smile just enough in return, inwardly wondering, *Now what in hell?*

"Does it?" Brass said mildly.

"It does," Atwater said. "Someone I want you to meet, up in my office."

Liking this conversation less and less, Brass tried to bow out. "I was just going to stop by my office for a second, then head over to CSI to check on some evidence. . . ."

Atwater's grin carried no mirth. "This meeting takes precedence."

The bell announcing the second floor interrupted any further explanation Atwater might have offered. Passengers scurried between and around them, all but two others getting off. The sheriff and his subordinate eyed each other as the doors whispered shut and the car again rose.

Brass twitched a noncommittal smile. "Mind if I ask who I'll be meeting?"

With his voice lowered almost theatrically, the sheriff replied, "Rebecca Bennett. . . . You recognize the name, of course."

Brass shook his head. "Can't say I do."

"I guess that's understandable," the sheriff said, as if forgiving the detective. "She hasn't been around for a while—most of the last decade, actually."

"Afraid you've lost me, Sheriff."

The doors opened on the third floor and the other two passengers got out to finally give the two law enforcement officers some privacy. As the door closed, Atwater said, "Well, you've no doubt heard of her mother."

No bells rang for Brass. "Bennett" was the kind of name the phone book had no shortage of.

The sheriff raised an eyebrow. *"Rita* Bennett?"

The third floor bell rang and so did another in the detective's mind—an alarm bell.

They stepped onto the third floor.

"The car dealer," Brass said. *And a major political contributor of yours, Sheriff,* he thought. "But didn't she pass away not long ago?" *Right after your election . . . ?*

"Yes, she did. She was a dear woman, a dear friend." The sheriff's grief seemed genuine enough; but perhaps any politician had the ability to truly mourn the death of a money source.

And Rita Bennett had been money, all right. She had won custody of one of her ex-husband's used car lots in their divorce settlement some fifteen years ago, after she'd caught hubby using his dipstick to check his secretary's oil in his office. She had turned the used car lot into one of the top GM dealerships in all the Southwest, leaving her ex in the dust.

The two men were walking down the hall toward the sheriff's office.

"Mrs. Bennett had a solid reputation in this town," Brass said, and he was not soft-soaping his boss. "But why is it we're meeting with her daughter?"

"Let's let the young woman tell her own story."

In the outer office, Brass saw Mrs. Mathis, the forty-something civilian secretary and holdover from Mobley's regime. Coolly efficient and constantly a step ahead of either boss, Mrs. Mathis ran the sheriff's office with a velvet hammer.

"Miss Bennett is in your office, Sheriff," Mrs. Mathis said as Atwater and Brass passed her desk.

Atwater thanked her and opened his door, going in ahead of Brass.

The room hadn't really changed since Mobley had called it home—different awards, different diplomas, different photos of the current resident with various celebrities and politicos. The most remarkable thing about the masculine office was the striking female seated in the chair in front of the sheriff's desk.

She rose and turned to them—a brunette in her late twenties, beautiful even by Las Vegas standards, though her clothing was decidedly not flashy: light-blue blouse, navy slacks, navy pumps. She wore her black hair short and in curved arcs that accented her high cheekbones; her eyes were wide-set, blue and large, conveying both alertness and a certain naivete. Her nose was small and well-sculpted, possibly the work of a plastic surgeon. And her full lips parted to reveal small, white teeth in a narrow mouth.

The smile, however, was joyless, like the sheriff's was in return. Also like the sheriff, the young woman showed no sign of the heat. *How did they do it?* Brass wondered; as he crossed the room toward her, Brass could almost hear himself sweating. But now he wondered if it was from the heat or in anticipation of whatever card Atwater was keeping up his sleeve.

"Rebecca Bennett," Atwater said, "this is Captain Jim Brass—if there's a finer detective in the department, I'd like to meet him."

This ambiguous praise sent another round of warning bells clanging inside Brass's brain as he stuck out his hand toward the Bennett woman. Atwater was about to spring some surprise, Brass just *knew* it—but didn't know where it would hit him.

Rebecca Bennett had a firm handshake and a no-nonsense cast to her eyes. And was there something predatory in those small, white, sharp teeth . . . ?

"Captain Brass," she acknowledged as they shook.

"Ms. Bennett," Brass said. "My condolences on your recent loss."

"Thank you, Captain. Actually, that's why I'm here."

Atwater moved behind his desk and motioned for her to sit and for Brass to sit next to her. "Miss Bennett," the sheriff began.

"Rory, you're a family friend. Just because you haven't seen me since I was a kid—it's still 'Rebecca'. . . ."

"Rebecca." His eyes narrowed. "I know this has been . . . difficult for you."

"I'm sure you do."

Atwater looked thoughtful, then assumed an expression that Brass knew all too well: sad eyes, soft frown, the staples of generic concern. "Rebecca, why don't you explain your . . . situation . . . to Captain Brass."

Odd way to put it—*situation*. Glancing sidelong at the woman, Brass could see Rebecca composing herself. Something was wrong here, or anyway . . . weird.

"You offered your condolences about my mother," Rebecca said, her voice strangely businesslike.

"I hope that was appropriate," Brass said, wondering if he'd committed a *faux pas*.

"Actually, it wasn't," she said with an odd little smile. "But you couldn't know that."

"Your mother was a unique woman," Atwater put in. "Larger than life—it's understandable that you'd be . . . conflicted."

What the hell was up, here?

Rebecca shrugged. "You could call it that."

"If you'll excuse me," Brass said, "maybe I'm the great detective the sheriff implied . . . maybe not . . . but I'm definitely not good enough to read between these lines. Please, Ms. Bennett—what's this about?"

"Excuse me, Captain Brass," the woman said. "I sort of . . . forgot that you were in the dark here. You see, I already filled in Sheriff Atwater, in some detail."

Brass shot a look at the sheriff who wore his politician's smile and shrugged, just a little.

Rebecca said, "You see, my mother and I had been estranged since I was eighteen. I moved in with my father after high school, and never looked back."

"Sorry to hear this," Brass said. A thought of his own estranged daughter, Ellie, flashed through his mind; but then something gripped him: Why was the *disaffected* daughter of a political contributor important to Atwater?

"Captain Brass," she was saying, "I do regret it . . . now. You get a little older and understand that you've probably held your parents to an unrealistic standard. But the bitterness between us was very real. She wrote me a letter, oh, seven years ago, but I never responded, and . . . Anyway, I always meant to reestablish contact with Mother, but the timing just never seemed right. And now, of course . . . it's too late."

She shrugged. No tears, not even wet eyes—just a shrug.

Atwater said, "You should give Captain Brass the background of this . . . situation."

Situation again.

"Captain, it wasn't long after my mother finagled my father out of his flagship car lot . . . in their divorce . . . that I learned her new boyfriend was actually someone she'd been seeing at the very same time my father was indulging in his own extramarital meanderings. . . . In other words, she was playing the violated wife in the divorce court, when she herself had been cheating. Her lover was one Peter Thompson, and they'd been seeing each other for months before Mother caught Daddy . . . what's the term? *In flagrante delicto?* . . . with that bimbo secretary of his. Would you like to know something interesting?"

Brass, fairly overwhelmed by this little soap opera, said, "Sure."

"My mother never fired the woman—Daddy's secretary, I mean. Don't you think it's possible the secretary was in on it? That it was a put-up job?"

Brass said, "Possible."

"Anyway, my finding out that Mommy screwed Daddy over was what drove the wedge between us. My father going broke, dying of alcoholism a few years later, didn't exactly . . . help. I didn't even go to the wedding when she married Peter. I was still in high school then—that was one of our four-alarm arguments, let me tell you."

"I can imagine," Brass said. "How long since you've spoken to your mother?"

"Over ten years." Another shrug. "As I said, since shortly after my eighteenth birthday . . . when I moved out. Not so much as a Christmas card."

"And, if you don't mind my asking," Brass said, "what have you been doing all this time?"

"I worked my way through Cabrerra University in Miami. Waitressing. Took six years to get the four-year degree."

"Why Miami?"

"That seemed about as far away from home as I could get without falling in the ocean. I majored in hotel/motel management—both my parents had business in their blood, and it got passed on, I guess. After that, I worked for a chain in Miami, last six years. Two months ago, I got transferred out here—the Sphere."

"Finding yourself in such close proximity to your mother—did you try to contact her?"

"Yes . . . yes, I thought fate had finally put me on the spot. Time to be a grown-up and make some kind of peace with the miserable bitch." She laughed harshly and then it turned into a sob. She got into her purse, found a tissue, and dried her eyes.

Brass and Atwater exchanged raised eyebrows.

Then Rebecca was talking again. "That was when . . . when I finally learned that she'd died. Just this May."

"You talked to your stepfather?"

"Yes—he said she died peacefully." She paused for a long, ragged breath. "In her sleep."

Brass glanced at Atwater, but the sheriff had his eyes on Rebecca Bennett.

"But you don't believe him," Atwater prompted.

"No, I don't."

"That's what brought you here today, isn't it?"

Hesitating, Rebecca glanced between the two men before saying, "Yes. I think my stepfather murdered my mother."

A prickle of anger tweaked the back of Brass's neck—so *that* was why Atwater had brought him in on this! With the daughter of a deceased major contributor battling the widower, who could say where the money would wind up?

Brass allowed himself to cast his boss a disgusted

smirk, but Atwater didn't seem to notice—he appeared placid, somberly so. Just a concerned friend of the family, trying to do the right thing . . .

"I want you to know right now, Rebecca," Atwater said, "that we'll look into this immediately . . . and thoroughly."

Brass had sense enough to tread carefully around the sheriff when Atwater was playing one of those cards from up his sleeve. Nonetheless, he asked, "Why don't you believe your stepfather, Ms. Bennett?"

She turned to Brass, her wide eyes like exclamation marks in her surprised face. Apparently it had never occurred to her that anyone might question her reasoning, much less her motives.

"There are several things," she finally said, as if that were explanation enough.

"What were the autopsy results?"

Rebecca's mouth formed a sarcastic kiss. *"What* autopsy results?"

"There was no autopsy?"

She shook her head. "In fact, that's one of the reasons I suspect Peter—he told me an autopsy would have been contrary to my mother's wishes . . . due to her *religious* beliefs."

"And you're skeptical of that reason?"

"I'm skeptical of that *excuse*—I've been away from Mom for a long time, and I understand that things can change, people can change . . . but she wasn't religious at all when *I* lived with her."

"Some kind of religious conversion, then. . . ." Brass offered.

"Yes, a conservative fundamentalistic church she

and Peter joined—the body has to be preserved for resurrection and all of that b.s."

"Not everyone considers that belief 'b.s.,' Ms. Bennett. . . ."

"I know, I know. . . . I don't mean to sound like some kind of religious bigot, but it just . . . seems very drastic for Mom. Out of character. But there are other things too. For example . . . Peter got *everything* in Mom's will."

Brass already knew why Atwater was here (to protect his ass, whichever Bennett inheritor wound up with the family fortune) and why he himself was here (to provide Atwater with a potential fall guy); and now, finally, Brass understood why Rebecca Bennett was here. Whatever contempt she might have felt for her mother, Rebecca wanted her share. Her piece.

She must have read what he was thinking, because she quickly said, "Understand, it's not about the money."

Keeping his face neutral, Brass nodded. Very little was certain in this wicked world; but one thing Jim Brass knew: Whenever somebody said it wasn't about the money—it was about the money.

"My mother's fortune was built on my father's used car business—a business she and Peter Thompson all but swindled Daddy out of. That after all these years Peter would be the one to benefit—it's just too much. Just too goddamn much."

"Ms. Bennett—"

She sat forward, blue eyes flashing. "There just seems to be so much . . . *secrecy* about my mother's death, and when I tried to talk to Peter? He shut me out."

"Which is why," Atwater said, with terrible casualness, "you want her exhumed."

Brass sat up like a sleeping driver awakened by a truck horn. "*Ex-*," Brass said, "*-humed?*"

"Yes," Rebecca said, with her own dreadful ease. "I want my mother exhumed, and an autopsy performed, so I'll know once and for all whether or not Peter Thompson killed her."

Brass felt the words tumble out: "Well, certainly your stepfather will fight you on this. . . ."

She laughed, head back, as if proud of herself. "He *promised* me he would. He hates me like poison . . . and he'll use my own murdered mother's money against me."

Softly, to try to bring the melodrama down a notch, Brass said, "We'll check him out."

"What about the exhumation?" she asked, sitting forward, excited now, nostrils flaring, tiny teeth clenched.

"Well . . ." Brass said, looking toward the sheriff, who would surely have the sense to call off this witch hunt. . . .

Atwater jumped into the *situation* with both feet . . . which of course landed on Brass, right where the sun didn't shine, even in a Vegas heat wave.

"The exhumation will be no problem," Atwater said, his gaze flicking for just a second to Brass, then back to his potentially lucrative audience. "As your mother's last blood relative, you have the right to an autopsy . . . especially with your suspicions about your stepfather. My best man, Captain Brass, will see to it . . . personally."

Here they were, murders up higher than the temp,

and Sheriff Atwater was assigning him a case that was little more than a political favor.

In his mind, Brass said, "Like hell I will. Do your own damn political bullshit!"

But what he said was, "Get right on it, Ms. Bennett."

He had to swim in these waters, too.

The Desert Palm Memorial Cemetery occupied a lush green space not far from the intersection of North Las Vegas Boulevard and Main Street. Two days had passed since Captain Brass met with Sheriff Atwater and Rebecca Bennett, and the detective stood with court order in hand, in the middle of the cemetery. Like most grave robbers, they were working in the wee hours—at the behest of the cemetery management, who requested that this effort not interrupt their regularly scheduled interments.

The desert was cool at night, it was said; and right now the temperature was all the way down to ninety-eight, with a slight devil's-breath breeze. Of course this was actually morning, about two hours from dawn, toward the end of the CSI graveyard shift . . . literally graveyard, this time.

Brass was well aware that CSI Supervisor Gil Grissom sympathized with his distaste for politics. But they all had a job to do, including two more nightshift crime scene analysts, Sara Sidle and Nick Stokes. The four of them cast long shadows in the light of a full moon as they waited while a backhoe tore open the earth over Rita Bennett's grave.

Two gravediggers were paid accomplices tonight

on this ghoulish mission. Joe, a lanky guy with stringy black hair and sky blue eyes, sat atop the backhoe. His partner, Bob, shorter but just as skinny, stood beyond the grave directing Joe to make sure the backhoe didn't smash the concrete vault that held Rita Bennett's casket. Both men wore filthy white T-shirts and grime-impacted blue jeans, appropriate for this dirty job that somebody had to do, if less than wholly respectful to the deceased they were disturbing.

Next to the backhoe, a flat bronze headstone with Rita's name, birth, and death dates carved into it, stood on edge, standing sentinel over the awkward proceedings. Brass and the CSIs stood well off to one side, watching the growling machine paw at the dirt.

Moderately tall with graying hair and a trim dark beard, Gil Grissom was dressed in black, head to toe, blending with the night. Even when the sun was out, though, the man in black gave no sign that the heat bothered him in the least. Brass, meanwhile, wore a tan sportcoat and light color shirt and had, all day, felt like he was walking around inside a burning building.

Grissom's two associates seemed dressed more appropriately for the weather. Sara, her dark hair tucked under a CSI ball cap, wore tan slacks and a brown short-sleeve blouse; her oval face had a ghostly beauty in the moonlight. Square-jawed, kind-eyed Nick Stokes stood next to her, a navy blue CSI T-shirt doing its best to contain the former jock's brawn; his dark hair was cut high over his ears and he seemed almost as at ease in the heat as Grissom.

Stokes said, "With the run of murders we been

havin', I wouldn't think the sheriff would want to go digging up new customers."

"If it does turn out to be a legitimate customer, Nick," Grissom said, in his light but pointed way, "we'll give full service."

"No autopsy," Sara said. "That doesn't smell right."

"Don't say 'smell' at an exhumation," Nick said.

"That's not inherently suspicious," Grissom said to Sara, meaning the lack of autopsy. "Some people want to get shuffled off this mortal coil in one piece. . . . Not unusual for religious beliefs to preclude an autopsy."

Sara made a face and shrugged. "I'm just saying."

But that was all she said.

They watched as the backhoe clawed another gouge in the earth. Before long, Bob the gravedigger waved for Joe, the backhoe operator, to stop. Joe climbed down off the machine and the two men met at the head of the grave, in executive session, apparently.

"Everything okay?" Brass asked with a frown.

Bob, hands on hips, looked over. "We've reached the vault."

Brass and the CSIs moved to where Bob and Joe stood at the edge of a hole that went down three to three-and-a-half-feet. Barely visible at the bottom was a sliver of something brown.

"Have to dig the rest by hand," Bob said. "Graves on each side are too close to use the backhoe, and 'course we don't want to damage the vault."

Brass knew this and so did Grissom, Sara, and Nick; but the gravedigger had never done an exhumation with this group before, and he seemed to enjoy sharing his wealth of information.

"Not our first time at the rodeo, Bob," Brass said dryly. "Do what you do."

"Could take some time," Bob said, cocking his head, relishing his power.

"This is a graveyard, Bob," Grissom said. "We'll reflect on the relative nature of time."

"Huh?" Bob said.

"Dig," Nick said.

Bob thought about that and then a grin appeared in the midst of his dirty face. "Yeah—yeah, *I* dig."

And the gravedigger scurried back to work, as Sara and Nick traded rolling-eyed expressions.

The detective and the three CSIs watched as the two men used tile shovels to carefully excavate around the concrete vault. Neither of the workers looked very happy as they gingerly pawed at the earth within their small hole.

"Where's the concerned daughter," Nick asked, "to watch us dig up Mommy?"

"Be nice, Nick," Grissom said.

Brass said, "She'll meet us back at CSI and be there when we finally open the coffin. Legal procedure requires her presence."

Sara said, "If I were forced to do this, with the grave of a loved one . . . ? I wouldn't want to be anywhere around."

Grissom looked at her curiously. "But you're a scientist."

"Even scientists have feelings," she said, with a mildly reproving glance.

Shrugging, Grissom said, "Nobody's perfect."

Sara and Nick took photographs of what followed. Grissom made field notes. Brass just watched.

The two workers finally got cables under the vault and, using the backhoe like a crane, they lifted the concrete box out of the ground and set it on a flatbed truck. Brass and the CSIs piled into the black Tahoe and followed the vehicle back to the station, where the flatbed backed in the tall door at the end of the garage behind the CSI building. Meanwhile, Nick parked the Tahoe, after which the quartet marched inside to get down to business.

The garage had spaces for three cars, beyond which was an oversized bay built to accommodate trucks even bigger than the one that carried the strapped-down remains of Rita Bennett. Essentially a concrete bunker with a twenty-foot ceiling and an overhead crane, the garage had a workbench along the back wall and two huge tool chests, one against each of the side walls.

First, Nick and Sara climbed up onto the truck and removed the straps from the vault. As they did, Brass went inside, to the office, to bring back Rebecca Bennett. As Brass disappeared through the door, Nick motioned for Grissom to come closer to the truck.

Keeping one eye on the door even as he and Sara undid the straps, Nick asked, "Don't we have better things to be doing than an exhumation to satisfy one of Atwater's contributors?"

Grissom's voice remained soft, but his face grew serious. "She's not a contributor—her late mother was."

"What, are we gonna quibble?"

"No, Nick, we're not going to quibble—this is a

woman who needs answers about the death of her mother . . . answers that we might be able to provide."

"Hey, all I mean, there's serious crimes—"

"Do your job, Nick."

Nick started to say something, but Sara cut him off: "It's a sealed vault! Gonna take us some time gettin' into it."

Nodding once, Grissom said, "No time like the present."

Using the overhead crane, Nick and Sara put the crane's metal runners under the frame of the concrete lid and tightened them down. Then, using the column of buttons on the hanging control box, Nick nudged the RAISE button a few times, until the slack was gone from the chain and the vault was just about to leave the bed of the truck.

Accepting a pry bar from Sara, Nick went to work on the sealed edge of one side of the vault while Sara worked on the opposite side. They had been at it for almost ten minutes, both perspiring despite the air conditioning inside the garage, when Brass reappeared with an attractive, slender, black-haired woman in dark-green slacks and a black silk blouse.

Grissom extended his hand as Brass and the woman approached where he stood next to the truck. The woman's eyes remained locked on the vault on the back of the vehicle, the two CSIs still plugging away with the pry bars.

"I'm Gil Grissom from the crime lab," he said, his hand still hanging out in space.

She finally tore her eyes from the vault, looked for a moment at his hand like she couldn't understand why it was there; then, with a visible flinch, she focused and shook it.

"Sorry," she said. "Rebecca Bennett. . . . I guess I wasn't prepared. . . ."

"As an abstraction, exhumation is just a word," Grissom said. "The reality is . . . sobering. You don't have to stay long."

"No, that's all right," she said, her voice cold, detached now, an attitude she assumed like a cloak she'd suddenly gathered herself in. "So that's Mother?"

"Yes. We've already started working on the vault, but it's sealed . . . so it's going to take a little time."

She nodded, her eyes returning to the vault.

At that moment the epoxy bond was broken and the vault settled back onto the truck bed, the shock absorbers and springs grunting as it did. The noise made Rebecca jump a little.

Brass walked the woman to a chair across the garage.

"Easier than I thought," Sara said, mopping her brow with her hand.

Nick gave her a sarcastic look. "Piece of cake."

Sara looked at him, smiling, but hard-eyed. "Nick . . . tell me you're not creeped out by this. . . ."

"What? Gimme a break. I'm a scientist, too, you know."

"Scientists have feelings, remember?"

"After all we've been through? Don't insult me."

Sara made a shrug with her face. "I wouldn't dream of it . . . but we all have our little, you know . . . bugaboos."

Nick grunted a small laugh. "Yeah, well help me open this one."

Rita Bennett had only been buried about three months and remarkably little odor crept over the sides of the vault and down to the trio on the floor.

Using the crane, Nick set the vault lid off to one side.

Brass walked over and asked, "How's the casket look?"

The two CSIs glanced down into the vault at the same moment.

Sara spoke first. "Looks good, surprisingly."

"Like brand new," Nick added. To Sara under his breath, he said, "Only one owner. . . ."

"Not much smell," Sara said quietly.

Their comments were *sotto voce*, to keep them from the daughter seated across the room.

Turning to Brass, Grissom said, "One of the good things about living in the desert—things decay slower, here."

"Personally," Brass said, "I'm decaying pretty damn fast these days, this heat."

Next, Nick and Sara worked straps around the casket and Nick used the crane to lift it out of the vault and swing it over the side of the truck. Lowering it slowly, Nick set the casket gently on the floor not far from Grissom and Brass.

Brass turned to the seated woman and said, "Ms. Bennett—if you'd join us?"

She did, and the five moved to the oaken box; then Grissom, Brass, and Rebecca watched as Sara and Nick released the locks and flipped up the lid of the coffin.

Within, Grissom had expected to find Rita Bennett looking much as she had when she'd been buried, just three months ago. The dress would be tasteful, her makeup in place but slightly over the top, like it always had been in her TV spots for the car dealership, and her hair would be dyed platinum blonde.

Looking into the casket, Grissom felt his stomach lurch a little.

He saw tennis shoes, jeans, a Las Vegas Stars T-shirt, painted fingernails, pierced ears, pink-glossed lips, and auburn hair surrounding a face that had to be younger than twenty-five. The young woman in the casket, younger than Rebecca standing next to him, looked very peaceful indeed.

She just didn't happen to be Rita Bennett.

Rebecca's hand shot to her mouth and her eyes opened wide.

Sara was the first to find her voice. "*Uh . . . oh. . . .*"

She looked at Nick, whose slack-jawed, wide-eyed expression mirrored her own.

"Gris," Nick said gingerly, "this doesn't look like a heart attack."

"What have you people done with my mother?" Rebecca demanded. She turned to Grissom and said, *"Where is my mother?"*

The shift supervisor turned to Brass, who seemed suddenly about three inches shorter, an invisible and very heavy weight having settled across his shoulders.

Sheriff Atwater was going to love *this. . . .*

Grissom faced Brass and asked, "We double-checked the grave location—right?"

"I went to the office myself," the detective said, his voice wavering between anger, confusion, and frustration. "And the damn headstone is even in the truck! Everything matched."

Holding up his hands, Grissom said, "No need to get defensive, Jim . . . just checking." Grissom turned to Sara and Nick with renewed energy. "If our paperwork was right, and the cemetery staff took us to the correct site . . . all of which seems to have happened, then we have ourselves a brand-new crime scene."

Rebecca Bennett got between them. "I'm thrilled for you! But where is my *mother?*"

Grissom raised a palm, as if trying to stop traffic. "I don't know, Ms. Bennett . . . but I can promise you we're going to do everything we can to find her."

"This isn't happening," Brass said, and sat on the bumper of the truck. "We come in to do a simple exhumation, and now we have a *murder?*"

"Not necessarily," Grissom said. "Could be a simple mistake."

The dead woman's daughter managed to open her eyes even wider. "Simple mistake?"

Covering his eyes, Brass was calling for a dispatcher on his radio.

"Forgive me, Ms. Bennett," Grissom said. He began to lead the stunned woman away from the casket. "We, as criminalists, have to approach this as a problem that needs to be solved. But we don't really mean to be callous."

"My mother, what the goddamn hell *happened* . . . ?"

"You have my word, Ms. Bennett—we'll solve this. All your questions will be laid to rest."

"Like my *mother* was?"

Grissom didn't have an answer for that.

Sara approached and said, "We're very sorry about this awful turn of events. This has been a terrible traumatic thing, but please believe me—we're going to help."

Grissom watched as a uniformed officer entered. Brass joined Grissom and the distraught young woman, showing up at the same moment as the uniform man.

"Ms. Bennett," Brass said, "I'm afraid we're going to have to ask you to step out now."

"Are you people trying to get *rid* of me now?" she asked, her voice, practically a shriek, careening off the cement walls.

Grissom stepped up. "No, Ms. Bennett—we're trying to preserve evidence. We have to find out what happened to the woman in your mother's casket."

"What . . . about . . . my *mother?*"

Shaking his head, Grissom said, "The only clues we have to what happened to your mother are inside that casket with this girl. You need to let us do our job."

Rebecca obviously wanted to put up a fight, but Grissom could tell she saw the logic of his argument; he read her as a strong, intelligent young woman. Hanging her head, sighing in defeat, she allowed the uniformed officer to lead her out of the garage.

Turning back to his charges, Grissom's face was tight. "Let's do it."

Sara was already bent over the coffin. "Blood on the pillow," she said. "I can't tell more until we get the body out."

Grissom said, "All right, then . . . Nick, you work the casket. Someone put her in there—let's see if we can't find out who. Sara, find out who she is and walk her through autopsy. Tell Doc Robbins this is a rush— we're already at least three months behind."

Brass added, "I'll start with the cemetery and work my way back to the mortuary." He checked his watch. "The staff should be there by now—you gonna work past the end of shift?"

Grissom nodded. "All the shifts are working overtime these days."

Sara asked, "What about Rita Bennett?"

"We can't find out what happened to her," Grissom said, "until we *find* her . . . and the only clue we have to her whereabouts is the mystery guest buried in Rita's grave."

"Blood on the pillow," Sara said. "Already looking like murder."

Nick shook his head slowly. "Doesn't *anybody* in this town ever die normal anymore?"

Grissom cast his charming smile on the younger CSI. "Where would the fun be in that, Nick?"

2

THE "RED BALLS," as high-priority murders were known in some jurisdictions, got the adrenaline flowing, and were the kind of cases that could build careers. But CSI Catherine Willows had come to prize the more normal calls, particularly in a period of record homicides and double shifts like the one she was in the midst of.

This morning—at a time when a nightshift criminalist like Catherine should by all rights be in bed asleep—she and her partner, Warrick Brown, were riding out to the Sunny Day Continuing Care Facility with the Tahoe siren blessedly off and the air conditioning whispering its soft song. In addition to less stress, such a relatively routine call provided Catherine a better sense of connection with the people she and the LVPD served.

For having worked all night, Catherine Willows looked surprisingly, if typically, crisp in cool cotton, a man-tailored white shirt, and khaki-color slacks; after twenty years of harsh Vegas sun, the slender, strawberry-blonde crimefighter remained blessed with the facial features and general architecture of a fashion model, though her past actually included runways of another sort. The journey of this former exotic dancer into this highly respected, demanding profession had been very much a self-made one.

Behind the wheel, Warrick Brown—with his restrained dreadlock Afro, creme de cacao complexion and arresting green eyes—did not reveal the long hours either. In the tan cotton pullover and cargo pants, he looked almost collegiate . . . or would have if his world-weary demeanor didn't convey something of the terrible things a CSI had to learn to live with.

The sun was already high, but the temperature hadn't risen to the broiler-like numbers it would register in another few hours; so the day still held the promise that perhaps the heat-soaked murder spree gripping the city might let up.

They had been summoned to Sunny Day by Detective Sam Vega, a veteran investigator with whom the nightshift CSIs had worked on numerous occasions. Routine or not, Catherine knew something must be up—the no-nonsense Vega neither spooked easily nor suffered fools lightly.

But as they made their way through traffic, Catherine forced herself away from pointless speculation about what might await them at the Sunny Day facility, and tried instead to concentrate on the very real sunny day all around them. Heat or not, she was enjoying it, particularly in thinking that she and her daughter Lindsey might get to the park later and enjoy some of this golden sunshine.

But Warrick, at the wheel, wouldn't let her evade

the reality of her . . . of their . . . job. "So what's this about, anyway? Vega say?"

Catherine shook her head, gave her partner half a smirk. "Vega was vague."

Warrick arched an eyebrow. "Actually, 'vague' is not Vega . . . he's usually one specific cop."

"Not this time. Just said he had something he wanted us to take a look at."

"What, scene of a missing bedpan?" Warrick took a left.

Catherine laughed in spite of herself. "Hey, don't be smug—we're all headed to Sunny Day, someday. You be nice, now. Respectful."

Warrick's easy grin seemed a little embarrassed. "Sorry, just kidding. I mean, with the kind of high-flyin' homicides we've been pulling lately, a rest home sounds, I don't know . . ."

"Restful? Would you rather have a dead scuba diver up a tree, or possibly a frozen corpse in the desert?"

Warrick nodded. "Maybe. Keeps you awake, on these endless shifts. . . ."

Tucked away in a quiet Henderson neighborhood, just off Lake Mead Drive, Sunny Day Continuing Care was a sprawling facility of the one-stop-shopping sort that seemed to be springing up in cities everywhere. Not merely a nursing home, Sunny Day offered the growing number of retirees invading the Vegas Valley everything from independent living to constant care.

Heading there, Warrick turned one more corner and they found themselves moving down a street with houses on the right side and an eight-foot wall down the left. Easing the Tahoe up to the guard shack outside the gate in the middle of the block, Warrick hit the down button on his power window.

A silver-haired guard, who might himself have been a Sunny Day resident, asked and received their names, inspected Warrick's ID, said he was expecting them, checked something off on a clipboard, and returned to his shack to hit the button that opened the wrought-iron gate.

The drive split in two around a green space occupied by park benches and, at the far end, a shuffleboard court. One side of the gated community was split between condos and duplexes, where the more active residents lived. The other was dominated by a pair of high-rises that housed the semi-care and full-care patients of the facility. Out in front of one high-rise could be seen Vega's Taurus, an ambulance, and a squad car.

"I think we've found the party," she said.

"I doubt I'll need my noisemaker," Warrick said dryly, referring to the automatics both CSIs packed on their hips, weapons that were rarely drawn, though a department mandate of recent years required carrying them—even on a nursing home call.

Warrick pulled the Tahoe up near the other vehicles, parked, and they climbed down. A single officer manned the door of the building.

"What about our kits?" Warrick asked, deferring to the senior officer.

Catherine shrugged. "Vague as Vega was, I say we get the story first, then come back for whatever we need . . . *if* we need anything."

"I like the way you think, Cath."

They approached the officer playing sentry. He was

a dayshift guy who Catherine had encountered a couple times, most recently on a love triangle murder in a Summerlin kitchen—Nowak was the name, if she remembered right. As they neared the tall, painfully young–looking officer, Catherine sneak-peeked at his nameplate.

Then with friendly familiarity, she said, "Hey, Nowak—what's the word?"

"Two words," the uniform said, giving Catherine a shrug and Warrick a quick nod. "Heart attack."

Catherine asked, "You know where we're headed?"

The officer gestured. "Doctor's office, second door down the hall. Administrative wing." He pulled the glass and steel door open for them. "On the right."

"Heart attack," Warrick said, shaking his head. He looked at Catherine and said, "And we're here why?"

Catherine said, chipper, "I don't know, Warrick. Why don't we ask Detective Vega?"

Officer Nowak said, "I think Vega's interviewing Doctor Whiting right now."

Warrick grunted, "Well, we'll try not to get in the way."

Warrick headed in and the officer raised his eyebrows and said to Catherine, "What's his problem?"

"Three days of double shifts." Catherine grinned. "Or maybe just his time of the month."

That surprised a laugh out of the officer, as Catherine stepped inside to catch up with Warrick.

It must have been even hotter outside than she thought, because this place felt like a walk-in refrigerator.

"Wow," Catherine said, head rearing back, almost laughing.

"What happened to senior citizens liking it warm?" Warrick asked with a little eye roll.

The long hallway was a pale institutional green, the overhead lighting fluorescent, the atmosphere sterile and decidedly unhomey—more hospital than hospitable. They walked past oversize, gurney-friendly doors that stood ajar, announcing a corridor where nurses and orderlies moved with joyless efficiency.

"Business must be good," Catherine said, pausing to note the plastic chart bins attached to the walls just inside.

Catherine could see beyond those double doors into the nearest room, to glimpse a bedridden woman with black-streaked silver hair, impossibly thick glasses, and an oxygen tube in her nose; her skin was the color of wet newspaper.

Across the way, a frail old man with wispy hair, his eyes closed, his countenance peaceful, made Catherine wonder if the old boy was dead or just asleep. Without more evidence, the CSI could not be sure.

Still, it was clear to Catherine that no one down that corridor would likely ever, under his or her own power, walk out of Sunny Day into any day, sunny or otherwise.

Warrick paused, and something flickered across those private, somewhat melancholy features.

"What?" Catherine asked with a gentle smile, as they walked on.

"Just thinking—we see all kinds of people end up all kinds of ways, most of them reeaaal bad."

"That we do."

His sigh came up from his toes. "This? . . . Is the worst."

The door with the nameplate "DR. L. WHITING, CHIEF OF STAFF" was closed, though muffled conversation within confirmed Vega's presence. Catherine knocked and a deep voice bid her to come in.

Catherine entered—there was no reception area— with Warrick just behind her, a formidable mahogany desk facing them. The office, also an institutional green, was less than spacious but not cramped, with a two-seater sofa next to the door, and the wall at left obscured by a credenza-style bookcase of medical tomes and family photos. On the wall at right, a few framed photographs taken on a golf course joined a handful of diplomas to intermingle with filing cabinets and provide this sparsely decorated office with a touch more warmth than a scalpel.

Pen and pad in hand, Vega occupied one of two chairs opposite the desk. The compact, broad-shouldered detective—he might have been a boxer or wrestler before his days on the force—was in his white shirt with the sleeves rolled up, his tie loose; only the over-the-top heat would inspire such casualness in this tightly wound cop. His black hair cut short, sans sideburns, his eyebrows dark and thick over sharply intelligent brown eyes, Vega had a serious visage that made a lot of his brother officers wonder if the man had had his sense of humor surgically removed.

The two CSIs, however, knew Vega well enough to

know that he did on occasion laugh—though seldom at work.

The man across from the detective had a build similar to Vega's, a handsome, even distinguished man of about forty-five in a white lab coat. His hair was the color of desert sand and neatly combed; he had dark blue eyes, high cheekbones, a deep Vegas tan, and the slightly remote expression of so many physicians. The straight, rigid way their host sat indicated he might have a bad back.

Physician, heal thyself, Catherine thought.

"Doctor Whiting," Vega said, without rising, swivelling toward the CSIs and gesturing with his pen, "this is Catherine Willows and Warrick Brown . . . from our crime lab. Catherine, Warrick—Dr. Larry Whiting."

The doctor rose stiffly, and Catherine and Warrick leaned past the seated Vega to exchange handshakes with their host.

"Good of you to come," Whiting said, his tone quiet, serious. He met Catherine's eyes and gestured toward the remaining chair.

"Thank you, Doctor," Catherine said, and sat next to Vega while Warrick settled his long frame onto the sofa just behind them, sitting forward, any double-shift tiredness wholly absent from his low-key keen attentiveness.

For a few moments, an awkward silence prevailed.

That happened frequently with CSIs, who often arrived in the middle of a police interview.

Vega decided to catch them up. "Doctor Whiting came to work today and found . . ." The detective looked toward the doctor. "Why don't *you* tell them what you found, Doctor?"

Whiting took a deep breath. He seemed very much like a man preparing himself to embark on a long, difficult journey.

"I've been here for almost a year," he said slowly. "That's not a terribly long time, of course, but I'm in charge of . . . how should I put it?"

Warrick said, "The last stop on the line?"

"We are indeed the last stop at Sunny Day—the terminal cases, and those so elderly that constant care is required. My point is that losing a patient is hardly cause for alarm. It is, I'm sorry to say, business as usual. Routine."

Catherine thought back to her own characterization of this call as a routine one, and wondered if her attitude had really been any better than Warrick's. . . .

"So today, when Vivian Elliot died, and then your assistant coroner, uh, Mr. uh . . ." He looked to Vega for assistance.

"David Phillips," Vega said.

"Today, when Mr. Phillips suggested maybe something wasn't *right* about Vivian's body, well I started thinking back, and wondering. . . ." His eyes went from Catherine to Warrick and finally settled on Vega, as if hoping he would not have to say any more.

"Doctor Whiting," Catherine said, with a smile that was really a frown, "with all due respect, sir—you're all over the map here."

Frustration tweaked the handsome features. "Well . . . isn't it obvious?"

Head to one side, Warrick said, "You're going to have to read us your prescription, doc, if you want us to fill it. We're just not making out what you mean."

The physician ran a hand through his dry sandy hair and looked at Catherine with a kind of helplessness. "You're right. . . . Obviously you're right. And I'm sorry, but this has just become almost . . . uh . . . surreal."

"A patient named Vivian Elliot died today," Catherine said. "Why wasn't *that* business as usual? Routine?"

"But that's just it—Vivian wasn't a typical resident of this ward. She doesn't even . . . I should say, *didn't* even . . . live at Sunny Day."

Warrick winced in thought. "How does someone who doesn't reside in this facility end up in your ward?"

"It's not frequent, but a certain number of our patients are not permanent residents. Mrs. Elliot, for example, came to us from St. Anthony's Hospital. She'd been in a serious car crash and was looking forward to a long, slow recovery."

Warrick said, "So she was transferred here? For the kind of long-term care you people do day in and day out."

"Exactly. And I can tell you, she's been doing well, very well!"

"Except," Warrick said, eyebrows lifting, "for today's little setback."

Dr. Whiting whitened. "Yes . . . yes. This morning I came in and—before I even got to rounds—she coded."

Catherine glanced at Vega, then turned back to the doctor. "Nothing could be done to save her? Don't people 'code' around here, all of the time?"

"Obviously, yes, but . . ." He shrugged and shook his head. "She was dead before I even got to the room."

Warrick said, "People do die of old age—natural causes."

Whiting gestured to a file folder on his desk. "Seventy-one years of age . . . that's young for Sunny Day. And before the automobile accident, Mrs. Elliot had been in good health and, after time and therapy, was making real progress."

Still confused, Catherine asked, "This is tragic, I'm sure, and unusual for your circumstances . . . but, Doctor—I'm still not sure I see why we were called in."

Vega turned to Catherine, gesturing with his notepad in hand. "What do you say we start by talking to David—this is his red flag."

"Fine," Catherine said, and patted her knees. "Where is David?"

Rising, Vega said, "Let's go for a walk."

The ward seemed a hive of activity, nurses bustling about in and out of rooms, the kitchen staff hustling along with trays of breakfast for those patients still able to feed themselves, and the odd visitor here and there coming to check on a loved one.

Vega took a left up a hallway and stopped in front of a closed room. The detective waited to knock until his little search party had caught up.

A vaguely startled voice said: "Who is it?"

Catherine and Warrick traded tiny smiles—she sensed her partner had also had the same mental image of David Phillips, jumping a little as he spoke. David was an assistant coroner assigned to Dr. Albert Robbins, with whom the nightshift CSIs frequently worked.

"It's Vega," the detective said, a little irritated. "Unlock the door, David."

The detective glanced sideways and gave Catherine a quick wide-eyed look that said, *Jeeesh, this guy.*

Soon a click announced cooperation and the door cracked open, David's bespectacled face filling the gap.

"Come in," David said.

Warrick whispered to Catherine, "What is this, a speakeasy?"

David, summery in a brown-and-white-striped short-sleeve shirt and light tan chinos, stepped aside and Vega entered with the others behind. With a touch of ceremony, David closed the door and turned to face them. Generally David had an easy if sometimes nervous smile, but right now there was no sign of it. His dark hair, getting wispy in front, seemed barely under control, as if wishing to abandon ship; and the sharp, wide eyes below the high forehead darted back and forth behind wire-frame glasses.

This was, Catherine noted, a fairly typical hospital room, though with just one bed. Under the sheet lay a body. Soft lighting emerged from behind a sconce at the headboard.

"Meet the late Vivian Elliot," David said as he drew back the sheet.

The woman's appearance confirmed the assistant coroner's opinion: She was dead, all right; her gray hair, though cut short, was splayed against the pillow, her eyes closed, her skin slack and gray, her features at rest, her torso lifeless.

"And?" Warrick asked.

"And . . . I don't know," David said, his voice solemn. He shrugged elaborate. "Everything looks fine."

"For a dead woman," Catherine said.

"For a dead woman, right."

Dr. Whiting stepped forward with stiff, strained dignity. "Sir—you indicated a problem. We called in a detective and crime scene investigators. *What* problem do you see here?"

David smiled weakly. Catherine knew that David had sought out his singularly solitary job among the dead in part because of the stress he could occasionally feel around the living. Though the hospital room was cold—any colder, their breaths would have been visible—Catherine could see beads of sweat popping out on the young assistant coroner's forehead.

"I said I *thought* there was something wrong here."

"You don't know?" Whiting asked, eyes and nostrils flaring.

"No! That's why we need, you know . . . an expert's read."

Catherine stepped forward and put a hand on Whiting's sleeve. "A second opinion never hurts, does it, Doctor? . . . If you'll excuse me, I'd like a private word with my colleague."

Now she took David by the arm and, in the corner of the room, spoke to him quietly. Even gently. "What's the matter, David?"

He moved his head side to side. "Catherine, I've been doing this job for a *while* now."

"Yes, you have. And you're very good at it."

"Thank you. . . . And you know, a person gets used to a certain routine. Mine is really like a lot of other jobs— life and death or not, it can be monotonous . . . and usually is."

Patiently she asked, "Point being?"

"I come to Sunny Day to make a pickup, once, twice a month."

"Yeah?"

A humorless half-smile tweaked his face. "This month? This is the *fourth* time."

Catherine called Warrick over and repeated what David had told her, still leaving Vega and Whiting out of the confab.

Warrick shook his head. "Whoa, dude—*that's* why you called the crime lab?"

Catherine gave Warrick a *take it easy* look.

David looked embarrassed. "That may not seem like such a variation from the norm to you, Warrick— but it struck me. I mean, I've *never* been here four times in one month."

Warrick's expression was skeptical, but something tugged at Catherine's gut. She asked, "How about three times?"

"Only twice—in four years on the job."

Warrick was considering that as he said, "David, four people dying in one of these places, in a single month . . . hardly unheard of."

David said, "Maybe not unheard of . . . I'd be lying if I said I knew what the statistical probabilities are . . . but it strikes me as strange, far beyond the norm as *I* know it."

"Better safe than silly," Catherine said, nodding.

David was getting in gear now.

"Then," he was saying, "you factor in Mrs. Elliot's relatively good health—at least compared to the other residents here—and you're running into odds worse than the casinos!"

Turning to Vega, Catherine asked, "You've heard all this?"

Vega's half-smile was uncharacteristically meek. "David's been like this since I got here. Frankly, that's why I agreed to call you guys in—I thought maybe you could talk him down off his ledge."

Catherine turned back to the assistant coroner. "What you have, David, is what we call around CSI a hunch—but we don't have them out loud. You know how Grissom would react, if we did."

David's eyes widened. "*Oooh* yeah."

She smiled sweetly and supportively at David, the way she did her daughter Lindsey, when the child had hit a homework brick wall. "Pretend I'm Grissom."

"That good an imagination," David said, "I don't have."

"I mean—convince me like you would him. If he were standing here, not me—tell me, what do you think we've got?"

David rubbed his chin as if it were a genie's lamp that might grant his wish for a good answer. Finally he let out a long breath and said, "Too many deaths spaced too close together."

"That doesn't suggest a crime," Catherine said. "Not inherently."

"Right . . . right. . . ."

"Think out loud if you have to, David."

"Well . . . I never considered it before today, but the four DOAs we picked up here this month?"

"Yeah?"

He smiled a little, raised one eyebrow, like a novice gambler laying down a winning ace. "*All* widows."

Ace or not, Catherine was not impressed, and said

so: "Women generally outlive men, David. No big surprise there."

David's face screwed up in thought. Finally he said, "We always mark the next of kin on the report . . . so we know who to call?"

"Riiight."

"Well, I was just thinking . . . I don't remember seeing that any of these four women had *any* family."

Catherine and Warrick traded a look. Warrick's eyes had taken on a harder cast, that steady unblinking look he got when something was really starting to interest him. . . .

Turning to Whiting, Catherine said, "Doctor, is what David thinks he remembers . . . true?"

The doctor shrugged. "I really can't say. I'd have to check the records."

Warrick said, pleasant but tight, "Why don't you?"

Catherine softened it: "Would you, please?"

Whiting nodded; but then he just stood there.

"Now would be good," Warrick said.

Sighing, Whiting said, "Anything to help, of course . . . but the truth is? . . . A lot of our residents at Sunny Day are widows." He cocked his head, raised an eyebrow. "As you sagely pointed out, Ms. Willows, it's hardly unusual for women to outlive men."

"Well," Warrick said, and smiled, "maybe you better check those records, before everybody passes away but CSI Willows here."

Whiting, obviously annoyed and probably not overjoyed leaving these investigators unattended in one of his rooms, nonetheless went off to do Catherine's bidding.

With the four of them alone now—but for the late

Vivian Elliot—Vega turned to Catherine. "You see why I called you?"

"You did the right thing." She sighed, rolled her eyes. "It's a little borderline, but—"

"But," Vega said forcefully, "if we're *not* chasing our tails, this is a crime scene."

Suddenly all four of them felt the ghost of Gil Grissom haunting the room.

"Yeah," Warrick said, "and if we don't investigate it *now* . . . no telling what evidence'd be lost forever."

"If it's natural causes, though," Catherine said, "think of the time we're wasting in the middle of this murder spike. . . ."

"I wish I had more for you, *right now*—" David said, "but until the autopsy, there's no way to know for sure."

Catherine thought for a few seconds, then said firmly, "We've got to treat it as a crime scene . . . and if we're wrong? We're wrong."

"Won't be the first time," Warrick said.

"I'll interview Whiting," Vega said. "If the Elliot woman was killed, that makes the entire staff suspects."

"Not just them," Catherine warned. "It could be any resident with reasonable mobility. But the staff is where to start."

"What can I do to help?" David asked.

Catherine gave him a supportive smile. "You can wait in the hall. If you are right—and you've discovered a string of homicides—you're standing in our crime scene."

By the time Catherine and Warrick returned with their kits, a small crowd of onlookers in the hall had gathered outside the closed door. A few were in robes and slippers, and two used walkers; but most were fully dressed and looked suspiciously chipper, for this particular ward. Some had already started to question David, really pressing him as he stood there, looking extremely ill at ease.

Noting this tableau up ahead, Warrick said, "Man, those gals are pretty aggressive."

"They've seen David here before," she said. "And always in the context of accompanying one of their own to a morgue wagon."

"Yeah. See what you mean. Not very often you get to turn the tables on the angel of death."

Striding into the middle of the group of seniors, most of whom were women, Catherine said, "I'm very sorry, but this is an official investigation, and we can't tell you anything right now."

"It's *Vivian*, isn't it?" asked a woman to Catherine's right.

Just under five feet tall, her gray hair short and straight, the woman wore a bulky gray sweater—the temperature outside may have been over one hundred, but it was, after all, chilly in here. Tri-focals peered up at Catherine, one bird studying another, new one.

"Vivian passed away this morning," Catherine said, "yes."

"Shame," another, more heavyset woman said. "She was a sweetie pie."

"You *knew* her?" Catherine asked. "I understood Mrs. Elliot didn't live here."

"She didn't," the first woman said, with a shrug. "It's just that . . . we're the Gossip Club, don't you know. We know everybody. And everything."

"That could come in handy," Warrick said under his breath.

Catherine said, "Gossip Club?"

"We visit the sick and dying," the heavyset woman said, matter of factly. "We considered 'Visitor's Club,' but it just sort of lacked pizzazz."

One of the few males in the crowd, from the back said, "I think Gossip Club is perfect!"

"You be quiet, Clarence," the heavyset woman said, good-naturedly, and general laughter followed.

Catherine focused on the bird-like woman, who appeared to be the leader. "And you are?"

"Alice Deams—I'm the president of G.C., and this is my vice president, Willestra McFee." She nodded toward the heavyset woman nearby. "And that's our treasurer, Lucille—"

Catherine interrupted the Mouseketeer Roll Call. "You're all residents here, I take it?"

Alice nodded. "Most of us live in the partial care building—next door? Dora and Helen . . ." Two women next to David waved. ". . . they live in the independent apartments down at the other end."

"You all come here every day?"

"Most of us," Willestra said. "Unless we've got doctor's appointments or Margie's arthritis is kicking up, in which case she'll spend the day in her room, watching her stories."

"And you've taken it upon yourself to visit the sick?"

"Oh my, yes. It's the Christian thing to do, and besides, someday we'll be in this wing, won't we? Wishing for a little company. These people are our friends and neighbors, you know."

Catherine raised her voice. "Did any of you know Vivian Elliot well?"

"I probably spent the most time with her," Alice said. "She was really a great gal."

Warrick asked, "Vivian have any family?"

Alice shook her head. "No, and that's tragic. Her husband just passed away a year ago and they only had one child, a daughter who was killed when she was just seventeen by a hit-and-run driver. Viv still mourned the girl."

Catherine asked, "No brothers or sisters?"

"No."

Warrick said, "You seem sure of that. You didn't know her that long, really. How is it—".

"Oh, well, she was like *me*, don't you know—an only child. It was sort of a more rare thing, back then, being an only child. Bigger families were the thing— everybody had brothers and sisters. So Viv and me, we made kind of a bond out of being only children. We decided we could be sisters—never too late, we said!"

"So, she had no family that you know of?" Catherine asked, just making sure.

"Not a soul—not even very many friends. I only saw one other person visit her the whole time she was here—another woman."

Warrick asked, "This woman, her name—did you get it?"

"No, no, I'm sorry. I never actually met her, you see. When the patients have visitors, we make a policy of not bothering them. The job of the Gossip Club is to lend support when no family and friends are around."

"Do visitors have to sign in here?"

Alice shook her head again. "No, this wing is like a hospital that way. During visitor's hours, people just sort of come and go."

Catherine made a mental note to tell Vega to alert the staff should the unidentified woman come back to visit Vivian Elliot in the next twenty-four hours. After that, the obituary would have run in the newspaper, and Catherine doubted that they'd have any chance of locating the mystery woman . . . unless she showed up at Vivian's funeral or someone on staff actually knew the visitor.

"When was the last time you saw this woman?" Catherine asked.

"Why, just this morning," Alice said. "In fact, she left just a few minutes before we heard the alarm coming from Vivian's room."

"Can you describe her?"

"Fairly young."

Warrick asked, "How young?"

"Oh—sixty-five or so."

That stopped Warrick for a moment; then he asked, "Description . . . ?"

"She had gray hair and glasses."

Catherine and Warrick looked at the group of women in the hall, and then at each other, confirming a shared thought: Alice had just described all of them.

"We don't usually have a fuss this big when one of us passes," Alice said, eyes making slits in her much-lived-in face. "Why now? Was she murdered?"

Trying to keep her voice and expression neutral, Catherine asked the woman, "Why would you think that, Alice?"

The heavyset woman, Willie, glowered at Alice, then turned to Catherine, "Never mind her—she watches way too much TV!"

"I do not," Alice argued back. "I swear there was a case *just* like this on *Murder, She Wrote.*"

Everyone in the hall stopped and eyeballed Alice for a long moment.

Behind her tri-focals, Alice's eyes widened and her chin rose defensively. "Well, there *was*. . . . Of course, it could've been *Barnaby Jones* . . . or maybe *Rockford Files.* Isn't that James Garner just adorable?"

As the woman prattled on about television, Catherine watched as the other members of the Gossip Club slowly eased away into real life, each suddenly needing to visit someone in a nearby room.

Taking the hint, Catherine and Warrick slipped back into Vivian Elliot's room, leaving poor David alone in the hall with Alice theorizing on what had happened to an old woman on some detective show she'd seen either last week or perhaps twenty-five years ago.

"What exactly are we looking for?" Warrick asked as they unpacked their equipment.

Catherine's eyes roamed around the room, stopping briefly on the body, then moving on. She prided herself on her ability to make the first read of a crime scene an important one. But she could only shake her head. "Warrick—I haven't a clue. . . ."

"I hate when that happens."

With a sigh, Catherine said, "We better gather everything we can. Now that we know that this was a murder."

Warrick's head reared back. "We do?"

"Suuuure," Catherine said. "It was on *Barnaby Jones!* Or was that *Quincy . . . ?"*

Shaking his head, smiling one-sidedly, Warrick got out his camera, pulled the sheet back, and began shooting pictures. Catherine started by taking electrostatic print lifts from the tile floor. Truth was, half the hospital had been in and out of here since Vivian Elliot had died; but if there *was* a killer, that person's shoe prints would be among the many, and Catherine hoped they (and the computer) would be able to sort them all out.

After he finished photographing the body, Warrick moved on and took shots of every piece of equipment, every machine, every piece of furniture in the room. Catherine bent at the plastic biohazard dump and pulled out the liner bag, marking it as evidence. When they finished, Catherine had a pile of maybe fifteen evidence bags and Warrick had shot at least six rolls of twenty-four exposure film.

And yet not a single thing had jumped out at either of them as saying, *This is a crime . . . I am significant. . . .*

David and his coroner's crew removed the body, while Catherine and Warrick took most everything else. When they departed, the bed had been stripped bare, including the pillows, and the metal stand that had held two different IV bags was empty. The biohazard dump was also empty, the closet too, and in separate containers at the bottom of one of the bags, Catherine had even collected the remnants of Vivian Elliot's last breakfast left on a tray that apparently had been shifted into the bathroom when the recovering woman had gone code blue.

Alice Deams peeked out a doorway as Catherine strode down the corridor with the last of her grisly booty.

"Was I right?" Alice asked, eyes wide behind thick lenses. "Is it murder?"

"We don't know," Catherine said, pasting on a pleasant smile. "Why would you even think that?"

"Oh! All the hubbub!" Alice said, as she moved into the hall, closer now, more confidential. "Besides . . . it isn't like we haven't *noticed* that more of us are passing away than usual."

Catherine's eyes tightened, but she kept her voice casual. "You think so?"

"Oh, my, yes. They're dropping like flies around this joint!"

A little stunned by Alice's no doubt TV-driven phrasing, Catherine managed to ask, "How long have you lived here?"

Alice shrugged; within the heavy sweater, her arms were folded. "Going on ten years."

"You have family that visits you?"

She beamed and nodded and withdrew a snapshot from a sweater pocket, holding it up so Catherine (whose hands were full) could see it plainly.

Alice said, "I carry this with me all the time—my son, daughter-in-law, and their boy and girl."

"Do they visit often?"

"Once or twice a week. They take me to the market—sometimes even out to a movie."

Catherine nodded. "It's good to have good kids. . . . You say, in ten years, you've never seen deaths bunched this closely together?"

"Not really. . . . The Gossip Club sends flowers to everybody's funeral. You know, we take up a collection, get everybody to sign a card. Our flower budget this month is already twice normal and there's still a week and a half to go in the month! The last few months have been hard, too."

"How so?"

"You get used to people dying in a place like this—in a way. But, still. . . . May I tell you something that will sound . . . awful?"

"Uh . . . sure. Go right ahead."

Alice moved closer; she smelled like medication. "When you live at a nursing home . . . and don't kid yourself, honey, this is a nursing home . . . and you see one or two people pass . . . you kind of sigh a sigh of relief, and think . . . *whew*. Odds are, not gonna be *me* this month."

"But lately . . ."

"Lately? All bets are off, kiddo."

Catherine drew in a breath. Then she said, "Alice, we're going to look into this—but I'm sure there's nothing to worry about."

Alice Deams trundled off down the hall, but she didn't look convinced; maybe that rerun of an old TV show was haunting her—more likely, it was seeing David show up with his coroner's wagon a little too often.

Catherine kept telling herself that four elderly people dying in one such facility was not unusual. The heat was at dangerous levels and, even though Sunny Day was air-conditioned, somehow that might be a factor.

Later, as Catherine moved down the hall with her gear, Vega came out of Whiting's office and approached her. He did not look like a happy man.

"No good diagnosis from the doc?"

"The guy's such a basket case over this," Vega said,

shaking his head, "he might as well be one of the patients."

"What's his problem?"

"The usual—all he can see is lawsuits, malpractice insurance, and a bunch of really, really bad news happening on his watch."

"Can he live through one more question?"

They knocked at Whiting's office door and were again admitted. Within they found the frazzled physician sitting behind his desk, head in his hands. He barely looked up as they came in.

"Doctor Whiting," Catherine said, leaning a hand against the desk, not bothering to sit. "Mrs. Elliot had a visitor, another woman, who stopped by this morning right *before* Mrs. Elliot died. Is there any way of finding out the identity of the visitor?"

Whiting shook his head. "Other than our guard gate, we don't have sign-in books or video security or anything. We spend the money we make on the residents, and maintaining a top facility."

"Wouldn't security be part of that?"

"We have security locks on the doors, but that's about it. If Mrs. Elliot buzzed the woman in, or if one of the other residents simply opened the door for her, the visitor would be inside, and we'd have no way of knowing it."

"Isn't that a little risky, Doctor?"

"I don't really see how."

"If your patients are being murdered . . . you may. Thank you for your cooperation."

Whiting was staring into space as Catherine and Vega left his office.

Back in the corridor, Catherine asked the detective, "What do you think?"

"I think David better hurry up and get that damn autopsy done." Vega locked his eyes on Catherine's. "The other three residents who died this month? All were without families, too."

"All?"

"Not so much as a long lost cousin."

"Sam, that still doesn't prove foul play. . . ."

"Well, we'd better find out from Vivian Elliot's remains, because we sure won't ever know with the other three."

"Why not?"

"As part of a cost-cutting measure here at Sunny Day, all three were cremated. No family to have an opinion, much less a service."

"Four people in a month? It's not that weird."

"Catherine, you were investigating that room for quite some time. That gave Dr. Whiting and me time to go over the records. Four this month, three last month, three the month before that, two each in May, April, and March, three in February, three in January—David isn't the only coroner making pickups, you know. That's a grand total of twenty-two deaths in less than eight months."

He opened the door and held it for her as she walked out into the heat. After the air conditioning, it was something of a shock. She braced herself for another.

Glancing back at the detective, she asked, "Is that a high figure for a place like this?"

"Almost *double* last year's total for the whole year."

"Ooooh . . . and you think someone's 'helping' these people to get out of Sunny Day?"

Vega shrugged. "I was hoping you'd find out for me."

"Well, let's start with Vivian Elliot first. You'll check with that guard, to see if our visitor's name got written down?"

"Sure. On my way out, I will."

Catherine loaded the last of the evidence into the Tahoe. Warrick was still inside, getting the last of his gear.

She turned to hold the detective's gaze with her own. "What do you make of David's hunch now?"

Vega rubbed his forehead like he was trying rub all thought away. "He did the right thing—but I still hope he was wrong. The number of deaths this could make suspicious? . . . Guess what *that*'ll do to the homicide stats that the sheriff is loving so much right now?"

Catherine decided to take that as a rhetorical question; even if it wasn't, answering would be too painful.

After Vega had disappeared into his own vehicle, Catherine sensed Warrick at her side.

"You think we have a murder, Cath? Give me your best guess—I won't tell Grissom."

"Well, Warrick, if it is a murder, we could be looking at a serial killer, and possibly, oh . . . two dozen victims? Most of whom have been cremated. . . ."

Warrick's eyes glazed over. "I'm sorry I asked. . . . Keep your damn guesses to yourself, Cath."

She chuckled and got into the Tahoe, rider's side. But the chuckle caught a bit.

Something very evil might be turning Sunny Day cloudy indeed, in which case Catherine Willows doubted in the foreseeable future that she'd be taking a "normal" call again.

3

THE COFFIN HAD BEEN PLACED on a trio of sawhorses in the CSI garage to provide Nick Stokes and Sara Sidle with easier access. As if at a bizarre funeral, Nick leaned over the coffin and gazed down at the woman who lay peacefully within.

No way this youthful corpse could ever have been mistaken for fifty-something Rita Bennett. Nick had never met Rita Bennett, but—like most Vegas residents—he'd seen her hawking cars in commercials often enough to recognize the woman; with her aging showgirl glamour, Rita had been a local celebrity with even a certain national fame, considering how many people came to Vegas and at some point switched on a TV.

This woman—girl, really—was barely in her twenties, if that. Even after three months in a casket, pretty features presented themselves, the airtight vault having allowed the exposed flesh to gain just the barest patina of white mold, as if a spiderweb draped the girl's face. For a moment Nick had an odd, even haunting sensation—it was as though the woman's features were coming to him in a dream, through a translucent veil.

Though the desert air didn't cause human remains to break down in the manner common to more humid climes, moisture left in the body sometimes would be enough to give the deceased that distinctive sheen of white. Slim and auburn-haired, the woman revealed no visible wounds, the small trail of blood droplets on the pillow the only evidence, thus far, suggestive of violence.

Jane Doe had a straight, well-formed nose, bangs that nearly covered large eyes closed over high, slightly rouged cheeks. Nick grunted and twitched a non-smile. Even in death, Ms. Doe seemed to glow a little, the desert conditions not having yet begun the mummification that occurred to so many bodies in the Southwest.

Nick started with his 35mm camera, recording the casket and body from more angles than a fashion photographer at a *Vogue* shoot. When he was done, Sara stepped up to check under the woman's scarlet-painted fingernails, looking for any evidence that this possible victim might have gotten a piece of an attacker.

When finished, Sara shrugged and said, "Nothing."

"Fingerprints next?"

"Fingerprints next."

While Sara inked the woman's right hand, Nick used his Maglite to carefully search the area around the woman's head. The blood droplets were small, even, and dried to a dark maroon.

"Looks like she dripped," Nick said, "while the killer loaded her into the casket."

"We don't know there's a killer yet," Sara reminded Nick, though there was something unconvinced and perfunctory about her tone. "Anything under her head?"

"Can't see for sure. . . . Doesn't look like it."

"Anything else on the pillow?"

Nick eased the light around to get a better angle. "No . . . no . . . yeah! Yeah, right here—a short black hair." He snapped a photo of the strand, then used a pair of tweezers to pick it up.

"Not our vic's," Sara said.

"Let's hope it's the killer's."

"If there is a killer."

"If there is a killer. You have that feeling, too, huh?"

Sara frowned. "What feeling?"

Nick grinned. "That Gris is always looking over your shoulder."

She half-smirked, then said, "If there is a killer, that hair could still belong to somebody other *than* the killer. . . ."

"Always a possibility. And I don't know enough about funeral homes and cemeteries to guess how many people might handle a casket."

Sara—after carefully cleaning ink off dead fingertips—slipped the corpse's hand back into the coffin. "I oughta load these prints into AFIS."

"Go ahead—I'll stay busy, and by the time you get back, we should be ready to pull her out."

Sara nodded. "Back in a flash—don't you two run off."

Nick gave her half a smile. "We'll wait for you."

*   *   *

With Brass behind the wheel of the Taurus, headed for the cemetery, CSI supervisor Gil Grissom sat quietly in the rider's seat, oblivious to anything but his thoughts, sunglasses keeping out much more than just glaring morning sunlight.

Barring the possibility that they'd exhumed the wrong corpse, the body in the casket could only have been exchanged for Rita Bennett's in a small and very finite number of places: inside the hearse, during transport, which seemed improbable at best; at the funeral home; or the cemetery.

"Soooo," Brass said, voice a little loud. "Do I take it, then, that you think the switch went down at the funeral home?"

"Huh?" Grissom asked, blinking over at Brass, who glanced at him, shook his head, then turned back to the road.

"I asked," Brass said, just a wee bit testy, "if you thought the bodies were switched at the cemetery. When you didn't answer, I figured—"

"Sorry, Jim. Thinking."

"And what brilliant insight do you have for me?"

Now Grissom shook his head. "None. Too early."

Brass's tight eyes indicated he'd been mulling the same possibilities. "Wouldn't it be hard as hell to trade bodies at the cemetery, if there was a graveside service?"

"Graves aren't filled in till after the mourners are long gone."

Brass considered that. "But the casket's already been lowered. . . ."

"What goes down," Grissom said, with a tilt of the head, "can come up."

The detective turned the Taurus through the gates and took a right into the gravel parking lot fronting the tiny office of Desert Palm Memorial Cemetery, which looked like a homespun stone cottage . . . which just happened to have had a cemetery spring up around it. Brass parked, then Grissom and the detective exited the vehicle and the blast of hot air was immediately withering. A little bell clinked when Brass opened the door and the two men entered into more blessed air conditioning.

The room was small and square with one window next to the door and another on the far facing wall, the green of the cemetery visible through both. A battered gray battleship of a metal desk lurked to their right, a woman of about sixty seated behind it in a short-sleeve rust-colored white-floral-print dress.

Due to the lack of space, the desk was shoved back close to the wall and, although the woman wasn't particularly large, she seemed almost jammed behind and under it; a phone, a large blotter/calendar, and a walkie-talkie were arrayed on the desktop, but no pictures or other personal items, although a little stand with free dog-eared pamphlets—*Grief Is God's Way of Saying Goodbye, Eternal Rest for Your Loved Ones*—perched at the front edge, next to a brass nameplate that read "GLENDA NELSON—MEMORIAL CONSULTANT." File cabinets separated her from another desk, empty at the moment, and the rest of the cottage served as a small shop where artificial flowers could be picked up for mourners doing some last-minute shopping.

"Welcome to Desert Palm Memorial, gentlemen," the woman said in a mechanically mellow voice, with a practiced smile and wholly unengaged eyes. "I'm Glenda—how may I help you?"

Brass flashed his badge. "This is Doctor Grissom from the crime lab; I'm Captain Brass. We were here early this morning—for that exhumation?"

"Yes, of course! Mr. Crosby informed me of that."

"Well, that's who we're looking for—Mr. Crosby. Is he here this early?"

Her smile disappeared but her eyes came alive. "I'm sorry, Captain, but he's not scheduled to come in today."

Had Crosby taken the day off, Grissom wondered, because the cemetery manager knew they might be back?

"Is there any way I can help you?" the woman asked.

"It's about the exhumation—there's a problem."

She frowned and seemed to Grissom a trifle alarmed, despite Brass's typically low-key manner; problems around here were fairly limited—the guests at this hotel didn't likely complain much.

The woman said, "Well—Joe and Bob didn't mention any difficulties. . . ."

Brass said, "Thing is . . . is it *Mrs.* Nelson?"

Grissom felt this guess on Brass's part was substantiated by evidence: The woman had on a wedding ring and diamond.

"Yes—it's Mrs. Nelson. But Glenda is fine."

"Mrs. Nelson, we opened that casket at headquarters, and we found the wrong body inside."

She blinked and thought about that and then blinked some more. "How in heaven's name is that possible?"

"Our question exactly," Grissom said.

The woman glanced at the phone on her desk. Grissom could tell *she wanted to pick it up*, probably to call Crosby, but she didn't reach for it. She'd been left in charge, and she would deal with it.

Finally, Glenda said, "You'll have to forgive me . . . I wasn't here earlier. . . . Can you tell me the name of the person you were supposed to exhume?"

Brass said, "Rita Bennett."

"Oh yes. From television." Glenda rose and went to a filing cabinet nearby; computers had not come to Desert Palm—not uncommon with such facilities.

"Rita Bennett," she repeated to herself. She opened the second drawer down in the file cabinet and thumbed through a few files before finding the right one. "Section B, row 3, plot 117."

Grissom restrained a smile. On the green grounds nearby, with their headstones, eternal flames, and floral arrangements, loved ones rested in serene dignity; but here in the office, a file cabinet would do as final resting place.

Brass was checking his notebook. "That's what Crosby gave me—section B, row 3, plot 117. . . . Mrs. Nelson, do you mind walking us over there?"

Glenda frowned. "I can't leave my post," she said, as if that desk really were her battleship. "What would happen if someone came in?"

Grissom and Brass exchanged quick looks, both thinking the same thing: No MO was on file with LVPD for perps prone to heisting artificial flowers from cemetery offices.

"I'll tell you what," she said. "I could call Bob on the walkie and have him take you back."

"Why don't you?" Brass said pleasantly.

Glenda called Bob.

While they waited for Bob's arrival, Brass asked a few more questions, beginning with, "Mrs. Nelson, is there any way one body could be . . . exchanged . . . for another?"

Glenda looked at Brass like he'd just blurted a chain of obscenities. "Captain Brass! This is not a used parts store—urban legends about organ thieves do not take into consideration such small factors as embalming!"

"I didn't mean to suggest—"

"We take our responsibility very seriously!"

Grissom bestowed a charming smile upon her and said, "Of course we understand that, Mrs. Nelson—but it's not impossible, is it?"

The gentleness of Grissom's tone calmed her, and she considered the question finally. "We would notice a disturbance in the ground. We are *very* particular about our landscaping. We're proud of the service we perform."

"As well you should be," Grissom said with a nod and a smile.

"But what about," Brass asked, "*before* the body is buried?"

Shaking her head, Glenda said, "The caskets are locked, for one thing; and for another, there are people at the graveside for the service. . . ."

"Always?"

"Usually. Then after that, the vault is sealed and the vault with the coffin is lowered, then covered. The only people who would have any opportunity at all, for what you're suggesting, are Bob and Joe, and they're both good men."

"Can you give us their full names?"

"Roberto Dean and Joseph Fenway," she said, "but you're wrong about them."

Grissom smiled again. "We don't have *any* opinion about them, Mrs. Nelson."

Brass was jotting the names in his notebook when Bob showed up on a rider lawn mower. They thanked Mrs. Nelson again, and she nodded rather coldly, and they went out to greet their old friend Bob, who already knew what they needed from Mrs. Nelson's walkie-talkie summons.

In the Taurus, Grissom and Brass followed the rider mower around to section B, row 3, plot 117—and found the open grave from which they had removed the vault this morning.

"Bob," Brass said out the car window, "you're sure this is plot 117? Section B, row 3?"

Bob, sitting on his mower, made a face, and not a terribly intelligent one. "Think I'm likely to make a mistake like that?"

"Of course not," Grissom said. "But do you have a map, or chart . . . ?"

Bob had both—a map of the entire cemetery and a chart of section B. He withdrew them from a back pocket of his dirty jeans and unfolded them and came over like a carhop to share them with the detective and the CSI.

"Bob," Grissom said, studying the folded sheets, "this *is* the right grave, right?"

Bob nodded, and there was pride in his voice when he said, " 'Round here, guy's gotta be careful what hole he sticks it in."

"Words of wisdom."

Waving at Bob from the Taurus, they drove back to the office and found Glenda fidgeting behind her desk and not terribly happy to see them return.

"Are you satisfied now?" she asked. "It was the right grave, wasn't it?"

Brass shook his head. "Right grave—wrong body."

Glenda's voice got very small. "This is terrible . . . this is awful. . . . Our reputation . . ."

His charming smile nowhere in sight, Grissom said, "Don't you think the loved ones of the deceased deserve better than your concern for your reputation?"

Glenda swallowed and stared at nothing. "You're right. . . . I should be ashamed." Then she raised bright, alarmed eyes, gesturing to herself. "Certainly you people don't think *we* had anything—"

Brass hesitated, and Grissom stepped in. "We don't think one of your employees did this."

Relief softened her features.

"But," Grissom added, "that doesn't mean they didn't. We just have no evidence to support that notion . . . so we'll be looking other places."

Cutting in, Brass said, "Like for starters, the funeral home that officiated over Rita Bennett's service."

"Which one was that?" Glenda asked.

Brass's voice stayed remarkably even and sarcasm free. "We were kind of hoping you could tell us."

"Certainly." The file was still on Glenda's desk and she thumbed through it, then said, "Mr. Black's establishment." She found half a smile somewhere. "I should've known—they're the biggest mortuary in Las Vegas. They do most of the funerals involving clients with money. And this Rita Bennett? If it's not too disrespectful for me to say so? . . . She was loaded."

"We know," Brass said.

"Does that make this more suspicious?" Glenda asked, eyebrows knitted.

"You know," Grissom said, "I think finding the wrong body in a coffin is suspicious enough."

She was pondering that as they went out.

Nick had bagged two more of the short black hairs, as well as a thin white fiber, and tested the maroon drops (just to make sure they were blood), before Sara finally ambled back into the garage.

"What does our friend AFIS have to say?"

Sara shook her head. "Not chatty yet—Jacqui loaded the prints into Missing Persons, too."

"Anything?"

"Not so far . . . but it was just getting started."

Nick sighed and gestured toward the girl in the casket. "Well . . . time for the coming out party?"

"Why not."

Sara pulled over a gurney and locked down the wheels. As she did, Nick put his latex-gloved hands under the body's shoulders and lifted her up and out; there was some resistance before the head finally tore loose from the pillow, leaving behind a glob of dried blood and some hair.

Looking at the back of the woman's head, Nick could see the reason for the blood: a small black hole, no bigger around than a ballpoint pen.

"Entrance wound," he said.

Sara snatched up the camera and snapped four photos of the tiny aperture. "No exit?"

"Doesn't look like it."

She raised an eyebrow. "Small caliber, huh?"

Nick nodded. "Twenty-two, maybe."

"Or a twenty-five? . . . No sign of defense wounds."

Nick twitched a grimace. "She didn't see it coming."

"Maybe that's not such a bad thing. . . . The killer—we agree there's a killer now, right?"

"We agree there's a killer now. Right."

"The killer? He or she went to a whole *lot* of trouble to get rid of the body. This wasn't some random act."

"Not hardly." Nick trained tight eyes on Sara. "If the killer didn't know her, if it was just a thrill kill or something . . . why not just leave her where she dropped?"

Sara set down the camera. "Point well-taken—the killer must have known her."

"That makes sense, but Grissom'll want more."

"He's not the only one."

"Yeah?"

Sara nodded at the dead girl. "She wants it, too."

The two of them lifted the girl out of the coffin and carefully laid her on the gurney. To Nick, even though he held the heavier end, the young woman felt feather light. It was said that when a person dies, their body weight drops by twenty-one grams; but this vic seemed to have lost much more than that.

Releasing the brake on the gurney, Sara prepared to take the body over to Doc Robbins for the autopsy. "Coming, Nick?" she asked.

"Not just yet. Now that it's empty, I want to go over this coffin. . . ."

"Good thought. You want me to come back, and help?"

"No, that's okay. I got it—not really room enough for two of us, nosing around in there anyway. You see what the autopsy has to tell us, and I'll catch up with you."

She said, "Sure thing," then pushed the gurney across the garage and through the doors into the corridor.

Alone with the coffin and vault now, Nick went to work. He started with the casket: They had been very careful about touching it while they worked, and so the first thing to do was to fingerprint the box; their own prints would be on both the casket and the vault—no helping that. They had expected to find Rita Bennett inside, so, obviously, hadn't been particularly careful about not leaving fingerprints. Once they found the other woman, though, they had pulled on the ever-trusty latex gloves. . . .

He dusted the coffin all down the lip of the lid, along the handles, and around the locks. Normally, the only prints he would expect to find would be his and Sara's; but with the sealed vault protecting the fingerprints from the arid desert air, he hoped to get luckier than that. It was a time-consuming job, but whenever he found something, he'd transfer it to tape and move on. In the end, he collected more than two dozen prints. How many would prove to be his and Sara's remained to be seen.

With the outside of the casket done, Nick moved back to the interior. Using his Maglite, he combed the satin lining, looking for any clue that might lead him to identify either the victim or the killer. Having gone over the head end of the coffin thoroughly (while the body was still inside), he now began at the foot. Several small pieces of something black—dirt, he decided—were visible, where they had probably hidden under the heel of the girl's shoes. It was possible the dirt had come from Rita Bennett's shoes, too, but the Bennett woman would likely have been buried in clean, perhaps even new shoes, whereas the girl had been murdered, not prepared and spruced up for burial. Either way, he took photos of the dirt, then bagged it.

Next, Nick moved on toward where her knees had been, then her waist, her back, and, finally, again to the pillow. He was going around the edge one final time when he saw a fiber hung up in a tiny flaw in the wood. Using his tweezers, he picked up the fiber and examined it more carefully—white, and less than an inch long. To Nick it looked like plain old-fashioned white thread; but he knew that David Hodges, CSI's resident trace expert, might well give him enough info to start a Plain Old-Fashioned White Thread website. He bagged the thread and then went over the casket one more time, this trip taking an alternative light source along for the ride. . . .

The blood showed up under the UV light, all right, but he found nothing else. Spraying Luminol on the pillow didn't help either: The blood that he'd already seen—the drops and the small patch under the woman's head—was all there was to find.

Finally finished with the casket, Nick stared at the empty vessel, as if waiting for a wraith to rise up and reveal all to him. Unlikely as that prospect might be, he sure could have used the help.

He had precious little to go on. He moved on to the cement vault, but there was even less there. The vault would have already been at the cemetery, and the casket sealed inside there. The possibility remained that the body could have been transferred right before it went into the vault; but the concrete wrapper had been exposed to the desert climate far more than the casket sealed within, and Nick was not confident of finding anything.

Still, he went over it inch by inch. He dusted for fingerprints, went over the outside and the edges for signs of blood, and examined the inside with both his Maglite and an ALS.

And came up empty.

He cleaned up, stored the evidence, then caught up with Sara in the morgue. Though the garage had been air-conditioned, Nick's hard work had him sweating, and when he strode into the morgue, the chill of the room gave him a shiver.

Sara stood opposite Dr. Al Robbins, the body on the steel table between them. The unknown girl was naked now, her clothes in evidence bags on a nearby counter, where Sara had put them.

Sara had put on a powder-blue lab coat and latex gloves as she assisted Robbins with his duties. Following suit, Nick took a blue lab coat off a hook and slipped into it. As he crossed to the table, he pulled on a fresh pair of latex gloves.

A rather tall, balding, salt-and-pepper-bearded man, Robbins was looking at less than twelve months before his tenth anniversary with the LVPD. A man who seemed composed of equal parts cool professionalism and warm compassion, Robbins moved with the aid of a metal cane, which now leaned, as it often did when he was working, in a corner near the table. The father of three and a devoted family man, Doc Robbins had a daughter whose age would not be far removed from that of their nameless victim.

Nick settled in next to Sara.

"Find anything?" she asked.

He shrugged. "Couple needles in the haystack. We'll see." Looking down at the body, Nick saw that their victim not only had been disrobed, but her face had been scrubbed clean. She was even prettier than he had originally thought. "How about you, Sara?"

"I'll want to go over her clothes more thoroughly, later," Sara said.

Nick looked at Robbins. "And you, Doc? She tell you anything interesting yet?"

Robbins glanced up at Nick, then turned his attention back to the woman on the table. "Cause of death was a single gunshot wound to the back of the head. Small caliber, probably a twenty-two. But you knew that.

"Here's what you didn't know," Robbins continued. "The fact is that the young woman is . . . was . . . pregnant."

Nick's eyes widened. He bit the word off: "Really?"

The ME nodded. "About nine weeks."

"So what we may have here," Nick said, thinking out loud, "is a father who didn't *want* to be a father. . . ."

"What we may have here," Sara added, "is an abortion."

* * *

Located on Valle Verde Drive in Henderson, Desert Haven Mortuary was about as far from Desert Palm Memorial Cemetery as you could get and still be within the city limits. Caught in the noon rush hour, Grissom and Brass had taken the better part of an hour making the trek across town. When they arrived, the parking lot was practically full and Brass had to pull the Taurus over to the far side of the building.

Through shimmering heat they walked around to the front. Done in tasteful brick with white painted trim and pillars, the mortuary was but a single story, though an endless, rambling affair. No matter how far Grissom felt like he had walked, the front door always seemed to still be in the distance; he knew that inside were at least six, and maybe more, visitation rooms, as well as a cluster of offices, the workroom where the bodies were prepared, and the crematorium.

As with so many businesses, the trend in mortuaries had become the big ones eating up the little ones; many mortuaries had started out as "Mom and Pop" shops, passed down from generation to generation, but the advent of chains was ending that, as corporations bought out family businesses. Dustin Black's Desert Haven Mortuary was an exception to that rule.

Still family-owned, Desert Haven was simply too big and flourishing for the corporations to buy out. The Black family had been in the business since the late thirties, when Daniel Black (Dustin's grandfather) had purchased a very early embalming machine. Even though at the time Vegas was little more than a wide spot in the road, Daniel had set up shop as a mortician and the family's course and fortune were set from then on.

Now the biggest mortuary between California and Arizona, Desert Haven was a pillar of the community and the mortuary of choice for those who could afford it. Anyone who was anyone wouldn't be caught dead anywhere but here.

The packed parking lot told Grissom that even though it was barely noon, visitations were going strong. Elegant double doors with etched glass provided entry into a large foyer area where the CSI supervisor and the detective were met by a quiet young gray-suited greeter with a loud tie, a handsome kid in his very early twenties.

Grissom was a little surprised to be met by such a young representative—often, funeral homes used older people with a comforting manner. This boy seemed anxious.

"Which family, please?" the greeter asked.

"The Black family," Brass said.

"I . . . don't understand. . . ."

Brass showed his badge, discreetly. "We need to talk to Mr. Black."

"We're really very busy." This request seemed to have thrown the greeter. "I'm not sure . . ."

Brass smiled—it was a particularly awful smile. "You're not very high on the food chain around here, are you, son?"

"Uh . . ."

"Why don't you fetch your boss and let *him* make this decision?"

Dark eyes beneath heavy brows tightened in thought; then the boy nodded and gestured. "Would you mind waiting over there?"

"Not at all."

They stood off to one side as the boy disappeared down a hall and an older man, with hair as gray as his suit, met incoming guests, and led them to the correct viewing room.

Three greeters moved in and out of the action like a well-oiled machine. People came and went, and always the three men—all of a certain age and bearing—were friendly, courteous, and helpful. One approached Brass and Grissom to make sure they'd been helped; they said they had.

Grissom was impressed—he'd seen casinos with less traffic. He knew the studies showed four million visitors a year, five thousand new residents a month . . . but how many deaths per month? How many funerals? How many cremations? Of course, Grissom knew better than most the certainty of death. The Black business was thriving, a dying business only in the literal sense, never in the financial.

Soon the young greeter delivered a tall man in his forties with an oval, pleasant face and a monk-like bald pate.

Probably at least six-five, almost heavyset, the man—distinguished in a well-cut gray suit with a blue-and-white-striped tie—moved with confidence and grace where many his size might seem oafish; a wreath of brown circled the back of his head and he had a full but well-trimmed mustache under a slightly crooked nose and wide-set, sympathetic dark eyes.

The tall man automatically stuck out his hand. His voice was mellow and he spoke softly, almost whispering. "Dustin Black—you gentlemen are with the police?"

Brass shook Black's hand, making short work of it. "I'm Captain Jim Brass and this is Doctor Gil Grissom, our top criminalist."

"That sounds impressive," Black said with a ready smile. "Nice to meet you, gentlemen." The mortician turned to Grissom and shook his hand also. "I'm a big supporter of you guys. I'm a member of the sheriff's auxiliary."

"Great," Grissom said with a forced smile, wondering why morticians always reminded him of ministers—or politicians. This one—both.

"I hope Jimmy wasn't too awkward with you, gentlemen."

Brass said, "Jimmy's your young greeter?" The boy had long since disappeared.

"Yes. It's his first time up front, but we have four showings right now. Kind of . . . bumper-to-bumper here today."

Grissom asked, "Jimmy's last name is?"

"His name is James Doyle. Why?"

The CSI shrugged. "I'm just curious by nature, Mr. Black."

"Ah. Well, Jimmy's been with me for years."

"Years?"

"Starting in high school, then as an intern during mortician's school, and since his graduation. But I have a big staff, Mr. Grissom, over a dozen employees. . . . How may I help you, gentlemen?"

Brass glanced around at the people milling in the

foyer, some on their way out, others on their way in. "Is there some place we can talk in private?"

"Concerning?"

"Concerning," Brass said, "something you won't want us talking about in the lobby."

Black led them into a spacious room that was obviously his office.

As Grissom had expected, the mortician's inner sanctum was as tasteful and staid as the rest of Desert Haven—a large gleaming mahogany desk, a wall of beautifully bound, probably unread books, lithographs of wintry scenes of cabins and barns in New England. Behind Black's desk were three framed diplomas and a window whose wooden blinds were shut. A banker's lamp threw a warm yellow pool of light.

Two visitor's chairs in front of the desk looked freshly delivered and the whole office had a mild patchouli aroma to it. Black gestured for Brass and Grissom to sit as he circled his desk and dropped into his high-back leather chair.

This, Grissom thought, had to be the fake office, this sterile, impersonal room out of a furniture ad, a place where Black met with the grieving to offer support and advice in a blandly soothing surrounding; somewhere else in this building, an office with clutter and real work had to exist.

"How can I help the LVPD?" Black asked as he steepled his fingers under his chin and rested his elbows on the desk.

"Did you handle the Rita Bennett funeral?" Brass asked.

A confident nod. "Yes, her husband—Peter Thompson—is a close personal friend of mine."

Grissom found that people who claimed many "close personal friends" seldom had anything but acquaintances.

"Losing Rita," the mortician was saying, "was a tragedy—such a vibrant woman. She was a two-time president of the Chamber of Commerce, you know."

Brass asked, "Which of this large staff of yours was in charge of the arrangements?"

Confusion creased Black's face. "Why are you asking me about *this* particular funeral?"

"It's come up in the course of an investigation. We'd like to know who was in charge."

He shook his head, eyes wide, half in thought, half in surprise. "I can't imagine *what* type of investigation would involve Rita Bennett's funeral."

"Bear with us," the detective said. "Who was in charge?"

"*I* was," Black said. "I oversaw Rita's arrangements personally. . . . As I said, Peter is a close personal friend. Rita was as well."

Grissom said, "Must be painful."

Black blinked. "What?"

"We recuse ourselves in cases involving friends or family. Must be painful, preparing a close personal friend at a mortuary."

"That presumes, Doctor, uh . . . Grissom? Doctor Grissom. That presumes a negative aspect to what we do."

Grissom's head tilted to one side. "Not at all. A physician does not operate on family, healing art or not."

"You're correct," Black said, his voice spiking with defensiveness. "But I consider it an honor, a privilege, to use my art where friends are concerned. I would stop short of *family,* I grant you."

"The Bennett arrangements," Brass said, trying to get back on track. "Everything go as planned?"

Black clearly was working to hold back irritation. "I'm sorry, Captain. Unless you can give me some idea about why you're here, I won't be answering any more of your questions today."

"Then I'll *give* you an idea, Mr. Black—at the request of her daughter, Rita Bennett's casket was exhumed this morning."

The mortician frowned. "Why was that considered necessary?"

Grissom said, "Actually, that fact is not pertinent."

Black grunted a non-laugh. "How could the reason for an exhumation not be pertinent?"

"When the body in the vault is the wrong one."

Black blinked. "What?"

Brass said, "The body in the coffin was not Rita Bennett."

Black froze, then recovered quickly. "Gentlemen, I'm sure you mean well, but there's clearly been a mistake. That's just not possible."

Grissom said, "You're right . . ."

The mortician gestured, giving Brass a look that said, *You see?*

". . . there *has* been a mistake."

"Well, the mistake was not ours," the mortician insisted, and folded his arms, rocking back.

Brass leaned forward a little. "Rita Bennett was how old?"

"Late fifties. But she looked younger."

"Did she look twenty?"

Black's mouth dropped open, but no words came out.

"The woman in the casket," Grissom said, "was at least thirty years younger than the woman whose name was on the headstone. Any ideas?"

"There's no way . . ." Black's eyes flashed in sudden alarm. "And you think I . . . *we* . . . had something to do with this . . . this switching of bodies?"

Brass said, "We're making no accusations, Mr. Black."

"We're just gathering evidence," Grissom said.

"What evidence do you *have?*"

"A body in a coffin. The coffin belongs to Rita Bennett. The body doesn't."

"Who the hell was in the coffin?"

"We don't know yet; we're working on identifying her now. You also have to agree it would be very hard to switch the bodies after the vault was sealed and the grave was filled in."

Grasping at straws, Black said, "But not impossible."

"The grave hadn't been disturbed," Grissom said, "and the vault was still sealed tight when we did the exhumation. . . . The evidence indicates the switch was made *before* the vault was sealed."

"I understand why you're here," Black allowed. "That fact makes you think that, somehow, we here at Desert Haven had something to do with this unholy travesty."

Brass leaned forward. "You were in our place—what would you think?"

"I see your dilemma, but I must assure you, gentlemen, there's no way that anything like that could have happened at this mortuary."

"You seem quite sure," Brass said.

Black straightened. "Of course I am. I trust all our employees—we're family, here. And none of them would do *anything* like this, and anyway . . . it's just not possible. There are always too many people around."

Grissom asked, "Can you offer us another explanation for the confusion of corpses?"

The mortician thought about it. "No—honestly, I can't. And the truth is . . . I've never heard of anything like this before. It makes no sense to me. Why would someone trade one dead body for another?"

"Possibly," Grissom said, "someone with something to hide, Mr. Black."

"Something like what?"

"Oh I don't know—a body, maybe?"

4

WARRICK WAS BONE TIRED. Beat. The long night he'd recently endured promised to be followed by what was developing into an equally long morning and afternoon. With two dayshift investigators out sick, and three others working a gang-related shoot-out in the desert, that meant overtime for everybody, which meant more money . . . but then you had to have a life to spend it on, right?

While the nightshift CSIs hung around and stayed on call for anything that might come up, they pursued their current cases.

Instead of drawing the shooting, which would have been enough to perk him up, Warrick (and Catherine) had been dealt some fairly unexciting cards—namely, following up on David Phillips's hunch at the Sunny Day Continuing Care Facility.

Not that Warrick would give anything less than one hundred percent. Beneath a surface of steady purpose that could be mistaken for boredom, despite a wry and dry sarcasm that might suggest lack of interest, an alert, brilliant criminologist lurked behind the green eyes of Warrick Brown.

The CSI took his job dead serious, even when it meant fingerprinting bedpans and photographing walkers. Exploring a suspicious death at Sunny Day rest home may not be as compelling as working a gang-banger shoot-out, but it deserved all due consideration and deliberation. If foul play had been done to Vivian Elliot, then it was Warrick's job to speak on her behalf.

As Grissom had said more than once, "We can't give them back their lives, so we have to find the meaning of their deaths."

By this Gris meant, in his oblique way, that the only thing left for a murder victim was justice—what could still be done for Vivian Elliot was to find her killer, and deliver that killer for punishment.

If Vivian Elliot had been murdered. . . .

Such idealistic notions didn't mean Warrick couldn't run out of gas, however, and he was definitely driving on fumes. Catherine had shut herself in her office to (quote) catalog the evidence (unquote); but on his way to the breakroom, Warrick noticed no light under her office door.

Cath had to be just as whipped as he was; but she had remarkable recuperative powers—she could nap fifteen minutes and be good to go for another eight hours. Warrick, on the other hand, was pumping coffee through his system in hopes the caffeine would help fight the sluggishness that had settled over him like damp clothing upon their return from Sunny Day.

Uncoiling his tall frame from a breakroom chair, he strolled to the counter and poured himself another cup of what had purportedly once been coffee (the lab results weren't back yet). He turned and looked at the table and chair he'd just vacated, and considered sitting back down and closing his eyes for what he hoped would be a short nap . . . only he didn't have Catherine's ability to quickly recharge, nor was the caffeine in his bloodstream likely to cooperate.

Instead, he would go check with David about the autopsy on Vivian Elliot.

Assistant coroner David Phillips often worked alongside Dr. Robbins in the morgue, but when Warrick peeked in, Robbins was in the midst of an autopsy with Nick and Sara looking on and providing whatever assistance might be necessary—no David. And Warrick could see just enough of the corpse's face on the table to know she wasn't their woman from Sunny Day; this corpse was young, if a corpse could be said to possess youth.

Warrick moved on in his search, which didn't take long—the assistant coroner was two doors down in X-ray.

As Warrick walked in, David was adjusting the placement of the X-ray tube over Vivian Elliot's remains. An X-ray had a multiplicity of uses where live bodies were concerned; and Warrick had seen such machines used even on dead bodies, to locate bullets or other foreign objects.

But the CSI wasn't sure he knew what David was up to, using the thing with the late Vivian Elliot. . . .

"Hey," Warrick said.

"Hey," David said. He smiled, glad for the living company apparently, and gestured. "Step into my booth. . . ."

"Said the spider to the fly?"

"Or not. And don't worry: That glow-in-the-dark rumor you hear is a buncha b.s."

"I'm coming, teacher," Warrick said.

David led Warrick into the control booth and hit a switch. Soon David shut it down, and moved quickly out into the main room to remove that film from under Vivian's body and to place another a little farther down.

"I could use a hand," David asked.

Warrick joined David. "I don't suppose you mean applause."

"No," David said, with his nervous smile.

Warrick turned Vivian slightly so David could get the film under her. "What are you up to, David?" he asked. "Not playing another hunch, are ya?"

"Not exactly. More . . . trying to confirm a theory."

"Which is?"

"That someone at Sunny Day injected Mrs. Elliot with air, causing an embolism that sent her heart into seizure . . . after which she died."

Frowning and nodding, Warrick said, "You think the killer did that, to make the death look like a heart attack?"

"I do—and this is something a bad guy could get away with . . . *if* the good guys weren't looking for it."

Warrick raised one eyebrow and gave David half a smirk. "First you think the woman was murdered, because you've been called out to that nursing home too many times. . . ."

"Yes, that . . . but also, that none of the last four people who died at Sunny Day had any family to notify, remember."

"I remember . . . and now you're telling me the murder weapon is air."

"Well, here's another fact for you. . . ."

"Facts are good. We like facts a lot better than hunches."

"I know you do. The *others* have all been heart attacks, too."

Warrick felt his skepticism fading and his interest rising; the facts were beginning to pile up like a winner's chips, and something in David's earnestness made Warrick want to trust the assistant coroner's instincts.

After all, a "hunch" from an expert, the "instincts" of a professional, could be as valid as a physician's diagnosis.

"The theory is really pretty simple," David began. "The killer injects a fairly large syringe full of air into the victim. In Mrs. Elliot's case, the IV catheter gave the killer an injection site that wouldn't even be noticed. The air embolism reaches the heart and the muscle seizes. The outward symptoms are that the victim is having a heart attack, but the truth is . . . she's been murdered."

"Dispose of the needle," Warrick said, "and it's like you were never there."

"That perfect crime you hear so much about."

"Not so perfect."

David frowned. "Where's the flaw?"

Warrick grinned. "Somebody smart like you, David, can see right through it."

David beamed, but Warrick didn't let him bask in the praise, asking, "What do you hope to accomplish with the X-ray?"

With a gesture toward Vivian Elliot, who posed under

the X-ray's eye, David said, "The cardiovascular system is a closed system. Despite the fact that there's over 60,000 miles of arteries, veins, and capillaries, the air bubble will show up on an X-ray. If there's an air bubble, Vivian Elliot was murdered. If not . . . I've wasted a lot of valuable time, and this poor woman is still dead."

"Dead not murdered."

"Dead but not murdered. . . . Only, doesn't this woman have a right for us to make a serious effort to find her cause of death?"

Warrick gave David the complete and profound answer the assistant coroner was hoping for: "Yes."

They moved the body and took more X-rays. Working in silence for a while, they finished their task in a relatively short order.

Holding up the last undeveloped X-ray, Warrick said, "Is this the only way to find out if she was murdered by an air bubble?"

Shrugging a little, David said, "There is one other way, but I don't think Doctor Robbins would ever go for it."

"Well, try me."

David's eyes flicked wide. "Well . . . you crack the chest and fill the cavity with water. If there's an air embolism, it'll leak out, and the ME will see bubbles in the water."

"That's nasty," Warrick said.

"So is murder."

"Good point."

"I've heard about this technique, but I've never actually seen anyone do it in practice. The X-rays are still our best bet."

"Well," Warrick said, "let's take these vacation pics to one-hour photo, and see if our next trip's gonna be to track down a murderer. . . ."

Catherine stretched her arms wide, yawning herself awake. The windowless office was pitch-black, the only light coming in under the crack of the door. She checked the iridescent dial of her watch and realized she'd slept five more minutes than the twenty she'd planned. Blessed with an uncanny internal clock, Catherine seldom had use for an alarm and only wore a watch for confirmation of what her body was already telling her.

She reached over to switch on her desk lamp. When her eyes had adjusted to the light, her gaze came into focus on the framed picture of her daughter Lindsey. The blonde-haired, blue-eyed girl smiled at her and Catherine smiled back. Not long ago, she might have felt a twinge of guilt over the many hours she spent away from the child.

But she had come to terms with her single-parent status, and dedication to her job was something to feel pride about, not shame. Catherine's nightshift work actually made it possible for her to spend more time with Lindsey than many a working mom . . . although in doubleshift marathons like this one, that notion was put to the test.

At a counter in her office, Catherine reached at random for one of the brown bags of evidence from Vivian Elliot's room. After breaking the seal, she realized she'd picked up the one filled with sheets. She set that aside, saving that for the layout room where she'd have more space. For now, she selected the bag containing Vivian Elliot's personal belongings; inside was a smaller bag of valuables as well, which she'd picked up from the Sunny Day office.

She carefully emptied the contents of the smaller bag onto the counter: three rings, a watch, a gold cross necklace, a wallet, and a cell phone. A few years ago, the cell phone might have surprised her, with a woman of Vivian's age; but now the whole world seemed to have one, and many seniors in fact carried cells for I've-fallen-and-can't-get-up emergencies.

The rings were a gold wedding band with an attached diamond engagement ring, possibly a karat, and a decorative number with a diamond-centered ruby rose. The rings weren't cheap, but they probably weren't from Tiffany's, either.

Likewise, Vivian's gold cross necklace was a nice mid-range piece that looked like she'd had awhile, but had taken good care of it, as with her rings. The watch was a Bulova that looked to be about ten years old; it seemed as well-maintained as the other pieces, and the band was a replacement one, fairly recent.

Nothing terribly significant—a woman with enough money to have nice if not lavish things, which she took care of and (as in the case of the Bulova) made last.

The cell phone was what really interested Catherine—cells often held a wealth of information just waiting to be tapped.

She jotted down the numbers from the speed dial—only three, but one might be the mystery woman who had visited Vivian right before her death. Next, Catherine checked the call log, which gave her the last ten numbers Vivian had dialed, the last ten calls she'd received, the calls she'd missed, and the in-box for text messages, though the latter was empty. Several of the numbers turned up again and again, most likely Vivian's closest friends. Women Vivian's age often rivaled teenage girls for phone time with their gal pals. . . .

In fact, one of the numbers showed up on the speed dial, the missed calls, the received calls (three times), and the dialed calls (four times). That would be where Catherine would start, figuring that number (keeping in mind the late woman's lack of family) probably belonged to Vivian's best friend.

Catherine was going through this list of cell phone numbers when she realized neither she nor Warrick had gotten a log of the calls to and from Vivian's room at Sunny Day. She made a mental note to ask Warrick about it, then picked up her own cell phone and dialed Vega.

"It's Catherine, Sam—got time for a question?"

"From you, always."

"Did you and Doctor Whiting discuss the telephone in Mrs. Elliot's room?"

She could hear the smile in Vega's voice as he said, *"I was wondering when the most diligent CSI in Vegas would get around to asking about that."*

Sighing her own smile, Catherine said, "Oh-kay, smart guy—don't gloat. *You* may pull a double shift someday."

"How about last week? . . . Anyway, there's only two numbers on the list, and frankly I haven't had time to run 'em yet."

"Got a pen or pencil?"

"Shoot."

Catherine gave him the number she figured belonged to Vivian's best friend.

"What are you, Catherine—psychic? That's one of the two!"

"The number comes up on her cell phone a buncha times. Give me the other one, would you, Sam?"

He did and said, *"If we have the best friend, we may have the mystery guest at Vivian's room."*

"Did that mystery guest sign in, Sam? At the guard shack?"

Vega sounded a little embarrassed as he admitted, *"When I went back to check, the shift had changed. I need to go back and talk to the guard who'd've been on duty. Sorry."*

"Hey, even the most diligent detective can get overworked, and tired. . . ."

Vega laughed. *"Okay, Cath. We're even."*

And they broke the connection.

Catherine set the phone numbers aside to run later. No point in getting too deep into this, until she knew what, if anything, they were into . . . and that she wouldn't know until after the autopsy.

The final item before her was Vivian's wallet.

A black nylon tri-fold number, the wallet had one zipper pocket on the outside. Catherine opened it, finding nothing. She undid the snap and laid open the wallet on the desk. The first section was the fold-over outside, the next a coin purse with what Catherine assumed was Vivian's spare car key and a dollar-and-a-half in change. The front of the coin purse was a four-pocket credit card holder with a cardboard educator's discount card from a bookstore chain, an insurance card, a Visa card, and an ID from a cost club superstore.

Not much help.

The final section held Vivian's driver's license and a clear plastic credit-card holder with four more credit cards—a department store, a house-and-garden store, a women's clothing store, and a MasterCard. Behind the three sections was a wider one with seventy-two dollars. Absently, Catherine wondered where Vivian Elliot's checkbook was. Other than that, everything seemed pretty normal with this woman—exceedingly normal.

Over the next two hours, Catherine cataloged the evidence and sent the biohazard materials off to the lab. She'd already spent the better part of a day on the Elliot case and still didn't even know if it was a crime.

Time to go to the morgue. . . .

There, she found David, Warrick, and Dr. Al Robbins hard at work. Robbins was performing the Vivian Elliot autopsy with David's help while Warrick looked on.

She slipped on a lab coat, gloves, and a paper mask, now matching her outfit to the others; they might have been a team of surgeons saving a life, not investigators probing a death.

Stepping up next to Warrick, across the table from David and Robbins, she asked, "Anything?"

Robbins said, "How about cause of death?"

"How about it?"

"Myocardial infarction."

"Heart attack." Catherine frowned in thought, looking at the exposed organ in question. "Caused by?"

With a facial shrug, Robbins admitted, "I think David's probably right . . . about the air embolism."

Warrick said, "Shared that theory, did he?"

This was the first Catherine had heard about it.

Robbins nodded, his eyes on his work. "I had gone through the autopsy already, and could find no good reason why this woman was dead. Her heart seized and stopped . . . but there was no real damage apparent before the event. She wasn't overweight, didn't have high cholesterol, minimal artery blockage— nothing, really, for a more or less healthy woman of her age."

"Natural causes maybe?" Warrick said with a silent chuckle. "A euphemism for 'who knows *what* killed her?'"

"A woman of her age could have a heart attack," Robbins said, "in the 'natural' course of events . . . but that doesn't really happen much. Something went very *wrong* with this woman's heart . . . and I can't find any reason for it."

David stepped forward. "Doc—I, uh . . . took X-rays of her when we brought her in."

Robbins looked surprised. "You did?"

David swallowed. "I thought, you know . . . you might want them."

The medical examiner gave David a sideways look. "Good idea."

David's relief was palpable.

"David," Robbins said patiently, his eyes on his assistant. "What do they say in Missouri?"

David thought about that. Then he asked, tentatively, "Show me?"

"Right. Why don't you?"

Spring in his step, David stepped out of the room, then came back in a flash carrying a large manila envelope. He handed it to Robbins, who grabbed his crutch and limped over to the light box on the wall.

Warrick flipped the switch and Robbins slapped the film up and began to study it. Moments later, he shook his head and moved on, taking that X-ray down and putting up another. On the second film, he found what he was looking for.

"There," he said, pointing to a dark spot near the center of a chest X-ray.

"What are we looking at, Doc?" Warrick asked.

"The dark spot in the pulmonary artery, Warrick. That's an air bubble."

Catherine drew in a breath, then asked, "And just how did that air bubble get there?"

Robbins gave her a grave glance. "I found no needle sites other than the IV catheter. . . . My guess is that's where it went in."

"Easy entry," Warrick said.

But Catherine was fighting the urge for immediate acceptance of the theory with a Grissom-taught insistence upon other options. "Could the air bubble be left over from the trauma of the car wreck?"

Robbins shook his head. "Doubtful."

"Possible?"

"Anything's *possible* . . . but my judgment is, in that case, it would have come up before, if it was going to. I think David is right."

Warrick's expression was grave. "You think we have an angel of mercy on our hands, Doc?"

"God knows it wouldn't be the first time someone killed the people they were supposed to be caring for."

Catherine turned to Warrick. "Get Vega on the cell.

Tell him it looks like murder and we're going to investigate it like one. Until or unless we find evidence that it wasn't . . . this case is a homicide."

"I'm with you, Cath. But what do you want me to tell Vega we're doin' next?"

Catherine thought for a moment, then said, "The lab work is going to take some time . . . and we've already been to Sunny Day. . . ."

"Vic's house?"

"Vic's house."

An hour later, Vega's Taurus pulled up and Warrick parked the Tahoe in front of Vivian Elliot's stucco home on Twilight Springs in Green Valley.

An average home for the neighborhood, pretty much matching the tile-roofed design of the others, the Elliot place had a lush green lawn that looked freshly mowed, a pair of well-tended small bushes on either side of the front door.

Catherine had gotten Vivian's keys from the late woman's purse. The missing checkbook hadn't been in there either, and Catherine could only wonder if someone had made off with it. She unlocked the door and the three of them entered.

The entranceway was small, a hallway, really, that led to the back. To her left, Catherine saw a short cherrywood table with a ceramic pot in which a peace lily bloomed.

"Lawn looked mowed," Warrick said, looking around. "That lily's healthy enough."

"Thriving," Catherine said.

"The Elliot woman was in the hospital for weeks,

before transferring to the rest home. Somebody's coming around to take care of things."

Catherine shook her head, half-smiled. "A little eerie, don't you think? Air conditioning on, everything so normal—like Vivian's going to walk in the door, any second."

"If she does," Warrick said, *"that* won't be normal."

The hallway was inlaid Mexican tile and Catherine could almost feel its coolness through the soles of her shoes. She turned to the right and found herself in a small but immaculate living room, a flowered sofa against one wall, two chairs framing the picture window onto the front yard. An entertainment center occupied the opposite wall, complete with Book-of-the-Month-Club–filled bookshelves on either side of the 27" TV. The wall to the left had a potted plant in either corner and was home to an array of photos at various heights in assorted frames—family photos, most taken before the death of Vivian's seventeen-year-old daughter.

The girl looked similar to Lindsey—same big blue eyes and wide, easy grin. Her hair was darker than Lindsey's, but that was the only real difference. Catherine felt as if she were looking into the future. Then, recalling the fate of this child, she felt a chill . . . that chill of dread that only a parent, contemplating the death of a child, can understand.

Off the living room was a small study, pine-paneling with nature prints beautifully framed, built-in bookcases with volumes on hunting, fishing, baseball, and football, and a desk with a computer, circa 1995.

"Husband's home office," Catherine said.

"Clean as a whistle," Warrick noted. "But not in use for some time, I'd say."

Back in the living room, the trio compared notes.

"Nice enough digs," Warrick said.

"Clean," Vega said.

"Think somebody went over it?" Warrick asked.

"It's not a crime scene, Warrick," Catherine said. "A cleaning lady cleaned it."

"Or her friend?"

"Or her friend. . . . Let's get the lay of the land before we get too carried away."

"You're the boss," Warrick said.

She looked at him.

"What?" he said.

With a wrinkled grin, she said, "It's just . . . every time you say that to me, I look for sarcasm and can't quite find it."

He grinned. "Maybe you're not good enough a detective to."

The house was only one story, and their tour didn't take long. When Catherine went back into the hallway, she followed it to the entrance of the combination kitchen/dining room, where another hall peeled off to the left. Catherine went that way, the other two right behind.

The first door on the right was a bedroom—a small tidy room with a sewing machine, bed, and dresser. A '70s vintage portable stereo was on a stand under a bulletin board adorned with David Cassidy pictures cut from teen fan magazines. On the pink bedspread were stuffed animals with big eyes that stared accusingly at the investigators.

"Daughter's room," Catherine said.

"Doesn't look like it's been changed much," Warrick said, "since the kid's death."

"Sewing machine is probably Mom's."

"I don't know, Cath. Kids sew, too."

"Mine doesn't."

Warrick lifted his eyebrows. "Neither does this one, anymore."

There were more green plants in here—three sitting on a ledge attached to the windowsill. Healthy looking.

Across the hall was the bathroom and, beyond that, another bedroom—this one rather anonymous with a desk with a computer and a plastic organizer filled with files; on a small table next to the desk, an AM/FM radio. Across the room the glass face of a small TV on a stand winked at them. Green plants dotted this room, too.

Next was a bedroom, obviously Vivian's. Two pictures sat on the far nightstand—her husband, her daughter. Yet another TV perched on a table on the wall opposite the bed. A giant armoire filled the wall next to the door and a long dresser consumed the far wall, leaving barely room to walk around the bed. Catherine managed, though, and beyond the armoire was a door to another, smaller, bathroom. Judging by the toothbrush, hair spray, toothpaste, and other products Catherine had seen no sign of in the other, bigger bathroom, this was the one Vivian had used most of the time.

"Big house like this," Warrick said, "nice, too—and she relegates herself to, essentially, a small apartment. Rest of the place is like a shrine to her lost family. Sad."

"A lot of older people make their lives simpler,"

Catherine said, "and keep to a room or two in the house."

"Maybe. That's not what this feels like."

Catherine didn't express her agreement with Warrick, but she felt it. Being alone wasn't always a good thing. . . .

More plants in the bedroom, everything freshly dusted.

"Someone was definitely taking care of this house while Vivian was laid up," Catherine said in the hallway.

"Who?" Warrick asked.

"This doesn't feel like the Merry Maids. I'll bet it's a friend."

The trio of investigators headed down to the living room to share their thoughts. Vega began by catching them up on what he'd found out already.

Referring to his notes, Vega said, "Husband's name was Ted, retired electrician, passed away last year at seventy-five. Daughter was Amelia, died in a car accident when she got hit by a driver who fell asleep from too much weed. That was 1970—they never had any more kids."

Shaking her head, Catherine said, "They went over thirty years without their child . . . a loss they obviously never got over . . . then Ted dies, and Vivian is left alone. Who would want to harm *her?*"

Vega shrugged.

"Hate to borrow trouble," Warrick said, a humorless half-smirk digging a hole in one cheek, "but how sure are we that Vivian's recent car crash was an accident, and not just the first attempt to kill her?"

"Pretty sure," the detective said. "She got hit by a drunk who ran a red light on Tropicana."

"You're positive," Warrick said.

"If it was a murder attempt, it was a lousy one."

"Why do you say that?"

Vega shrugged again. "Drunk ended up dead."

Warrick's eyebrows lifted. "Guess that qualifies as 'lousy.' "

"Also qualifies as freaky," Catherine said.

Vega frowned. "Why's that?"

"Two deaths in one family? Both getting hit by impaired drivers?"

"I've seen weirder," Vega said.

They all had—and they let it go. For now, at least.

Warrick said, "So—Vivian wasn't a target, in the car crash . . . but could she have been trying to kill herself, in the manner her daughter died?"

"That's sick," Vega said.

"I've seen sicker," Warrick said.

They all had.

"What are you saying, Warrick," Catherine said, shaking her head, smiling in a glazed fashion, "that Vivian waited, engine idling, till a drunk came by, to pull out in front of?"

And they let that go, too.

"Maybe it was just bad luck," Vega said. "In this town, I've seen worse."

And indeed—they all had.

Catherine said, "Only now, Vivian's luck's finally turned from bad to just plain shitty."

"Got that right," Warrick said.

"No disagreement here," Vega said. "Now what?"

"Now," Catherine said, glancing at Warrick, "we really get to work."

"I'll take the living room," Warrick said. "You wanna start with Vivian's bedroom?"

"It would seem the most promising place, yes."

"Sounds good."

Vega said, "I'll canvass the neighbors and see what I can come up with."

"A best friend, maybe?" Catherine said.

"A best friend, maybe."

The two CSIs unloaded their equipment and went back inside while Vega headed for the house next door. Warrick and his crime-scene kit took the living room while Catherine and her kit entered Vivian's bedroom.

But Catherine started with the dead woman's private bathroom, going through the medicine chest first. Other than some Paxil, which treated anxiety disorders, she found nothing stronger than ibuprofen. The Paxil made sense—a seventy-one-year-old woman living alone in a house with shrines to the family taken from her, her only child gone at an early age. Who the hell wouldn't have anxiety attacks?

In the bedroom, Catherine went through the dresser and came up with nothing in particular, then the armoire, where she found some of Ted's old clothes; she got no help from the TV stand or the bed either. She moved on to the other, larger bathroom and discovered nothing that seemed pertinent. The sewing room-cum-Amelia shrine gained the CSI nothing. Finally, she went into the bedroom/office.

Though she expected little in the way of help from the computer, you never knew what information lurked inside those devious little boxes. She photographed the machine and all its connections, then called Tomas Nunez, a computer expert who had worked with her and Nick on several cases—not a cop, but an outside specialist on the LVPD's approved list.

When she finally got him, Tomas said, "Hola, *Cath—good to hear your voice!*"

"That's just because you know my voice means greenbacks. . . . Where are you, anyway? Sounds like a circus!"

"Sports bar at the Sphere, doing a favor for a friend."

"How long are you going to be?"

"You got business for me?"

"Yeah."

"Well, business trumps favors. What's the sitch?"

She explained and gave Nunez the address.

"Twenty-five minutes," he said.

He was there in twenty.

If the neighbors had seen Tomas Nunez arrive, they were now busy locking themselves in their houses, assuming the Hell's Angels had invaded this quiet respectable 'hood. Six feet and rangy, the top computer expert in Vegas had slicked-back black hair, a mustache that looked like an old shoelace, and a face with the color and sheen of your favorite brown leather belt. He wore black motorcycle boots, black jeans, a black leather vest, and a black T-shirt with the logo and name of a band called, provocatively enough, Molotov.

As she walked him back to the bedroom office, Nunez cased the place.

"You say she lived here alone?" Nunez asked.

"Yeah—husband's been gone almost a year."

Inside Amelia's shrine, Nunez looked at the computer on the desk and shook his head. "I'll buy you dinner at the top of the Sphere, if the old gal has anything more exciting than a cake recipe on this puppy."

Catherine said, "Prejudging, are you?"

"Hey, I'm an expert. That's an expert opinion."

"We don't do 'opinions' at CSI."

He gave her a sideways look. "You gotta hang with somebody besides that Grissom character, Cath; you're gettin' contaminated. Hey, you know I'll do a first-class job."

"For first-class pay."

"You want the best, don't you? You ready for me?"

She nodded. "I took pictures of everything. The husband's computer is in his study, but it's unlikely to have anything of interest."

He unhooked the monitor, keyboard, mouse, speakers, and phone line. Then he packed the CPU under his arm and headed for the door. "I'll put this in the truck," he said.

Fifteen minutes later, the process had been repeated with the computer in the study. He hauled that CPU to his vehicle, then returned to the living room to tell Catherine, "Two days." he said.

"Two days for *cake* recipes?"

"Two days for two computers."

She just looked at him.

He said, "You think I've got nothin' else on my plate? Nothin' and nobody else in my life but Catherine Willows, girl detective?"

She kept looking at him. She was using her best half-smirk and single arched eyebrow.

So, of course, finally he caved. "Give me a call to-morrow. I might have something."

She beamed at him. "I know you'll come through. *Adios,* amigo."

He grinned and waggled a finger at her. "Patronize me, *chica,* and see where it gets you."

Then he and the two CPUs were gone.

With the computers out of the way, Catherine went back to the bedroom office and started going through the desk and all the files. Soon she found Vivian's checkbook in a drawer. That was something, at least.

The balance was just over a thousand dollars. Catherine found paperwork from a lawyer and a financial advisor, as well as envelopes with statements from June that Vivian had evidently opened just before her car accident.

Vivian had a money market and an annuity. It wasn't a lot, but it was far from nothing. Murders were committed in Vegas for pocket change every day. And Catherine estimated the value of Vivian's estate at just about a hundred thousand, not figuring in the house.

She joined Warrick in the living room. "Anything?" she asked.

He shook his head. "Not unless you count chicken pot pies in the freezer or a half-bottle of Canada Dry in the fridge. How about you?"

She told him about the money.

"With hubby and baby gone," Warrick said, "who inherits?"

She shrugged. "Don't know yet. The mysterious guest? The best friend? Who are maybe one and the same."

"None of this makes sense," he said, shaking his head. "Why would anyone go to all this trouble to kill this woman?"

Catherine said, "The money isn't chump change—but other than that, I can't see *any* reason to do it."

"Where's the money now?"

"Still invested, I'd assume. I'll call the financial guy and the lawyer when we get back to the office."

Warrick looked at her for a long moment, then his voice grew quiet and serious. "Please tell me we're not on a wild-goose chase."

"Wouldn't be the first time."

"Yeah, but as backed up as we are right now, can we *afford* chasin' wild damn geese?"

"Doc Robbins thinks it's murder. That air bubble says so. Can we afford not to chase what might be a wild goose, if somebody murdered the nice old lady that lived here? She may have had a sad little life, in the end . . . but it was hers. And she deserved to finish it out at her own speed."

Warrick's expression had sobered. He nodded. "Yes she did . . . and she deserves our best damn effort."

"Yes she does."

Vega came in through the front door.

"What did you find out?" Catherine asked.

Vega had that wide-eyed look he got when he finally had something. "The neighbor to the west thinks Vivian was the most wonderful person she ever met. She's a widow lady, too. Her name's Mabel Hinton—*she's* the one that's been watching the house."

Jazzed by this news, Catherine asked, "Did she visit Vivian early this morning?"

"Like, right before she coded?" Warrick put in.

Vega said, "She says no. But do we buy it?"

Catherine held out open hands. "Who else could be our mystery lady? And now we have a suspect."

"Yes we do," Warrick said.

"Hold those horses, gang," Vega said. "This gal's a basket case. She hadn't even heard about Vivian's death before I *told* her. She came frickin' un-*glued!*"

Warrick said, "She could be acting."

"If she is, Meryl Streep could take lessons."

But Warrick pressed. "Was this Hinton in line to inherit any of that dough?"

"No! That's the crazy thing—*no one* was. Several neighbors told me Vivian planned to leave everything to some charity!"

"We'll have to confirm that," Warrick mumbled.

Catherine said crisply, "Anybody say *which* charity?"

Vega shook his head. "No one knew that for sure."

"Another reason for me to call the lawyer," Catherine said, almost to herself.

Vega threw up his hands. "Everybody said Vivian Elliot was the *grandma* for the whole neighborhood! Everybody's kids were welcome and accepted here. She baked more cookies than Mrs. Fields."

"Greeaat," Warrick said.

"Well, *somebody* didn't accept her," Catherine said, hands on hips. "Where there's a murder, there's a motive."

"We look for evidence, Cath," Warrick said.

"The evidence can show us the motive."

"True."

Vega's and Warrick's skepticism was understandable to Catherine. It certainly seemed like they had a crime—someone had to have administered Vivian her deadly shot of air . . . but who in hell would want to murder the neighborhood's grandma?

And why?

5

DUSTIN BLACK HAD about as much color as his clients before the makeup; unlike the dead he served, however, he was sweating.

Right now the obliging mortician, leading them down a hallway at Desert Haven Mortuary, was assuring Brass and Grissom that he could not understand how they might think the bodies had been switched here at Desert Haven; and, still, the answers Black gave to their questions all sounded just . . . off.

"Gentlemen!" Black said, up ahead, holding open a door for them. "This is the preparation room. . . ."

They stepped into a large chamber that might have been a morgue—three steel tables in the middle, walls lined with countertops and cupboards. Over to the far wall was a double door; three embalming machines lined up against the near wall. At this moment, the room was empty of either the living or the dead—not counting Brass, Grissom, and Black, of course.

Brass asked, "What's the procedure, exactly?"

Black frowned in confusion. "I'm not sure I know what you're asking."

"The whole deal—the funeral home routine."

"We don't really think of it as a 'routine,' Captain. . . ."

Vaguely uncomfortable, Brass tried again: "What happens when, say, my ex-wife dies?"

Grissom gave Brass a quick arched eyebrow, as if to ask, *Wishful thinking?*

The mortician tented his fingers; his voice assumed a slow, calming cadence. "You would call us, of course. We would arrange to pick up the body of the deceased, wherever the final moments took place—her home, perhaps, a hospital. . . ."

"Keep walking me through, Mr. Black."

"All right. We would bring your ex-wife here . . . you'd be handling the arrangements yourself, despite being divorced?"

"Let's say we're *not* divorced."

Black frowned again. "But you indicated this was your ex-wife. . . ."

Fighting exasperation, Brass said, "Hypothetically speaking, Mr. Black—make it my wife."

"Sorry. . . . In that case, you and either myself, or one of my staff, would make decisions concerning the disposition."

"Disposition? Of the body, you mean?"

A solemn nod. "Either burial or cremation. We offer both services here."

"Always nice to have options," Grissom said pleasantly.

Brass winced; his headache was coming back. He

managed to get out, "Let's say I decide to bury her."

"Then," the mortician said, "the next step would be embalming, which would happen in this room. . . . Did you want me to go into that process, in detail?"

Brass held up a palm. "No."

Black nodded again, exhaled, gestured to one of the trays. "After embalming, your wife would be dressed in clothing selected by you or other family members, and our cosmetics expert would make her up for viewing, probably using photographs you provided for reference as to her preferred style. May I assume there'd be a viewing?"

"You may."

"The viewing would probably be the afternoon and/or evening before burial, with visitation, followed by the service, perhaps in the morning or afternoon, after which your wife would be laid to rest for eternity."

The only thing creeping Brass out more than the mortician's Addams Family demeanor was Grissom's little smile; the CSI was standing there, arms folded, lapping up the information.

Black was saying, "As you can see, gentlemen—the deceased would always be with someone . . . and frankly, in this controlled environment and situation, I don't begin to know how someone could ever have exchanged the bodies."

Grissom's smile disappeared. "You don't see anywhere in this process when the corpse would be left alone for a significant time?"

"We don't use the term 'corpse' in this facility, Doctor Grissom. It's disrespectful."

Grissom's brow knit. "It is?"

Brass said, "Could you answer Doctor Grissom's question, Mr. Black?"

"Certainly. I don't see any window of opportunity for this ghoulish thing to have occurred."

Grissom asked, "Obviously, the visitation is attended by friends and family, looking at the . . . body in an open casket? So a switch can't have occurred until afterward."

"Yes, of course."

"So, any switch would have to have been made after that. Visitation for Rita Bennett was the night before the service?"

"Yes."

"Is there anyone here after hours?"

Black looked uncomfortable. "No, but obviously the mortuary is locked for the night and our security is first-rate."

"You use a service?" Brass asked.

"Yes—we have a contract with Home Sure Security. They drive by on a regular basis . . . and all the doors and windows are wired. No one gets in without the security code."

"Who has the code?"

"Myself and five employees."

"Which gives us at least six suspects," Grissom said, almost to himself.

"Suspects?" Black's eyes and nostrils flared. "I cooperate like this, and you call me, and my people, suspects?"

Grissom, innocently, said, "Why? Is that another disrespectful word here at the facility?"

"You have no right—"

"We have every right, Mr. Black," Grissom said, his tone as gentle as his words were not. "Someone switched those bodies, and the best opportunity was right here in your shop. The body that replaced Rita Bennett's was that of a murder victim . . . and that makes this a homicide investigation. So, yes—you and your people are all suspects."

Black's eyes darted around the empty room, as if confirming no one was hearing Grissom's accusations.

"Now," the CSI said, "let's get back to how and when the bodies could have been switched."

"I . . . I *still* don't see how . . ."

"The visitation is usually the night before the service—was that the case with Rita Bennett's funeral?"

"Yes."

"You're sure."

"Positive."

"That means her body spent the night in here . . . with no one watching over it."

Black shrugged dismissively. "That's a question of semantics—yes, no one was in the building; but Home Sure Security was on the job every second. Besides, in Rita's case, a second, shorter visitation took place an hour before the service."

Grissom frowned in thought. "The coffin was open?"

"Yes."

"Do you close the coffin *before* or *after* the service?"

"Generally, before."

"Specifically," Grissom said, "in Rita's case . . . before or after?"

Obviously struggling to control his temper, Black said, *"Before."*

"Good. All right—what happens after you close the coffin?"

"I need to back up a step. . . ."

"Please."

The mortician folded his hands in a dignified manner over his slight paunch. "Behind the curtain, the family has one last opportunity to privately say goodbye to their loved one before the coffin is closed. The family is escorted to their seats and we then shut and lock the coffin, and open the curtain to begin the service."

Brass asked, "You were personally with Rita's body during that entire time?"

Impatience edging his voice, the mortician asked, "Why don't you follow me to the chapel? I can show you in detail."

"Please."

The trio walked across the preparation room and out the double doors, which took them to a short, dark corridor. A few steps more led them to another set of double doors, one of which Black opened, and bid Grissom and Brass to pass through, which they did.

Brass found himself facing the pews of the chapel, as if he were officiating the service. He was standing near where the coffin would have been.

Grissom and Black flanked the detective.

"That," the mortician said, gesturing, "is my station during most services . . . and I was here for Rita's."

Brass said, "But you could see Rita the whole time until the coffin was closed."

"Yes."

"How did it proceed from there?"

"The family left after the service to gather in a receiving line. While that took place, we wheeled the casket out the back, through the doors we just entered . . . to the hearse."

The detective frowned. "Who's we?"

"Myself, Jimmy Doyle . . . you met him . . . and the new guy, Mark Grunick."

Brass jotted down the names. "And the three of you loaded the coffin into the hearse?"

"Yes, then Jimmy drove the hearse and I chauffeured the limousine, conveying the family to the cemetery."

"No stops along the way?"

Black shook his head. "Short of a flat tire or some other emergency, that's just not done. One does not make a detour from a funeral procession into a 7-11 for a package of gum."

"Everything, as you remember it, went off without a hitch?"

"Yes."

"And yet, somehow, some way . . . Rita Bennett's body was not in that casket."

Black held out his hands, palms up. "There's always the cemetery, you know. All I can say is, I spent the whole day with Rita—she was in the casket from the time we got her into it."

Brass turned to Grissom. "Any thoughts?"

After considering for a moment, Grissom said, "Not now. We just keep gathering information, which will lead us to more evidence and eventually we'll find Rita Bennett."

Black said, "She deserves a proper burial. To rest in peace."

"Mr. Black," Grissom said, "we also have a murdered woman who took Rita Bennett's place in your casket—and she deserves to rest in peace, too . . . with her killer tracked down, and punished."

Any sign of anger or irritation banished behind his calm facade, Black said, "I wish you gentlemen nothing but good luck in your endeavors. I only wish I could be of more help."

Grissom smiled. "Oh, Mr. Black—you will be."

As Brass and Grissom found their way out, the detective could almost feel the mortician's uneasy eyes on them.

Sara and Nick were in the breakroom, huddling over a file folder, when Brass and Grissom strode glumly in.

The usual exchange of "hey's" was foregone as Brass poured himself some coffee and Grissom went to the refrigerator for a bottle of water.

"I'm not feeling a good vibe," Sara said. "No lucky streak in Vegas this morning?"

Grissom was in the middle of a long pull on the bottle and Brass, stirring in creamer, answered her question. "Nothing at the cemetery—less at the mortuary."

"Come on," Nick said. "Somebody has to know something."

Brass offered up half a smirk. "They knew all kinds of things, both places—just nothing useful."

Grissom said, "We don't know enough yet to make that call—something important might be right in front of us, and we don't have the context yet to make sense of it."

Brass said, "It would be nice to *at least* know who our girl in the box is."

"I can brighten your day, then," Sara said. She showed them a photograph. "Meet Kathy Dean—before she stowed away in Rita Bennett's coffin."

Grissom and Brass came over to view the snapshot of a smiling, pretty teenage girl.

"Came in just a few minutes ago," Sara said.

"Fingerprints do it?" Grissom asked.

Nick said, "Naw—AFIS was no help. Missing Persons matched our morgue photo of her with this one."

"So who is Kathy Dean, exactly?" Brass asked, the young woman's photograph in one hand.

"A nineteen-year-old, just out of high school, getting ready for college."

"And never made it."

"No. Disappeared about three months ago."

Grissom's eyes widened. "Around the time of Rita Bennett's funeral?"

Sara smiled without humor. "Actually? Within twenty-four *hours* of Rita Bennett's funeral."

Grissom asked, "Disappeared from where?"

Sara glanced down at the report before answering. "She came home from a babysitting job, talked to her parents for a few minutes . . . they both said she seemed fine, normal, so on . . . then she went up to bed. Her parents woke up the next morning, her bed was empty, what she'd been wearing in her hamper, and her nightgown on her bed . . . and no Kathy."

"When we found her," Grissom said, "she was fully

clothed. . . . Did she change clothes and sneak out, or was she forced to get dressed, and abducted?"

Sara lifted an eyebrow. "The parents say they didn't hear anything unusual during the night."

"And what does the evidence say?"

"We've just started going over the reports in detail, but what it looks like? She sneaked out. Bedroom window showed no signs of forced entry . . . and the only sign that anyone other than the family was in that house was a semen stain in her bed."

Grissom found that interesting. "Fresh?"

"No. Predating the disappearance."

Brass asked, "So there was a boyfriend?"

Nick shrugged. "Hard to say."

Brass's eyebrows rose. "There was semen in her bed but it's hard to say if she had a boyfriend?"

"The parents don't think she had a regular boyfriend. Matter of fact, they thought their daughter was still a virgin."

Sara picked it up. "According to these reports? Mom and Dad had no idea who Baby Bunting was seeing, or for how long."

Nick was nodding sagely. "These are parents who kept their daughter on a pretty tight leash."

"She was nineteen," Grissom said.

"And just out of high school, and an only child, still living at home. Gris, parents of a girl that age don't always know what their 'little girl' is up to."

"Tell me about it," Brass said.

"It gets worse," Sara said. "During the autopsy, Doctor Robbins discovered a pregnancy—just over two months."

"Let me get this straight," Brass said. "She disappeared, when . . . around Memorial Day?"

Nick nodded. "May twenty-ninth."

"And was buried on . . . ?"

"Same day . . . at least that's when Rita Bennett was buried."

"But she'd been pregnant since . . . ?"

Sara said, "Sometime around the end of March."

Brass shook his head. "And her parents didn't know she was seeing anyone?"

Nick gave up half a wry smile. "You know how it is."

"Yeah," Brass said gloomily. "Little too well."

Sara said, "A nineteen-year-old girl who's been sheltered like that? Out in the world but living at home? Sometimes, she can lead a double life. She could have multiple boyfriends . . . guys . . . She could be breaking loose, and throwing caution . . . and birth control . . . to the wind."

Grissom said, "Let's lay off on the speculation. Back to the facts—what are the parents' names?"

Sara checked the report. "Jason and Crystal Dean. He owns and manages half a dozen strip malls. Pretty well off, but not rich. They live on Serene Avenue in Enterprise."

Brass said, "Anybody tell them about their daughter yet?"

Nick said, "Not yet. We just identified her right before you two showed up. We decided we better read the report first, familiarize ourselves with the Missing Persons case."

"Good call," Grissom said.

"All right," Brass sighed. "Hell. . . . I better go tell

them." He turned to Grissom. "You want to come along?"

"I'm going to pass," Grissom said. "Everybody says my people skills are weak, so I'll leave it to the master."

"Gee thanks."

"Anyway, I need to see what I can find out about Desert Haven Mortuary."

Sara said to the detective, "Hey, I'll go . . . if you want someone to tag along."

"Wouldn't mind," Brass admitted.

Hair ponytailed back under a CSI ball cap, Sara followed Brass out into the parking lot where another scorcher of a day awaited. She wasn't looking forward to the long drive out to Enterprise, but the CSIs were the ones who had found Kathy Dean and Sara felt a responsibility to be there when the news was delivered to the victim's parents.

The Taurus's air conditioning fought valiantly, but with the sun beating down, the car interior remained barely bearable. At least it was a straight shot down Rainbow Boulevard from the CSI lab on Charleston to Serene Avenue, if they could survive the stoplights and traffic.

By the time they made the turn onto Serene, despite the air conditioner's best efforts, Sara could feel sweat trickling down. Vegas had a lot to offer those who came here for more than a few days vacation; but today would not make a good argument for it.

The Dean home was an impressive two-story white stucco with a tile roof and many windows, shades down all round; a two-car garage to the right of the house seemed buttoned up tight, and the yard was dirt with scrub brush, similar to the xeriscaping so prevalent these days in Vegas, but rather more barren-looking. Though the house said its owners had money, the place possessed a forlorn, even vacant look.

Sara hoped that someone was home, or she and Brass would have to sit in the car waiting and roasting.

As the detective and CSI strode up the driveway, Sara wondered if the desolate look of the house was a response to Kathy's disappearance; or perhaps the Deans had always liked their privacy. Brass rang the bell more than once, but no one answered.

"Check the back?" Sara asked.

Brass shook his head glumly, and pointed. "Fenced-in yard."

"Talk to the neighbors?" Sara hoped Brass would say yes just so they could step inside an air-conditioned home.

Before Brass could answer her question, though, a white SUV pulled into the driveway. They watched as two people got out—the driver a tall, big-shouldered man in a green Izod shirt and jeans, his wispy blond hair combed straight back, making no attempt to disguise a high forehead; his female passenger wore khaki cotton shorts and a v-necked peach-colored T-shirt. She came around to join him, a good seven inches shorter than his six-three, probably about a hundred pounds shy of his two-twenty, with long curly hair whose auburn color was at once remindful of Kathy Dean's.

There could be little doubt that this was Kathy's mother, Crystal, whose big, dark eyes mirrored her daughter's as well (though Sara had only seen Kathy Dean's eyes open in the Missing Persons report). Not surprisingly, the couple stared openly at Sara and Brass, but with the seasoned look of parents whose shared tragedy had put them in enough contact with police to know that this was an official visit.

Showing his badge in its wallet, Brass approached them, saying, "Captain Jim Brass—CSI Sara Sidle. You're the Deans?"

"I'm Jason Dean," the man said, crisply solemn. He shook hands with Brass. "This my wife—Crystal. Kathy's mother. . . . That's why you're here? Kathy?"

"Yes. Yes it is."

Crystal Dean was staring at them with unblinking eyes, understated but unmistakable fear in her expression.

"Do you think we could go inside and talk?" Brass asked.

Before anyone could take a step, tears began to trickle down Crystal Dean's cheeks. Her husband slipped an arm around her, and she said, her voice trembling, "We've been waiting for over three months. Can't you just . . . tell us? Tell us *now?*"

"Darling," Jason Dean said, "let's go inside and talk to these nice people."

He was gently trying to steer her toward the house, but she was having none of it.

Her unblinking eyes were frozen in something near rage. "Tell us what you know—*please!*"

"We have found your daughter . . ." Brass began.

Sara edged closer to Mrs. Dean, without the woman noticing (she hoped).

"If Kathy was all right," the mother said, "you'd say

so, wouldn't you? You'd be smiling! You wouldn't look like . . . like you were going to cry."

"Your daughter is gone," Sara said. "I'm so sorry."

"What . . . what right do you have to be sorry? You think we didn't know she was dead? After all this time? You think . . . you think . . ."

Crystal Dean started to fold in on herself, but both her husband and Sara were ready. They each caught her under an arm, then guided her toward and onto the front walk. Mr. Dean tossed his keys to Brass, who caught them with one hand. The detective moved out in front of the procession and somehow managed to pick out the right key on the first try; he flung the door open and stepped out of the way as Sara and the husband drunk-walked the distraught Crystal Dean inside the house.

The front door opened on the living room and Sara helped Dean get his wife to the couch, where he plopped down next to her.

He said to Sara, "Thank you," and seemed terribly composed as he slipped his arm around his wife's shoulder and drew the crying woman to him. Then he shattered into tears and Sara, though she had just met these people, felt her own eyes well up and she turned away.

She and Brass moved to the far side of the spacious living room, which was furnished in white leather, the tables and entertainment center a dark, polished cherry. Family pictures adorned the walls and end tables, like an audience for a prominent high school prom-dress portrait of Kathy that presided over the fireplace. To Sara, the room told the story of a fortunate family, successful, even affluent, blessed with closeness and everything an American household could hope for—except a happy ending.

Sara whispered, "Are they up to this?"

Brass whispered, "Give it a few seconds. We'll follow their lead."

Perhaps two minutes later, Jason Dean called them over to the couch, where they stood before their host like defendants awaiting a jury's decision.

With his wife's face still buried in his shoulder, Jason Dean asked, "Where is she?"

"In the coroner's care," Brass said.

Sara could only admire the delicacy of the detective's phrase; how horrible it would have been for these parents to have to hear, *At the morgue.*

Pulling away a bit from her husband, her face slick with tears, Mrs. Dean asked, "Can we go to her?"

"Of course," Brass said. "But it would be helpful if we could talk now, here, first."

But both parents were shaking their heads.

Firmly, Dean said, "We want to see our daughter—*right now.* This ordeal has lasted over three months—anything else . . . *everything* else . . . can wait."

Brass glanced at Sara, who shrugged.

"Would you like us to drive you?" Brass asked.

In his office, Grissom sat at his computer going over Clark County records pertaining to Dustin Black and Desert Haven Mortuary. He wasn't sure what he was looking for, but he was reasonably certain that he would know it if he saw it. He would seek the business's financial records next. Evidence wasn't always a fingerprint on the murder weapon or a tire track on the shoulder of the road. Sometimes, Grissom knew, evidence could be far more subtle—it wasn't always tangible. . . .

A knock at his open door alerted Grissom.

Sheriff Rory Atwater leaned there, with a casualness that was as studied as his mild smile.

"Hope I'm interrupting some real progress you're making," he said, his tone friendly, "on the Bennett case."

"Sheriff—actually, it's the Dean case."

"That's the young woman in the casket?"

"Right. Kathy Dean."

"Spare a second to talk?"

"No," Grissom said.

Atwater chuckled, as if Grissom had been kidding, and ambled in, the closing of the door behind him signaling just how un-casual this meeting was. Then he dropped himself into the chair opposite Grissom, leaning back, tenting his long fingers.

"Have you found Rita Bennett?"

"Not yet."

"Where are you with that?"

"She's not the priority, Sheriff."

"Her body is missing, and she's not a priority?"

"I didn't say she wasn't 'a' priority—I said she wasn't 'the' priority. The murdered teenager we found in her casket is."

Atwater nodded knowingly, then said, "Rebecca Bennett is quite distraught over this."

"Really. I didn't think she and her mother were close."

"How close would somebody have to be to their

mother, Gil, to be upset about having her body go missing?"

"That would probably vary."

Atwater sighed. "Look, I'm not trying to tell you how to do your job—"

"Good."

"But I don't know how long we can keep this from Peter."

"Peter Thompson? Rita Bennett's husband?"

"Right."

Grissom never failed to be surprised by the behavior of the human animal. "You haven't told Mr. Thompson that his deceased wife is missing?"

Atwater sat for a long moment before shaking his head. "When Brass told me Rita was missing, I hoped you and your crew would solve this quickly, and we could avoid telling Peter . . . you know, until we'd recovered Rita's body. I mean, why cause him any needless aggravation or grief?"

"Because he's a contributor to your campaign, you mean?" Grissom blurted. Immediately, he wished he could withdraw the words.

Surprisingly, Atwater took no offense. The smile was gone, and he merely seemed weary. "Politics is a dirty word to you, Gil—I know that. You found my predecessor, Brian, far too political for your taste."

"We worked well enough together. You know our arrest and conviction record."

"I do. But your conflicts with Sheriff Mobley are frankly legendary. Let me explain something to you—in the kind of clinical, even scientific manner you should understand. Look around you—look at the technological wonders at your fingertips—look at a crime lab, a facility, that is among the finest in the nation."

"I don't take that for granted," Grissom said.

"With all due respect, Gil—I think you do. You disdain politics—but where do you think facilities like this come from, in a state where there's no damn income tax? Figure it out, man."

Faintly chagrined, Grissom said, "You have a point, Rory. Easy enough for me to criticize, while you're in the trenches, trying to get me my toys."

"Thank you. Now, you may not like it, but the outcome of this case has political ramifications."

"What are you asking me for, Rory?"

"Just your best."

"No problem," Grissom said.

Atwater nodded, then his eyes narrowed. "Do you think Peter Thompson could have killed Rita . . . and then somehow switched the bodies to keep us from exhuming Rita and doing a proper autopsy?"

"You mean, is he a suspect?"

"Yes."

"Everyone related to the case is a suspect. But I would say, doubtful."

The sheriff fidgeted and Grissom wondered how big a campaign contributor the Bennett-Thompson family had been.

"Talk me through it," Atwater said.

"Well . . . not to bore you with details about the funeral home and its layout and how they do things . . . Thompson would literally have had to smuggle his wife's dead body in and out while he was with the funeral party. Seems absurd on its face."

Atwater nodded. "I just want to make sure we're covering our—"

"Bases?"

"Right. Gil, could it have been a mistake? You know, a mix-up, either at the mortuary or cemetery?"

"On any given day there's, what? Maybe two dozen funerals in Vegas, spread over a dozen or more mortuaries? Then on top of that, we have two corpses in the exact same casket at the exact same time? The odds would seem astronomical."

"Who is this Kathy Dean?"

"A young woman someone killed—we're working on why and who. But someone intentionally put her where she was, so she wouldn't be found. What better place to hide a body?"

"But what about the damn body that had to be *displaced?* What good does it do to get rid of one body and have another on your hands?"

"That would seem to be the question. But the answer is wrapped in somebody hoping to get away with murder . . . who won't, if we have anything to say about it."

"And that someone isn't Peter Thompson."

"I don't think so. But if it is—and even if he's your biggest contributor, Sheriff . . . he will go down for it."

Atwater slapped his knees, then rose. "Wouldn't have it any other way."

And the sheriff was gone.

The four of them got into the Taurus, Brass driving, Sara in front, the Deans in the back. As they pulled away from the forlorn stucco house, Brass knew he would have to steer the conversation as much as the car. Sara would expect this and just sit quietly and follow his lead. They were less than a block when he started offhandedly in.

"What kind of student was Kathy?" he asked.

"Straight A's since junior high," Mrs. Dean said. "Never anything lower than a B before that."

"Involved in a lot of activities?"

"Band, chorus, drama club, Spanish club . . . in the spring she ran cross-country on the track team."

Looking in the rearview mirror, Brass could see that he was already doing well—Crystal Dean wasn't thinking about where they were going . . . the morgue . . . or what they would see when they got there . . . her daughter's body. She was, instead, answering his questions, keeping her daughter alive.

"She liked cross-country?"

In the rearview, Mrs. Dean actually smiled a little. "She said she loved the quiet of running alone."

Brass said, "Really into it, huh?"

The father finally spoke up. "She was, but she always kept her grades up. That was her number-one priority."

"What about college?"

Mrs. Dean sniffed, said, "She was . . . was going to start at UNLV. This fall."

Dean added, "She had a dual scholarship. Track and academics."

"Wow. How often does that happen? . . . Lot of her friends going to UNLV, too?"

"Not really," Mrs. Dean said. "Kathy didn't have all

that many friends. Don't get me wrong—she was no wallflower, she was popular, in her way."

Sara smiled and glanced over her shoulder. "Lovely girl."

Her mother went on: "Kathy knew lots of people, had many acquaintances, she just wasn't . . . close to a lot of them. She was more of a loner. Focused on her studies."

Sara asked casually, "She have a boyfriend?"

"No!" Dean said.

The response was loud (and surprising) enough to make Sara jump a little.

Brass wondered why the reaction had been so strong, but decided not to push it. He glanced over at Sara and gave her a signal with his eyes to keep carrying the ball for a while.

Sara said, "I know how it is. I was into my studies so much I just didn't have time for boys."

"That's how it was with Kathy," Dean said. "She had her studies and her running to concentrate on. Anyway . . . do I have to tell you what boys are after? Just one thing. One thing."

At this moment Brass decided that today would not be the day to inform these parents that their daughter had died pregnant.

A silence fell over the car and Brass wondered if he'd pushed too hard. The couple seemed to be clamming up now, and that wasn't going to do any of them any good, including the late Kathy. With another glance in the rearview, he saw Mrs. Dean pat her husband's knee. Dean's tears were flowing again and Brass figured he'd blown it.

He had needed to get as much as he could out of them, on the ride over. Once they saw their daughter on a morgue slab, they would be in no shape or mood to give Brass the information he so needed.

Then, out of nowhere, Mrs. Dean said, "You know, on top of school and her running? Kathy had several jobs, too."

"Jobs?" Brass asked. "Really? Busy as she was?"

"Yes! She worked as a waitress at Habinero's Cantina, and she still had some people she babysat for. She even volunteered at the blood bank."

"Habinero's Cantina?" Brass asked. "Is that—"

Dean said, "On Sunset. In Henderson."

And then the Taurus was pulling into the CSI HQ parking lot. As Brass ushered the Deans out of the car, Sara went quickly inside to set things up with Dr. Robbins.

Soon Brass was escorting the grieving parents into a small tile-walled room just off the morgue. A curtain covered the upper half of one wall—a big window. The only furniture were two chairs and a metal table against a wall, a box of tissues at the ready.

The Deans huddled together in front of the curtain, his arm around her shoulder, her arms around his waist. Brass had already explained what would happen—that when he opened the curtain, Sara would uncover the face of the victim for confirmation that this was indeed their daughter.

There really wasn't any doubt, but this was a formality that could not be avoided.

"Ready?" Brass asked as gently as he could.

Dean let out a breath and tightened his grip on his wife's shoulder. He nodded.

Brass pulled the drawstring and the curtain slid away to reveal Sara standing on the other side of the glass; she was no longer in the baseball cap and her expression was solemn, dignified. A body under a sheet on a gurney was between Sara and the picture window.

When Brass nodded to her, Sara pulled the sheet back to reveal Kathy Dean from the neck up.

Jason Dean groaned and his wife lurched into his arms. Then the mother took a quick step forward, hand splayed against the window opposite her daughter's face, the mother's breath fogging the glass. They were both crying now, Mrs. Dean whimpering and her husband's lip quivering, though neither spoke.

Brass was a hardened homicide detective; but he was also a father. And right now he hated his job almost as much as he would love that job when Kathy Dean's killer was in his custody.

When Brass nodded again—his signal to Sara to cover the body—Jason Dean waved for her to stop and she froze, the sheet not yet up over the dead girl's features.

His eyes still locked upon his daughter's still countenance, Dean said, "She looks so . . . beautiful . . . normal . . . natural, almost as if she could just . . . sit up."

"My baby," the mother said.

An edge in his voice, Dean said, "What killed her?"

"Gunshot to the back of the head," Brass said.

"Ooooh," Mrs. Dean said.

"She felt no pain," the detective said.

Both parents looked at him, though Mrs. Dean's hand remained touching the glass.

"Is that . . . is that true?" the mother asked.

"It's true," Brass said. "She never knew what happened. I will say to you as the father of a girl not much older than your daughter . . . that's a blessing."

"Where did you find her?" Dean asked.

"Why don't we sit down and I'll give you all the information," Brass said.

Dean turned back to face the window, as did his wife. They looked at their little girl for another long moment before Sara finally covered Kathy Dean's face with the sheet and—as Mrs. Dean reluctantly broke contact with the glass—Brass pulled the curtain, banishing the image that neither parent would ever forget.

"Sit—please?" Brass gestured toward the table and the tissue box.

Both parents shook their heads, holding their ground, standing there waiting for more, when they clearly had already had more than enough.

Brass had no choice but to give it to them. "As to where your daughter was, we found her in a grave in the Desert Palm Memorial Cemetery."

Dean was understandably incredulous. "Cemetery . . . how the hell . . . ?"

Brass filled them in quickly, giving them the broad strokes of the fantastic situation.

"We're doing our best to find out how she ended up there," Brass told the startled parents. "Obviously we suspect the one who took her life did this thing as well."

Brass eased the stunned mother and father out into the corridor.

"You can understand," he said, "why we'd like to talk to you about Kathy's activities around the time she disappeared."

Before the door closed, Mrs. Dean stopped, looking back toward the curtained window. "When can we take her out of that dreadful place?"

"Just a little longer," Brass said. "Now that Kathy's case is a homicide, we have to make sure we have all the evidence we can before we release her body."

Mrs. Dean recoiled. "I want her out of there *now!*"

"Mrs. Dean, please, I can certainly understand your feelings . . . but your daughter's body is our only link to her killer."

"I don't care! I want her out of there!"

Jason Dean kept an arm tight around his wife. Wild-eyed, Mrs. Dean strained to get back into the viewing room; finally, Dean got control of her and looked pleadingly at Brass.

Keeping his voice low, his tone even, Brass said, "Our crime scene people are the best. You met CSI Sidle—she cares deeply about this case, I promise you."

Dean said, "What kind of 'evidence' can you hope to find at this late date? We need to deal with this—we have arrangements to make. We want our daughter, Captain Brass."

"Sir—there might be some microscopic clue that can lead us to her killer. Finding that piece of evidence might be the only way to stop whoever did this from doing it again . . . to someone else's daughter."

Mrs. Dean turned toward him and her expression had an alertness, as if Brass had slapped her awake. "You really think you can catch whoever did this?"

"I can't promise you. But our CSIs are the best, anywhere. And I promise you I will do *my* best. I see your daughter and, frankly . . ."

Something happened to Brass that hadn't happened to him on the job for a long, long time: He felt his eyes filling with tears.

He swallowed and said, "I see your daughter and I see my daughter. Do I have to say more?"

Mrs. Dean studied Brass for a moment, then she touched his cheek, very gently, and allowed her husband to steer her away from the viewing room door.

They were still trudging toward the exit when Sara came out of the morgue and rejoined the somber parade.

They all got into the Taurus for the long ride back to the Dean home. More traffic made this ride slower than their initial trip to the house on Serene Avenue. Brass watched in the rearview mirror as the Deans huddled in the backseat. Now, though, Dean seemed to have gone inside himself while his wife stared out the window, seeing nothing.

Finally, Mrs. Dean turned to look at Brass in the mirror. "I don't know what we can tell you that we haven't already told the other officers. When Kathy was a missing person."

Brass smiled mildly. "Well, let's go over it again and see what we can see."

Mrs. Dean nodded slightly. "What do you want to know?"

"How about her job at Habinero's Cantina? How did she get to work?"

"She had her own car."

Dean said, "2003 Corolla. Your crime scene people impounded it after she disappeared."

Sara caught Brass's eyes and mouthed: *Dayshift.*

Dean was saying, "They found Kathy's Corolla abandoned in a parking lot on Maryland Parkway. We still haven't gotten it back."

Brass ignored the small jab and asked, "How'd Kathy like her job? Been there long?"

Mrs. Dean gave that some consideration, then said, "She worked there for two years or so—started right before her seventeenth birthday."

"Did she enjoy it there?"

"Most of the time."

"Not all of the time?"

In the mirror, Brass saw Mrs. Dean wipe her nose with a tissue. "She did have some trouble . . . with a boy she dated there for a while?"

"What kind of trouble?"

"I said it was a boy."

Dean piped in to say, "He couldn't take the hint that she had other, more important priorities in her life than dating."

Definitely not the day to tell the Deans that they had almost been grandparents. . . .

Brass said, "What kind of trouble *exactly?*"

"He wouldn't stop calling her," Mrs. Dean said, "but that was right after she started at the restaurant. She'd only been there a month or so when they began dating. It must have been over in, oh . . . two months?"

"Did you tell the Missing Persons detectives about this?"

Mrs. Dean thought for a moment. "I may have mentioned it, but maybe not—it was such old news."

Brass stopped for a red light and turned to look at Mrs. Dean. "Do you know if the detectives looked into it?"

"They never said."

"The boy's name?"

The light turned green and Brass got them moving again.

"Gerardo Ortiz."

"Did the trouble with this boy come to any kind of a head?"

Dean harumphed. "Kid must have finally taken the hint. He stopped calling. I was just about ready to track him down and beat the ever-living crap out of him."

Brass glanced in the mirror and saw the anger reddening Dean's face. "But you're over that now . . . right?"

Rubbing his forehead and obviously forcing himself to calm down, Dean said, "Yeah . . . yeah, I'm over it. Anyway . . . that kid quit the restaurant, disappeared, far as I know."

"No idea where he is?"

"No! And good riddance, too."

Brass pulled into the Deans' driveway and they all got out.

As they walked up the sidewalk, Brass fell in alongside Dean, whose arm was around his wife. "Do you think the Ortiz boy was capable of harming your daughter?"

Dean paused and looked hard at Brass, eyes glittering. "For his sake? . . . I hope to God not."

They went inside the house and sat in the living room, the Deans on the sofa again, Brass and Sara in two wing chairs angled next to the couch. The grouping was great for facing the entertainment center, but not wonderful for eye contact during conversation, much less a police interview.

"We'll look into Gerardo Ortiz," Brass assured them. "But now I'd like to hear more about her other jobs. She have any problems at the blood bank?"

Both parents shook their heads.

Mrs. Dean said, "She handed out cookies and drinks to the people who gave blood. Everyone loved her."

Someone didn't love her, Brass thought; *or maybe somebody had loved her too much. . . .*

Sara asked, "What about the babysitting jobs? Isn't that more a job for junior high, middle-school girls . . . ?"

"Maybe so," the father said. "That's when Kathy started, and she held on to some of her 'clients' . . . mostly people who were friends of ours, who Kathy knew and got along with well. She *loved* kids, so she was a natural at babysitting."

Sara asked, "Would you mind if I took a look around her room?"

Nonconfrontationally, Dean said, "The other officers did that, already . . . when she first disappeared?"

"I understand, but fresh eyes might turn up something."

"Be our guest," Mrs. Dean said. "Her room is upstairs—last on the left."

"Thank you. Jim, could I have the keys? I need to get my kit."

Brass passed her the car keys.

"Kit?" Dean asked.

"Crime scene kit," Brass said. "Sara doesn't want to contaminate any evidence, should she find something."

"I see. But her bedroom isn't a crime scene, surely."

Brass thought, *If she was abducted, it could be,* but said instead, "Just routine."

Sara went out the front door.

"Let's get back to her babysitting," Brass said.

Mrs. Dean said, "Well, as I say, she didn't have that many regulars anymore—she was down to, oh, one or two nights a week? Usually, just helping out so a couple could go to dinner and a movie away from the kids. She was hardly ever out past midnight."

Sara came in carrying her silver crime scene kit and headed up the stairs.

"Didn't she have a sitting job," Brass asked, "the night she disappeared?"

"Yes," Dean said, "but she was home around twelve and in her room by twelve-thirty. She said everything went great. She really liked David and Diana."

"David and Diana," Mrs. Dean said, "kids she sat for that night."

"But she was home after that and everything seemed fine?"

"Yes, she closed her door, like my husband said, before twelve-thirty. She'd had a long day and was really tired. Jason had gone to bed about eleven, but I stayed up until Kathy got home—one of us always did. Anyway, she went to bed and, about ten minutes later, I went up."

"And that was the last time you saw her?"

Mrs. Dean swallowed; her eyes were very red. "Until today . . . yes. Kathy told me she was tired and that it had been a long day . . . those were the last words she ever said to me."

She stared into her lap; no tears—she was, for the moment at least, past that. Her husband's arm remained a comforting presence around her shoulder.

"Well, we'll start in her room and with that last day," Brass said, checking his notebook. "Uh, one more thing—what was the name of the family she sat for that night?"

"The Blacks," Dean said.

Brass's gut tightened. "Excuse me . . . ? The Blacks?"

"Why, yes."

"*Dustin* Black?"

"Dustin Black," Jason said, nodding. "Do you know Dustin? He and his wife, Cassie, own Desert Haven Mortuary. . . . In fact, I'll be calling Dustin soon, about Kathy."

Me too, Brass thought. *Me too. . . .*

6

THE HEAT WAVE HADN'T BROKEN YET, but at least Catherine Willows had gotten some time in with her daughter Lindsey yesterday; and the CSI felt more rested than she had in weeks.

Grissom had given both Catherine and Warrick the graveyard shift off to enable them to catch up on sleep and work the Vivian Elliot case in the daylight it called for.

Catherine was comfortable enough in her ponytail, sleeveless dark brown T-shirt, and pinstriped brown slacks; and Warrick, at the wheel of the Tahoe, in his light green T-shirt and blue jeans, looked cool in several senses of the word.

But it was early—they'd walked from the air conditioning of the police station to the air conditioning of the SUV. The hot day hadn't really had at them, yet . . .

They pulled up to the gate of the Sunny Day Continuing Care Facility. Detective Sam Vega had tagged along and was in the backseat, leaning up like a kid wondering how-many-more-miles-Daddy. The same silver-haired guard from yesterday was on duty, and Warrick had barely come to a stop when the guy waved them through.

"Hold up, Warrick," Vega said, hand on the CSI's shoulder. "We still need to talk to him. First chance I've had . . ."

The guard came out of his air-conditioned shack, frowning and clearly worried; this was apparently the biggest commotion he'd had to handle in some time.

"Hey!" he said to Warrick, who'd powered down the window. "Didn't you see me wave you through?"

Warrick nodded. "Yeah—we're Crime Lab, remember?"

The guard peered into the vehicle, his eyes finding Vega. "Yeah, I remember you people. . . . How are you doing, Detective? You need some backup?"

Catherine couldn't hold back the grin, but Vega remained stony as he unhitched his seat belt to lean even farther up, talking to the guard past the back of Warrick's headrest.

"We do need to ask you a few questions, sir. Starting with, what's your name?"

"Fred Mason. I'm an ex-deputy from Summerlin. Retired ten years ago."

"Meant to check with you yesterday, Fred, but you'd gone off shift. The other gentleman said that you each lock up your own clipboard. That right?"

"We each have our own responsibilities, yes."

"Could you check yesterday's sheet, and tell me if anybody signed in to see Mrs. Elliot?"

"Mrs. Elliot died yesterday morning. *You* know that."

"Before she died, Fred. Could you check?"

"Sure."

The retired deputy—*did he have a single bullet in his pocket*, Catherine wondered, *like Barney Fife?*—went back to his shack, got his clipboard and returned, flipping sheets. "Yeah, yeah, here she is . . . Martha Hinton."

Warrick and Catherine exchanged looks, Catherine mouthing: *the neighbor.*

"Fred," Vega was saying, "I'll need that sheet."

"Well—I'll have to get it photocopied before I hand 'er over."

"No problem, Fred. But if you go off shift, leave the original in an envelope with the guard who comes on after you. I'll give him a receipt for it."

The guard nodded.

Behind them a car honked.

"Anything else?" the guard said. "They're really starting to pile up."

One car was waiting.

Vega said, "Thank you, Fred. Appreciate your professionalism."

Fred liked hearing that.

Warrick pulled ahead. "Martha Hinton, huh? That's the best friend, right? But she said she *didn't* visit Vivian, right?"

"Said she hadn't been to see Vivian," Vega said, "for a day or so."

"Could she have been confused?" Warrick asked.

"Possible." Vega shrugged. "She was upset, hearing about her friend's death. Could have rattled her a little."

Catherine said, "In any case, you'll be talking to the good neighbor again, then."

"Yes . . ." Vega's eyes narrowed in thought. ". . . but we're here. Let's deal with what's in front of us."

"Agreed," Warrick said.

Catherine nodded, ponytail swinging.

Within five minutes the detective and the CSIs were again seated in Dr. Larry Whiting's office.

The doctor did not look thrilled to see them, but he remained professional and polite. Again, he wore a lab coat, his tie brown-and-white striped and neatly knotted. Vega and Catherine sat in the chairs opposite Whiting while Warrick opted not to sit on the couch this time and leaned against the door.

The detective wasted no time. "Our crime lab has conducted an autopsy. The evidence indicates that Vivian Elliot was murdered."

"That's terrible," Whiting said, obviously surprised.

Catherine wondered if the doctor considered it "terrible" for Vivian that she'd been murdered, or for the Sunny Day facility?

Sitting forward, the doctor asked, "Do we know how it happened yet?"

Catherine noted the doctor's editorial "we"—as in, a doctor on rounds greeting a patient with, *How are we feeling today?*

"I'm not at liberty to say at this point, Doctor," Vega said. "But the CSIs and I will be looking into the backgrounds and records of all the employees here."

Whiting sighed, but said, "I understand."

Getting out his notebook, Vega asked, "I'll need the names of Vivian's caregivers."

"I would have to pull the records to know for sure. When do you need that?"

Catherine said, "Now would be good."

Whiting reached for a file on his desktop; he had vaguely implied it would take some doing finding the file, and here it was, at his fingertips—clearly he'd anticipated needing it.

He read, "Kenisha Jones . . . Rene Fairmont . . . and Meredith Scott." He lay down the file. "Those were the main ones. Various nurses might enter for assorted small tasks."

Vega was writing down the names. "What shifts did these three work?"

"Kenisha works days, Rene is second shift, and Meredith works overnight."

"What can you tell us about them?"

"Nothing beyond that they're professionals," Whiting said, gesturing with open palms. "Frankly, I don't know what kind of information you're looking for. Do I think any of them killed Vivian or any of the others? No. Of course not."

"Can you be specific about their individual performance?"

"I don't work with Meredith that much, as you might imagine—I'm seldom here overnight. As for the other two, Kenisha is a first-rate nurse; I've worked with her for as long as I've been here. Rene, the second shift nurse, strikes me as a dedicated caregiver as well. Never had a bit of problem with either of them."

Looking up from his notebook, Vega asked, "And how long have you been here, Doctor?"

"Two years last April."

"Any particular reason you're at Sunny Day, and not at a bigger hospital?"

Catherine added, "Or in private practice?"

Whiting closed the file on his desk and shunted it aside. "I view medicine as my calling," he said, choosing his words carefully. "But, temperamentally, I crave a slower pace than a bigger hospital or a private practice would grant me. I prefer the tempo of Sunny Day or, I should say, I preferred it before the last eight months."

"How so?"

"*You're* here, aren't you? . . . Things have been getting further and further out of hand, and until your assistant coroner noticed certain suspicious trends, I think we were all simply writing these deaths off as a streak of bad luck."

Catherine asked, "People dying? Streak of bad luck?"

"I don't mean to sound flippant," Whiting said. "I'm anything *but*. . . . It's just that this isn't the first assisted care facility I've worked in, and over the years you notice that sometimes deaths seem to come in . . . yes, streaks."

"Life and death," Catherine said, "just another game in Vegas?"

"I told you I didn't mean it in any kind of flip way. It's just . . . sometimes you'll go *months* without a death . . . then suddenly . . ." He snapped his fingers, once, twice, three times. ". . . three people go in a single month. Then we'll go a month with nothing, and get one or two in a row again. You have to understand— over five hundred people reside in the various wings of Sunny Day. Twenty-two seems like a lot of deaths but, truth is, there are extenuating circumstances."

Catherine arched an eyebrow. "Such as?"

"Sunny Day doesn't have an overnight physician,

understand. There's a four-hour gap in service, with what you might call a skeleton crew on hand. Any crisis after midnight, the nurses call nine-one-one—just as you might at home. Myself, along with Doctors Todd Barclay, Claire Dayton, and John Miller . . . we're the only doctors on staff full time."

Warrick asked, "How are the shifts split up?"

Whiting said, "We split the two shifts, seven days a week. Claire and I are a team, as are Todd and John. We do three ten-hour shifts, then we're off two days. A few of these patients are visited by their own personal physicians . . . but not many."

Vega frowned. "You work fifty hours a week?"

"Plus overtime," Whiting said. "And there's plenty of that to go round, too."

"Sounds brutal," Warrick said.

"It is," Whiting said.

Catherine said, "What about that slower pace you say you crave?"

A grin blossomed—the first sign of spontaneity from this controlled interview subject. "Compared to having a private practice, and seeing thirty to forty patients every day, six to seven hundred a week? I prefer to see fifty patients today, the same fifty I saw yesterday, and the same fifty or so I'll see tomorrow. Where a physician in private practice will have a roster of over a thousand patients, mine is fifty and I get to spend considerably more time with each one of them."

"More personal," Warrick said.

"Much," Whiting confirmed. "The pace is a lot different than private practice. The vast majority of these patients never walk out of Sunny Day, remember.

Those of us who work here do our best to provide them care and comfort before they are, frankly, rolled out."

Flipping his notebook closed, Vega said, "We'll likely be in touch again, Doctor."

"Let me know how I can help," Whiting said.

The trio marched from the administrative wing and back down one of the hallways lined with patient rooms. An attractive African-American woman in white slacks and a floral smock came out of a room, head lowered, studying a chart as she walked right into Warrick, the chart popping out of her hands.

Warrick caught it.

"Oh, I'm sorry!" she said, a hand shooting to her mouth. "Didn't see you there." The hand came away and revealed an attractive smile. "Nice catch."

Catherine read the woman's nametag: *Kenisha Jones.* Since Warrick was closer to the nurse, Catherine waited for him to say something. He didn't—he was looking at the woman with the glazed, dazed expression of a hypnotist's volunteer on stage in a casino lounge.

The power of a beautiful woman over a man had always amused Catherine, and for a number of years, she'd made a good living taking advantage of that male trait. And this was a handsome woman so Warrick could hardly be blamed.

The woman's long neck—a stethoscope her necklace—rose gracefully to a heart-shaped face dominated by full lovely lips, a straight nose, and wide brown eyes with dark, narrow brows. Tight banana curls erupted out of the nurse's upswept black hair—she was a lovely Medusa who had turned Warrick Brown to stone.

Finally, Warrick managed, "Hey, no problem," and handed back the chart, as if presenting her with an award.

Cutting this mating dance short, Vega stepped forward and flashed his badge. "Kenisha Jones?"

Her head reared back. She gestured to the nametag, saying, "Uh . . . yes." The "duh" implied. . . .

"I'm Detective Vega and this is Catherine Willows from the crime lab. You've already met Warrick Brown—he's also from the crime lab."

The nurse nodded sagely. "Ah—you must be here about Vivian."

"That's right," Warrick said.

They smiled at each other, and Vega—who appeared to have no romance in his soul, at least right now—said, "Somewhere we could talk?"

"Look," she said, her eyes finding Vega's past Warrick, "I'm fine with answering questions about Vivian; but this is not a good time. I'm the only dayshift nurse for this wing."

"If you get called away," Warrick said, "we'll wait for you."

"Well . . ." She smiled, shrugged. At Warrick. "All right . . ."

She led them into a small breakroom with just room enough for three round tables, a counter (with a microwave and a coffeepot), a refrigerator, and the four of them.

"Help yourselves to coffee," the nurse said. "Water and soda in the fridge."

No one took her up on it, but Kenisha got herself a bottle of water. "Gotta stay hydrated," she said.

"I hear that," Warrick said, rather nonsensically, since he hadn't bothered to get anything to drink.

They sat around a table.

The nurse asked, "What can I tell you about Vivian?"

The detective said, "First, you need to know—Vivian Elliot's death was a murder."

Kenisha Jones shrugged. "And?"

Warrick and Catherine traded raised eyebrows; Vega just stared at the woman in his cold unblinking way.

"You don't seem terribly surprised," Catherine said.

"Figured as much."

The woman had known from jump that they were here to talk about Vivian; since the CSIs and Vega had been here yesterday looking into the death that assumption made sense. But knowing that it was *murder* . . . ?

Vega said, "You . . . figured as much?"

"Do I sound cold?"

Warrick said, "A little."

"Don't mean to be. But this wing is not home to a lot of happy endings, right? . . . People come here to take their time dying, to not suffer while they're doin' it . . . but nobody's making big plans, post–Extended Care wing."

"Granted," Warrick said. "But you don't get murders every day."

"Not *every* day. . . . Hey, she was a healthy woman—plus, she was gettin' better. Suddenly, she has a heart attack and dies? There was not a damn thing wrong with Mrs. Elliot—hell, she was in better shape than me. Up and died? I didn't buy it. I don't buy it. And if you're here saying she was murdered, *you* don't, either."

Catherine watched Warrick as the young woman got a smile out of him with her sassy, smart attitude. With the barest nod of her head, Catherine signaled Warrick.

Without missing a beat, Warrick said, "Ms. Jones, you're right. We are here looking into it. Which is why we need your help. You were on duty, when she coded?"

"Yes," Kenisha said, adding emphasis with several nods. "I looked in on her, then went down the hall to check on Mrs. Jackson. Vivian was fine when I left her, and less than ten minutes later . . . damn. She coded, all right. All the way."

Catherine and Vega were hanging back now, letting Warrick talk to the young woman, who seemed to feel as comfortable with him as he did with her.

Warrick asked, "And what'd you do then, Ms. Jones?"

" 'Kenisha.' Your name's what again?"

"Warrick."

"Warrick, the whole damn crash team came in. First team, off the bench and in the game—Doctor Whiting, myself, and the two staffers from the other wing, Nurse Sandy Cayman and Doctor Miller."

Vega checked his notebook and put in: "Doctor John Miller?"

"Yes."

Warrick resumed the lead. "So, Kenisha—what happened next?"

"Well, I was the closest," Kenisha said. "Got there first. Only . . . she was already gone, poor thing. Only 'poor thing,' that's not right, really. . . . Warrick, that woman was healthy as a horse. No way she shoulda died. Vitals were strong just, what . . . *ten* minutes before. She was one of the handful, ya know."

"Handful?"

"The handful who had a future. The handful who walk outta here into some more life. No walker, no wheelchair—under her own damn speed. We *savor* those. This . . . this . . . should *not* have gone down like that."

"Place like this," Catherine put in. "Don't these things happen?"

Kenisha's eyebrows rose. "Little too many of these things are just 'happening' round here, you ask me."

Catherine said, "We are asking you, Kenisha. And I'm Catherine."

"All right, Catherine. I'm just saying, I had my suspicions, way before this."

Warrick picked it up again. "Then why didn't you call us in, Kenisha? Or say something to that assistant coroner who comes around?"

"And say what?" Kenisha asked, her voice rising now. She did a mocking voice: " 'Too many old folks dyin' out here at Sunny Day, come runnin' '?"

Looking sheepish, Warrick said, "Well, yeah—I see your point."

"In a world of malpractice, you learn not to make waves, unless you are very damn sure of something." She shook her head. "You point the finger, then they'd be all . . . where's your proof? And what do I have to offer, except a feeling in my gut."

Gently, Warrick said, "And what is your gut telling you, Kenisha?"

"Telling me, something's wrong here, only . . . nobody seems to know what it is, or how to stop it."

Warrick's expression was somber. "Kenisha, if something wrong *is* going down here, I promise you: We'll find it."

Her eyes were moist. "You know it's so easy to hide a murder in a place like this—another old fogey dies, and who the hell cares? Well, *I* care."

Catherine said, "Kenisha . . . trust me. So do we."

Kenisha's face showed that she wanted to believe her.

Before they left, Kenisha gave Warrick her cell phone number, "In case you need to contact me . . . about the case."

Warrick gave the nurse his cell, too.

On the way out, Catherine said, "Wow, very thorough . . . that exchange of phone numbers. You're really trying to stay on top of this."

Warrick gave her an uncommonly shy grin for such a confident man. "Cath—don't even go there."

Her chin crinkling with amusement, she raised her hands in surrender as they walked out of one Sunny Day into another.

At the office, they split up.

Vega went right back out, this time to interview Mabel Hinton about her visit to Vivian Elliot the morning she died. While the lab techs worked on the evidence, Warrick and Catherine, each pursuing separate courses, concentrated on doing background checks on the doctors and nurses who worked at Sunny Day.

Catherine had been at it for hours when finally Greg Sanders interrupted. Probably the brightest among the rising stars of the crime lab, Greg was young, ambitious, if sometimes scattered, his streaked blond hair giving him the appearance of a man who had just stepped off a Tilt-A-Whirl.

"Hey, Catherine," he said, hovering over her desk, his hands behind his back.

Catherine scooted her chair back and looked up at him. "So Greg—spill."

"I . . . found . . . your . . . murder weapon."

She grinned. "Really?"

A quick nod, and Greg explained: "We went through everything in the biohazard bag you brought in."

"We?"

He gestured with a thumb over one shoulder. "I had help from a couple of interns. Just a small tip? Any time you gotta go through the contents of a bio-hazard bag? Call an intern."

"Noted."

"When your vic coded, they gave her a throm-bolytic agent."

Catherine nodded that she understood. "To break up a clot if there was one."

"Exactly. Streptokinase, in this case. They also gave her dopamine and nesiritide—Natrecor as it's called."

"Natrecor?"

"It's a vasodilator. It's the synthetic version of BNP, a hormone manufactured in the heart."

She'd followed this for a while, but now was lost. She'd become a CSI, not gone to medical school.

"Oh-kaaay," she said finally. "So the murder weapon was . . . ?"

"After going through all the different syringes," he

said, "I found *this* homeless puppy." He produced a plastic evidence bag from behind his back.

She took the bag from him. Within, a large, nasty-looking syringe looked as clean as when it had come out of its protective wrapper.

"How can you know it was this specific needle?" she asked.

Greg held up one finger, said, "Ah! . . . That's why you come to an expert for an opinion. Because you'll get an expert opinion."

"Greeeggg . . . ?"

"There were traces of both blood . . . Vivian Elliot's, by the way . . . and saline from her IV on the needle."

"And on the inside?"

"Not so much as a molecule of dust—not . . . a . . . particle."

Catherine frowned. "But there should have been traces of something, right?"

"There were in all the others," Greg said, with an affirming shrug. "*And* in every syringe I've ever looked in. This one? This one has never held anything more than . . . air."

"Fingerprints?"

"Not on the plunger, not on the tube, not on the needle, nothing."

Catherine said, "All right—maybe we can track it some other way."

"Just let me know if you need anything," Greg said. "Always happy to solve your cases for you."

"Do you want me to say it?"

"I wish you would."

"Greg—you're the best."

He was gone less than a minute when Warrick rolled in, Catherine still staring at the plastic evidence bag.

"And what have we here?" he asked.

"You know that old cop expression? All we've got in this case is a pound of air?"

"I've heard it."

"We've got it . . . only we're happy to have it."

She held up the bag and explained what Greg had said.

"Murder weapon," Warrick said. "Always nice to have."

"So far it's a dead end, though."

"Plenty other leads."

Catherine nodded. "So. How go the background checks?"

"Kenisha Jones came up clean."

Catherine laughed once. "And Warrick Brown's heart skipped a beat."

"Cath . . . I said don't go there. . . . As for Kenisha, she went to UNLV, put herself through school. Hard worker, and never so much as a parking ticket. What'd you come up with?"

"Meredith Scott?" Catherine said.

"Third shift nurse?"

"Right. She wasn't so lucky."

Warrick pulled up a chair, his eyes perking with interest. "Really?"

"Really. Got busted just after high school for shoplifting. Then, while she was still in college, there was a petty theft beef with the boss of the restaurant where she worked. He said she was pocketing money out of the register."

"How did that one turn out?"

"Scott pled to misdemeanor theft, repaid the money. At the time, she claimed she'd intended to pay the money back. Just a youthful error of judgment. And truth is, other than that, her jacket's clean. Since college? Solid citizen."

"How about Rene Fairmont?" Warrick asked.

"I'm passing her off to you. Plus, you've still got the doctors to do, right?"

"Yeah, but now that we established *my* plate's full, what are you gonna be up to?"

Catherine leaned back in her chair. "I'm taking that proverbial fine-tooth comb to Vivian Elliot's finances. . . . If our killer is picking these people because they have no family, to me that signals a financial-gain motive."

Warrick nodded. "Can't argue that. What about the other vics?"

Catherine heaved a sigh. "Bodies long gone, crime scenes cleaned up past the point of no return. Only thing left is the records of those that have died over the last eight months. Vega's over there picking them up for me now. Once I've gone through Vivian's finances, I'll start on those."

"Never a shortage of fun things to do around here," Warrick said, putting his feet up on the edge of her desk. "How do you like dayshift?"

"In this heat? Is it fair to have an opinion?"

Warrick, staring at the ceiling, said, "You've seen the security out at Sunny Day."

"Yeah—Deputy Dawg. Not exactly the vault at Mandalay Bay."

Warrick looked at Catherine. "What if our killer's not one of the staff?"

Shaking her head, Catherine said, "Then he or she better screw up soon, or we're gonna have trouble making a collar. If this isn't about money, how does the killer pick a victim? If it *is* about money, and the killer's not one of the staff . . . the neighbor, maybe . . . she or he's got to have an accomplice on the inside."

"You sure about that? An outsider with medical knowledge might've shot that air in that IV, right?"

"I don't think so. This syringe matches the ones from Sunny Day. . . . Maybe somebody doesn't like old people . . . and their hobby is taking one out every now and then . . . and I don't mean for lunch."

"Ah, Cath, you can't—"

"I can. It's always a possibility, you know."

"What is?"

"Being up against a killer who is well and truly around the bend."

Warrick had no response to that.

After he ambled out, Catherine began going through Vivian Elliot's personal papers.

The CSI had brought in all the things she'd found at the Elliot house. The checkbook, with more than a thousand dollars in it, hadn't been used since the morning before Vivian's car wreck. Looking through the register, Catherine saw that Vivian had purchased a brake job, radiator flush, and oil change with check #9842. That had been from the dealership that had sold her her 1999 Chrysler Concorde.

The next day, Vivian had been traveling south on Nellis Boulevard when the drunk ran the red light and plowed into her. Since the woman hadn't written a check thereafter, the top check in the book should be #9843. Flipping past the register, Catherine saw the correct check on top.

She wondered why Vivian hadn't carried the checkbook with her on the day of her accident. Thinking it through, she thought she had the answer: Catherine knew that many older folks, especially those raised during the Great Depression, believed in paying most things with cash. Three hundred dollars, the price of Vivian's auto repairs, was probably more cash than the woman liked to carry . . . hence the check.

Vivian's financial advisor was Christian Northcutt, whose office was in a new complex on Robindale near Las Vegas Boulevard, the same office park as Newcombe-Gold, an advertising company Catherine had investigated just last year.

Looking through the statements from Northcutt, Catherine discovered that Mrs. Elliot had a money market with about three thousand dollars, a mutual fund program with a shade over fifty thousand, and an annuity valued about forty-five thousand dollars. In no way could Vivian Elliot have been considered rich, but she hadn't exactly been standing in the government cheese line, either.

If someone wanted to steal Vivian's estate, how would they go about it? Was there a will? There was only one way to find out: Catherine would have to talk to Vivian's lawyer.

Before Catherine could take that thought any further, however, Vega entered her office, hauling a monstrous cardboard box, the sleeves of his suit straining to contain his biceps as he brought the thing over and dropped it unceremoniously on her desk.

"The hospital records," he said. Fit as he was, the heat had him sweating and even panting a little.

"What took so long?"

He cut her a look. "Court order, Cath—you know how it is."

"Yeah, I sure do. Doctor Whiting give you any trouble?"

"Naw. Once he saw the paperwork, he pretty much fell all over himself trying to help. He would've been fine without it, personally, he said—but Sunny Day's a business like any other."

"I think," Catherine said, gesturing to the financial records spread out elsewhere on her desk, "we need to talk to Vivian's lawyer."

"Do we know who the lawyer is?"

"Yeah—Pauline Dearden." She handed Vega an invoice the attorney had sent Vivian. "Know her?"

"No."

"Me either."

"Let's get acquainted then," Vega said.

Next thing Catherine knew, she was riding in Vega's unmarked Taurus, headed south on Boulder Highway. She filled him in on the news of the murder weapon, and he was pleased, though frustrated that it didn't seem to lead anywhere.

Just north of Flamingo, Vega waited for a break in traffic and turned left into a strip mall parking lot. A two-story stucco building, the mall was home to a variety of offices. The bottom floor included an insurance company, a loan company, a bail bondsman, and a pawnshop; top floor held another insurance company, a baseball card and comic book store, a vacant storefront, and, at the very end, PAULINE DEARDEN, ATTORNEY AT LAW.

They went up the stairs and entered the office. Catherine expected to find the firm of Drab, Dreary, and Dubious practicing here; to her surprise, the office was spacious and the decor bright and cheery—blond furniture, light green walls, waiting area with mini-sofa covered in a floral pattern, three chairs, and a coffee table scattered with glossy magazines. Beyond was a good-sized desk, two client chairs, and a high-back leather number for the attorney—the one who didn't seem to be here. A computer sat on a smaller desk next to the main one, and beyond that was a closed door, from behind which came the sound of a flush and then running water.

That door opened and a tall, wide-shouldered woman in a high-collared navy blue jacket and skirt stepped out, patting her hair, as if it could be out of place. Catherine knew the latter was unlikely, as the woman wore enough spray to shellac her obviously dyed red hair into a tight helmet. The blue-eyed red-head wore a great deal of scarlet lipstick, too, and when she saw her guests, the woman looked up and smiled with bright, white teeth—something slightly predatory about it, but then . . . this *was* a lawyer.

"May I help you?" she asked cordially enough.

Vega showed the badge and introduced them both. The woman studied the IDs carefully before handing them back. Then the attorney shook hands with them and gestured to the client chairs. "I am, as you've surely guessed by now, Pauline Dearden. What's this all about, Sam?"

Catherine glanced over toward Vega, to see how this no-nonsense professional was taking this woman he'd just met using his first name.

Vega let the comment pass without a ripple in his impassive expression. "We'd like to talk to you about one of your clients—Vivian Elliot."

Pauline Dearden leaned forward a little. "Within bounds of client confidentiality, I'm of course happy to help the police. But why Vivian?"

"Haven't you heard, Pauline?" Vega said. "She's been murdered."

The attorney's eyes opened wide, then she sagged a little. "Hell. . . . No. No, I hadn't heard anything about it. I seldom read the paper and almost never watch television." She sat for a long moment, her manner suddenly morose.

"Ms. Dearden?" Vega prompted.

"Sorry. . . . Vivian was a good client, and a nice woman."

Catherine asked, "Can you tell us a little about her?"

The Dearden woman opened a drawer and withdrew a tissue and dabbed at her eyes. "What . . . what would you like to know?"

"What legal work had you done for her recently? I noticed an invoice from your office among her financial records."

A humorless laugh coughed out of her. "Normally, I'd have to rail on and on about attorney-client privilege . . . but since she's been murdered . . ."

Catherine waited.

Gathering herself, the attorney said, "She was considering suing Doctor Larry Whiting for malpractice."

Catherine blinked. "Doctor Whiting? First we've heard of that."

"Well, it's true."

Vega was still trying to wrap his mind around this. "Doctor Whiting at Sunny Day?"

"Uh huh—the very one."

Catherine sat forward. "Why did Vivian stay under his care, then—if she was considering suing him for malpractice?"

A grunt of a laugh preceded the attorney's answer: "She thought all the *other* doctors at Sunny Day were even bigger problems than Doctor Whiting!"

Catherine said, "She could have moved to another facility, if she thought the care was subpar. It's not like Sunny Day's the only game in the valley."

"She was an old woman," the attorney said matter of factly. "Set in her ways, and not willing to listen to anything I had to say."

"You're not saying she was senile, or that Alzheimer's was setting in—"

"Oh, no! Far from it." The attorney sighed. "But Vivian could be very stubborn. Hell—bullheaded is more like it. She liked the *people* at Sunny Day, though—the nurses, the other residents, those Gossip Club ladies. She thought of them as friends, and even Doctor Whiting she actually even liked. She just thought he and the other Sunny Day doctors were, as she put it, overrated quacks."

"Frustration with doctors is common for patients enduring long hospital stays."

"No argument there. But you should've tried to tell Vivian that."

Catherine couldn't think of an easy way to ask the next question. "Pardon me for asking, and this is strictly off the record . . . but was Vivian's lawsuit frivolous?"

The attorney sat back a little, possibly trying to decide whether to be offended or not. "I didn't think so or I wouldn't have taken the case. She had back trouble from the accident and that's always a touchy area. She said Whiting had added to her pain and suffering by not listening to what she had to say about her condition."

"Did he know she was considering suing him?"

"Of course," Pauline said. "He thought he was doing the best he could with her. They had a couple of confrontations."

Catherine wondered why Whiting had neglected to mention this little fact. Trying to cover it up, or just an innocent omission?

"All right," Vega said. "Let's move on. . . . Did she have a will?"

The attorney seemed a little alarmed. "You think Vivian might have been killed for her money?"

Vega shrugged. "We're not ruling out anything— not the doctor, not the money, nothing."

The attorney's eyes glittered now, anger replacing sadness, at least momentarily. "She was in a full-time care facility. She should have been safe there. What the hell *happened?*"

"She was murdered," Vega said.

"You said that before, Sam. *How?*"

Catherine gave it to her straight: "Someone gave Vivian a syringe full of air creating—"

"An embolism." The attorney's exhale had controlled rage in it. "Yes, I could see how someone thought they might get away with that. And you think Doctor Whiting did it?"

"Please!" Catherine said, holding up a hand. "We haven't found the killer—we haven't even ascertained a motive yet."

Best not to trust the lawyer with the theory that they just might be dealing with a serial killer. . . .

"But the potential motive you're exploring," the attorney said, "is money?"

Catherine shrugged. "When people are murdered . . . unless the killer's insane, the four main motives are money, love, sex, or drugs. Do any of those fit Vivian?"

"I see where you're going," Pauline Dearden said. She leaned down to withdraw a file folder from the bottom right-hand drawer of her desk, then scanned the folder's contents quickly. "Vivian did have a will and she changed it recently."

Catherine and Vega exchanged glances.

The CSI said, "Changed the beneficiary, you mean?"

The attorney nodded. "Originally, her estate was going to go to several charities. In the end, she gave it all to something called D.S. Ward Worldwide."

"Never heard of it," Catherine said, and Vega nodded the same.

"Neither had I," she said. "According to Vivian, it's a charity that feeds children overseas. Possible, I suppose, but I did some digging anyway."

"What did you find?" Catherine asked.

"Not a thing."

"Nothing?"

"At all, and when I look, Catherine, I look hard. D.S. Ward Worldwide doesn't even have a damn website."

Vega said, "Even *scam* charities have websites."

"Exactly," Pauline said. "That's what sent my red flags flying."

Catherine asked, "Did you discuss this with Vivian?"

"Till I was blue in the face. She refused to listen to reason. I said it before—a nice woman, but stubborn."

"Did she tell you how she'd come to hear about this D.S. Ward Worldwide?"

"No. And I asked repeatedly."

"She didn't mention a contact with the charity, who'd approached her?"

"Well, she did tell me a friend had told her about the cause, but she didn't want to elaborate. Someone had prepped her, apparently, that I might give her a bad time. She kept saying she had a right to do what she wanted to with her estate. Which of course she did. And since she had no close surviving relatives, well . . ."

"Was this advisor a friend at Sunny Day?" Catherine asked.

"I gathered as much, but I can't confirm it. But I do know, this hunger charity talk all started after she landed in that place."

"What about the disposition of the estate?"

Picking up the file again, Pauline read the top page, then flipped it over and took in the next page quickly. "Once the house is sold, I'm to cash in the entire estate . . . roughly a quarter of a million . . . and, after taking my fee and expenses, I forward the rest in a certified check to D.S. Ward Worldwide."

Catherine asked, "How are you supposed to forward the money?"

"Certified check sent to a PO box in Des Moines, Iowa."

"Can you give me the address?"

Pauline Dearden wrote down the address. "Think you can get a line on these people?"

"Good chance," Catherine said. "I've got a CSI friend in Des Moines. Can you stall the disposition of the estate, at least until we can get a court order to stop it?"

The attorney's scarlet mouth formed a sly smile. "I'm not in any hurry."

7

THE DOOR TO KATHY DEAN'S room was closed.

Though she knew the bedroom had been compromised as a crime scene in numerous ways, Sara Sidle slipped on latex gloves before gingerly opening the door onto darkness relieved only by a fraction of afternoon sun filtering in pale blue curtains.

She stepped inside and flipped the light switch, illuminating a blue-and-white room that immediately invoked memories of childhood friends with similar adolescently feminine quarters: a double bed with a floral bedspread and frilly pillows in the midst of which a big brown teddy bear wallowed; a poster, looming over the bed, of Justin Timberlake in concert; and a small white nightstand with half-a-dozen bookended horror paperbacks (Stephen King mostly), as well as an alarm clock and a remote control for the 13" TV sitting atop a dresser on the wall opposite.

Above the TV and dresser, a UNLV pennant slanted; nearby was the girl's desk, a two-section corner affair whose nearest section—over which loomed a poster of long-distance runner Mary Decker Slaney—was empty but for a plastic file organizer with a dictionary and thesaurus leaning against it. The other section was home to a computer monitor with keyboard, speakers on either side, sub-woofer on the floor, printer on a raised triangular shelf. Farther along that wall was the window and, beyond that, a bookcase crammed with paperbacks and hardbacks.

Although the room appeared spotlessly clean, gaps stood out where the original investigators had taken certain items, and not yet returned them, most obviously the computer tower that went with the monitor/keyboard/speakers/printer.

Judging by the severe angle of the dictionary and thesaurus, Sara surmised the absence of another book. There would be other missing stuff, too, as Conrad Ecklie's dayshift CSIs had already been through this room . . . meaning ninety-nine and-a-half percent of anything useful would already be in the evidence locker.

Her job would be to find that final half percent; but first, a call to Nick at HQ seemed in order. She got out her cell.

"*Stokes,*" Nick's voice said, after the second ring.

"It's me. . . . Listen, I'm in her room, Kathy's room."

"*And you're looking for what Ecklie's people missed.*"

She grinned in spite of herself at Nick's cocky assumption that nightshift could always find something at a crime scene that dayshift overlooked.

"No," Sara said, "actually, I was thinking that we should get the evidence they took . . . and go through it?"

"Once again, CSI Sidle, I'm a step ahead of you. Already got the box right here."

Shaking her head, grinning again, Sara said, "Okay, smart-ass—what have you found?"

"Hey, nothin' yet. Even miracles take time."

"But have you been through the stuff?"

"Just in a cursory way, making sure everything is there."

"Still . . . spot anything good?"

"Haven't studied it; just verified the catalog."

"Everything's in order?"

"Yup," Nick said. *"No puzzle pieces missing . . . unless you find some missing ones."*

"Hey, uh . . . is there a diary, a journal . . . ?"

"I don't remember seeing one."

Sara made a click of frustration in one cheek. "Something missing on her desk . . . next to her dictionary and thesaurus? And I was hoping it might be another book—diary, maybe."

"There's an address book. Ms. Sidle, you betray your age."

"I do?"

"Diaries are so last century. If you were a high school girl, keeping a journal today, where would you keep it?"

Her eyes moved to the vacant spot where the computer had been and she nodded. "Yeah, yeah, you're right—electronically. Anything of interest in the address book?"

"Haven't looked yet. I figured we'd go through it when you got back."

"Ah. CSI Stokes, where would you be without me?" Sara clicked off before Nick could answer, and her smile faded as she went back to searching the dead girl's room.

She began with the dresser, going through the drawers and finding nothing but clothes of Kathy's: underwear, T-shirts, jeans, socks. Next, she checked under the TV; then flipped the pages of the dictionary and thesaurus. The file organizer held no clues, nor did the single drawer in the desk have any revelations to share. Nothing on or under the bed.

She thumbed through the pages of the novels on the nightstand and found nothing. The bookcase and a double-door closet were all she had left when Brass came in, an alertness in his eyes telling her something was up.

Something big.

He said, "Guess who Kathy Dean was babysitting for the night she disappeared? Dustin and Cassie Black."

Sara's head reared back. "Whoa. . . . The mortician you and Grissom went to see?"

"One and the same."

Her eyebrows rose and she exhaled. "Now that's interesting. So, I'd guess you kinda wanna go back and have another talk with him . . . ?"

"Kinda."

Nodding, Sara gestured around her. "Can it wait forty-five minutes or so, till I'm done here?"

"No need. You're on your own. Grissom's on his way here now to pick me up."

"Why's that?"

"He was with me last time I talked to Black. Wants in on it. He'll ride with me, and leave the Tahoe for you."

"It's a plan." She moved to the closet.

Brass said, "I'll wait downstairs—let you know when Gil gets here."

"Sure," she said with a shrug.

The closet held nothing of interest and she finally turned her attention to the monster bookcase in the corner, five shelves high and brimming with books. The CSIs before her no doubt had gone through each volume, but she would do the same. Tedious work, and after three shelves of nothing, she was expecting to end this exercise disappointed.

Then a small slip of paper tumbled from the pages of the book she was fanning through. It wafted back and forth, feather-like, before coming to rest on the floor.

With a pair of tweezers, she picked the paper up by its edge, a folded note from what looked like a restaurant receipt pad. Resting it on the desk and using a second pair of tweezers (so as not to damage any possible fingerprints), she carefully unfolded the note.

Across the top were stamped the words *Habinero's Cantina*. The message—hastily scrawled in pink ink on the light green lined sheet—was both simple and cryptic: *FB @ your place, 0100, A.*

Sara had no idea what this meant, nor when Kathy might have received it. But the note must have been meant for Kathy, or at least held significance for her, otherwise why would she have folded it up and stuck it away? Question was: What did the note mean?

And when had Kathy received it? Could've been the day she disappeared, or (considering how long she'd worked at Habinero's) any time in the last two years.

She went to heft the book that had held the missive and checked the spine—*Lady Chatterley's Lover*, D. H. Lawrence.

Sara half-smirked to herself—a classic all right, but

probably not on the preferred reading list of Mr. and Mrs. Dean. . . .

She placed the book in an evidence bag, then carefully did the same with the note.

Grissom appeared in the doorway, Brass in the hall.

"Anything of note?" Grissom asked.

"*A* note, in fact." She held up the bagged evidence.

Grissom took the bag with the note and read it through the plastic, handed it to Brass.

The detective asked Sara, "Mean anything to you?"

Sara shook her head. "I'll run it past the parents before I leave."

Grissom glanced around the bedroom. "How close are you here?"

Sara shrugged. "Half an hour?"

"Good work," Grissom said, and he and Brass were gone.

Downstairs, twenty-five minutes later, Jason and Crystal Dean—seated in their kitchen having coffee—read the note, then gave each other a puzzled look.

"So," Sara said, "neither of you know who FB might be?"

"No," Dean said.

"Or A?"

They said, "No," at the same time.

"Are you sure? Could you think about boys she was seeing, or even was just friendly with?"

Dean gave her a cross look. "Young lady, I told you, I told *all* of you, a hundred times—our daughter had different priorities. She wasn't seeing anybody, wasn't dating anyone."

Sara suddenly realized it was time to take off the

kid gloves and give Kathy Dean the informed investigation she deserved.

"Mr. and Mrs. Dean, your daughter was pregnant when she died."

Mrs. Dean's face was a white mask with huge eyes. Her husband's face reddened.

"That's a goddamn lie," he said. "That's impossible!"

"Impossible . . ." the mother moaned.

"No," Sara said, "it isn't. The coroner's report has confirmed this. Her pregnancy may well have been a factor in her murder, so it's imperative for you to try to recall any young men who may have been friendly with Kathy."

The father's mouth was a harsh straight line; his eyes quivered with dampness. "You don't have any right to call her by her first name."

"Mr. Dean. I am only—"

"Leave. Right now. Leave us alone." He was comforting his wife, an arm around her shoulder.

He still was, when Sara went out.

Brass had parked in the Desert Haven Mortuary lot, and he and Grissom were just getting out of the Taurus when a late-model Cadillac Escalade pulled past and took the lot's prime reserved space.

Dustin Black, again in a well-cut gray suit and tie, emerged from the shiny new car, not noticing (or at least not acknowledging) their presence, as he headed into Desert Haven. The detective and CSI entered the funeral home perhaps thirty seconds behind the tall, bald mortician.

Fewer people milled in the lobby of the mortuary

today and Dustin Black himself, and not one of his assorted flunkies, was the greeter who held out his hand as they entered.

When the mortician recognized the representatives of the LVPD, his mouth dropped open, and that hand hung in space awkwardly until Brass shook it, smiled, and said, "We'd like a private visitation, Mr. Black . . . with you."

Eyes wide, mustache rabbit-twitching, with a furtive glance around at mourners heading in and out of doorways, Black said, "Right this way, gentlemen."

He led them through the same side door as before and down the corridor. The young greeter they had met on their last trip here was sitting at a desk in the office opposite Black's. He was eating a sandwich, reading a magazine and—judging by the way his head was bouncing to a private beat—listening to music through the earbuds of a pocket gizmo. The boy—his own gray suit coat over the back of his chair, his tie slung over his shoulder while he ate—did not notice their presence. Seemed lost to the world.

"A moment," Black said, frowning to his guests.

The mortician went to the office, rapped loud on the open door, and the young man sat up, mildly startled, and took out his ear pieces.

"What's up, Mr. Black?" the boy said.

"Jimmy, if you're going to eat lunch in, keep your door shut."

"Oh. Sorry."

"I could have been coming through with clients, and music and fast food don't suit the mood."

Black returned to open the door to his office for Brass

and Grissom, who went in. Black watched reprovingly as the young man across the way shut himself inside.

"What are you going to do?" he said, and closed his own door. He waved a hand toward the chairs in front of his desk. "You know how kids are these days."

Brass and Grissom sat.

"Yeah," Brass said. "Imagine you do, too—you've got two of your own, haven't you?"

Black appeared puzzled by the remark, his eyes moving to the framed family photo on his desk, then back to Brass. "Yes, I do."

Brass referred to his notepad. "David and Diana, right?"

The mortician shifted nervously in his swivel chair. "How . . . *why* would you know my children's names? . . . And what on earth could it have to do with anything?"

Brass folded his arms. "You remember of course that we told you the body in the coffin was not Rita Bennett's?"

"Yes, but I'm sorry, I'm not following your line of . . . I don't see how my kids . . ."

Grissom placed the Missing Persons photo of the deceased Kathy Dean on Black's desk in front of the mortician.

Who was pale to begin with, yet managed to whiten further; his mouth sagged open—it was as if he'd had a minor stroke. "Oh . . . my God . . . you're not . . . no. *This* is who . . . ?"

"Your babysitter, Kathy Dean," Brass said, "was the woman in Rita Bennett's casket. Yes."

"Oh, Lord, what a horrible . . . Her poor parents . . .

I knew she was missing, obviously, but I . . ."

"You spoke to the police when the Dean girl first went missing, correct?"

Black nodded numbly. He was staring at the photo of Kathy Dean on the desk as if she might have been one of his own kids; but he never touched the photo.

Brass said, "You drove her home—after she babysat for you that same night she disappeared?"

"Yes," he said, and he pried his eyes from the photo, and shrugged, his tone working unsuccessfully at playing this down. "The Deans don't live far from us, but it was dark outside. Dangerous for a girl her age to walk home alone."

"I guess," Brass said.

Grissom asked, "You didn't pick her up?"

"No," the mortician said. "No—Kathy had walked over, but the sun was still up then."

Brass asked, "Was it normal, typical . . . for you to drive her home?"

"Yes. She felt uncomfortable, walking alone at night. This can be a dangerous city."

"So we hear," Brass said. "What time did you drop her off at home?"

He shrugged. "Midnight, maybe."

Brass nodded. "You watched her walk into the house?"

"Yes," the mortician said, with a decisive nod, "whenever I dropped her off, I never left until she was safely inside her parents' house and had closed the door."

"Then you went straight home?"

"Yes, of course." Black swallowed. "Might I ask you . . . *how* she died?"

"She was shot," Brass said, "in the back of the head."

He covered his eyes with a hand. "Oh . . . oh God."

"Do you own a gun, Mr. Black?"

The mortician's hand dropped to the desk and his surprise morphed to shock. "You can't think . . . *I* killed her?"

Brass offered the tiniest shrug. "You said Rita Bennett was never out of your sight. This is what we call in police work an inconsistency."

The mortician leaned back in his chair. His expression would have been no less pained had Brass just punched him.

"I'll ask again," Brass said patiently. "Do you have a gun?"

"No! I *don't* have a gun. I've never owned a gun."

"You were aware that Kathy Dean disappeared within twenty-four hours of Rita Bennett's funeral— am I right?"

Black's eyes widened in indignation. "Why would I ever put those two events together? This is a funeral home, Captain—*whenever* Kathy disappeared, I would have been attending someone who had passed."

"It didn't strike you as odd that you were burying one woman you knew at the same time another was disappearing?"

"Please! I know a lot of people—this is a prominent business, and I have a certain prominence in the community, myself. I deal with deceased individuals who were acquaintances of mine all too frequently. Comes with the territory, as they say."

Grissom said, "You do understand we're raising this

issue because one woman turned up in the other's Desert Haven casket?"

With a frustrated sigh, Black said, "It wasn't like the two events happened simultaneously. Rita died on Thursday. I talked to her husband, Peter, about holding the funeral in our mortuary on Friday, Kathy babysat for us on Saturday night, then disappeared sometime after midnight. I didn't hear about the disappearance until Sunday night, when the police stopped by the house to talk to my wife, Cassie, and me about Kathy. Rita wasn't buried until Tuesday morning. Why would I assume any connection between these events?"

"Was your wife with you when you drove Kathy home?"

"No—obviously, we wouldn't leave our kids alone. When we got home, the kids were asleep on the couch and Cassie got them up and was walking them upstairs, when I left with Kathy . . . and when I got home, Cassie was in bed asleep already. So, the police just asked Cassie general stuff about Kathy."

"What did they ask you?"

"Their questions were more pointed to me—after all, I'd driven the girl home. Haven't you spoken to them about it?"

Actually, Brass had assigned Sergeant O'Riley to that very task, but the report hadn't come back yet.

"That's not your concern, Mr. Black," Brass said. "Now, if Rita Bennett died on a Thursday, why did the funeral wait till the following Tuesday? Isn't that an unusually long time?"

"It varies quite a bit. In this case, the husband,

Peter, had a sister flying in from Atlanta for the services. She couldn't get in until Monday night."

Brass's gut was twitching. Something was wrong here. For now, the detective would keep this feeling to himself; hold it close to himself, actually, nurturing it. . . .

"One last question," Brass said.

"Yes?"

"Were you aware that Kathy Dean was pregnant?"

For just a moment, Black stiffened, the man's eyes tightening. It wasn't much of a reaction, but enough for Brass to note.

Recovering quickly, the mortician said, "How sad . . . but how would I have known that? *Why* would I have known that?"

"The young woman's parents are under the impression that she didn't even have a boyfriend. A problem like pregnancy, she might have wanted to turn to an adult she trusted for advice. A father figure."

"We were friendly, but I can't honestly say she confided in me."

"Okay. Just wondering."

In the parking lot, walking to their car, Brass said to Grissom, "You weren't exactly chatty in there."

"You were doing fine."

"Was I?"

"He knows something he's not telling us."

Brass stopped and turned to Grissom. "Then you saw it, too. He's guilty of something."

Grissom twitched a smile. "Aren't we all? Question is, in Black's case . . . guilty of what? Let's get some evidence, Jim, 'cause *what* he's guilty of is something you might want to know before you read him his Miranda."

Sara came into a lab at CSI to find Nick bent over what she assumed was the box of Kathy Dean's belongings, courtesy of an evidence locker. Smaller items were spread across the table, but most of it was still in the box.

"Anything?" she asked.

Nick gave her half a smile. "How about, Kathy Dean had sex the night she disappeared."

"She did?"

"According to the lab report on her clothes."

Sara frowned. "There was nothing at the autopsy. . . ."

A raised eyebrow cut into Nick's forehead. "She went home and changed clothes, remember, maybe took a shower, and God only knows what was done to her before she went into that coffin."

Sara withdrew the bagged note from her crime kit.

"What's that?" Nick asked.

"Give me your opinion."

Nick examined the note, leaving it in its plastic home. "Parents have any idea who 'FB' is?"

"No," she said. "They still think their daughter was a virgin. . . . They didn't know 'A' either."

"What Cracker Jack box did you find this prize in?"

She pulled out the bag with the book. "In her room."

"*Lady Chatterley.* . . . Not exactly virginal reading."

"Maybe it was research. Anyway, Nick, I'm going to take the note to the document examiner—maybe she can do something with it. What else have you found out?"

"Tomas Nunez went over Kathy Dean's computer, back when Ecklie's people brought it in."

"What did Tomas find? Knowing him, he came up with something. That electronic diary, maybe?"

"No—nothing that helps us. Mostly lots of songs. She was downloading digital tunes like there was no tomorrow."

"Legally?"

"Ninety-five percent of them."

"Anything else from the Internet?"

"There were some e-mails from a couple of people, but they were in that same 'almost' language as your note."

Sara pondered momentarily, then asked Nick, "Did Tomas trace the sources of the other e-mails?"

"Yeah, but only a couple were local, and we got nothing from them. They translated the e-mails, but it was nothing helpful. Girlfriends from high school days. Stuff's still in the box, if you care to read them."

"Anybody called 'A'?"

"Nope, not even an e-mail handle that started with A."

Sara rubbed her forehead. "She's downloading music, only . . . there's no stereo in her room."

"No, but she had the computer."

"I suppose. Was there a stereo in her car?"

Nick picked up a report and read it. "AM/FM, CD player. CD burner on her computer, too."

"But if music is so important to her, don't you think she'd have a way to play it?"

"Besides the CDs?"

Sara thought back on the room. "I didn't see any CDs. You got some among this stuff?"

"No."

Sara shrugged. "Then either they've disappeared or they never existed."

"So she's downloading strictly to her hard drive, you think?"

Sara shook her head. "Seems to me she'd have something that would play 'em."

"IPod? Rio player?"

"Something like that, and there was no phone in her room either."

"Meaning?"

"Meaning the Deans were good parents with money and yet there was no phone in their daughter's room."

"She had a cell phone," Nick said, checking the Missing Persons info. "It must've been her only phone."

"Do we have it?"

Nick gestured with empty hands. "No. Just the phone records indicating she had one."

"Well, where is the thing?"

"With her MP3 player?"

She pointed a finger at Nick. "If somebody *used* the cell, phone records could lead us somewhere."

"Sara, that phone's been dead since the day she disappeared."

Sara made a face, then tried again: "Ecklie's people get anything useful from those phone records?"

"Just the names of some of her friends that the parents didn't know about, mostly girls she worked with either at the Mexican restaurant or the blood bank . . . but they didn't know jack about Kathy's disappearance."

"Any 'A' names among the friends, or 'FB'?"

Nick shook his head.

"How about Gerardo Ortiz?"

Nick reared back, smiled a little, and said, "What are you doin' there—pulling names out of a hat?"

"No, he's a guy she used to date."

"Yeah, he's in here. Name's crossed out with a black marker, though. And there's a Post-It from one of the detectives that has the guy's name and an address."

"My guess is he doesn't live there anymore."

Nick frowned. "And why is that, Kreskin?"

"You read the Missing Persons file on her, right?"

"Yeah."

Sara grinned. "*You* didn't know who he was. If he was mentioned in the report, if they had found him . . . you would have recognized the name. Simple deductive reasoning."

Nick just stared at her for a long moment. "That's scary—you're starting to sound a *liiittle* too much like Gris. . . ."

"Yeah, well I could use a *liiittle* more of his reasoning power right about now. I might know what we should do next."

"I don't know about you," Nick said, "but I'm going to Trace, to work on the fibers and hairs I culled from Kathy Dean's clothes and coffin."

Sara looked at her watch. "I'm going to drop off the note, then catch some dinner."

"Eating. Yeah, I remember that. I used to do that now and then. Anywhere special? Maybe I'll have you bring me something back."

"Pretty special," Sara said with a smile. "I was

thinking of trying this Mexican place I keep hearing about . . . Habinero's?"

Brass passed the Dean home on Serene Avenue, took a right on Redwood and cruised down several houses before he and Grissom saw a massive two-story brick home, the backyard surrounded by a six-foot wooden fence, the top of a swimming pool slide visible above it.

The detective stopped in front of Dustin Black's castle, which seemed to belong in Georgetown or a Connecticut country estate, not the Clark County desert. On a pole in the front yard, near the three-car garage, flapped an American flag. A small red, white, and blue sign near the pole said: "We support the Pledge." A massive white front door awaited the visitors under a portico supported by four gleaming white columns.

"Quite the all-American little bungalow," Brass said.

Grissom shrugged. "Morticians are just like us, Jim."

"That right?"

"Long as people keep dying, we're in business."

"And you say I'm the cynical one."

Grissom gave him the charming smile. "You are, Jim. I'm just stating a fact."

The front walk wound through a lushly green lawn that might have been hand-trimmed with scissors, two perfectly coiffed bushes standing sentinel on either side of the entrance. The other houses on the block all had healthy grass and shrubbery, too; perhaps the neighborhood hadn't gotten the memo that Clark County was suffering through a major drought.

Brass used the huge brass knocker in the midst of

that white door. Thirty seconds or so later, the door opened and a tall brunette looked at them accusingly.

The dignified beauty was in black high heels, tan slacks, and a v-neck black sleeveless blouse showing just a hint of cleavage. Her overly large brown eyes might have seemed cartoonish had they not been glinting with intelligence. Her curly hair rolled to her shoulders like a cresting wave. She had a slightly beakish nose, hinting ill-advised plastic surgery, and collagen-full lips rouged a deep red.

More work had been done on this forty-something woman than on one of her husband's average corpses; but the result was nonetheless striking and, Brass thought, she probably looked quite lovely, in low lighting.

"May I help you?" she asked, her voice a rich alto.

Brass displayed his badge. "Mrs. Black?"

"Yes."

"I'm Captain Jim Brass and this is Gil Grissom from the crime lab. Might we have a moment of your time?"

"I'm busy right now. But if it's important, I could spare you a few minutes."

"If it wasn't important, ma'am, we wouldn't be here."

She frowned in concern. "What's it about?"

"We're looking into the murder of Kathy Dean."

Her hand shot to her mouth; the too-large eyes got larger. "You found the poor girl? She was . . . murdered?"

"I'm afraid so, Mrs. Black."

"Nice-looking girl like that, when she disappears . . . you have to think the worst. So many awful people in this world. Values such as they are."

"Right. Could we come in?"

"Where was she found?"

"Desert Palm Cemetery."

"Oh my God. . . ."

She opened the door farther and stepped back so the two investigators could enter.

To Grissom, the living room looked more like an *Architectural Digest* layout than somewhere a family actually lived, everything perfect, magazines fanned out on the coffee table, furniture arranged more for show than for ease of use. Only Mrs. Black's tan suit jacket on the arm of the couch, and her black purse nestled in the corner next to it, clashed with the color scheme of dark green and beige . . . which Grissom figured a top-ticket decorator had probably referred to as "spruce" and "champagne."

"You say the poor dear was found at the *cemetery?*" Mrs. Black asked, waving them to wing chairs that looked far more comfortable than they actually were. She perched on the edge of the sofa as if sitting back might overwear the couch material.

"Yes, under frankly bizarre circumstances," Brass said. "She was in a casket we exhumed a couple of days ago."

Mrs. Black, clearly confused, asked, "She was buried . . . in a casket?"

"Yes, someone else's casket. Rita Bennett's, actually."

The hand went to Mrs. Black's mouth again. "Oh, my God . . . Rita of all people!"

Grissom asked, "Your husband didn't mention this to you?"

"No, no. When I married a mortician, some years ago, I had only one hard and fast rule—Dustin must leave his work *at* work. I feel I hardly need to justify that wish."

"No." Grissom shrugged. "But then . . . having two corpses switch places is probably not business as usual."

"The reason we're here, though," Brass said, perhaps afraid Grissom was moving the woman down the wrong path, "is to talk to you about that last night . . . the night the Dean girl babysat for you and your husband."

"Well . . . I've already talked to the police about that night. Ad nauseam."

Brass nodded. "That was a fairly cursory conversation, I'm sure. . . . To tell you the truth, Mrs. Black, I haven't reviewed the interview with the officers involved, so quickly are we moving forward on this homicide. Which is why we'd like to talk about that night in a little more detail."

"Well, obviously, I want to do anything I can do to help. These animals who kill young girls, they should all receive lethal injection, as far as I'm concerned."

"No argument," Brass said, and smiled.

"All right, then, Captain . . . Bass was it?"

"Brass."

"Captain Brass." She settled her hands in her lap, like a Catholic school girl about to pray. "What would you like to know?"

"Well—why don't you just walk us through it from the beginning?"

She thought back for several moments, then said, "I

had talked Dustin into coming home early that day—
it was a Saturday."

"Yes, ma'am."

"Saturdays . . . if there isn't a funeral . . . Dustin
usually likes to work with the staff on getting everything around the mortuary spiffed up for the next
week."

"Spiffed up?"

"The hearse and limo get washed and waxed, and
the mortuary is cleaned from top to bottom."

Grissom said, "For insisting your husband leave
his work behind, you seem well-versed in the business."

"I *own* half of the business, Mr. Grisham."

"Grissom."

"Grissom. As co-owner, there's much I'm aware of.
That doesn't mean I want to talk about the rising cost
of hearses and caskets, or the latest in embalming
techniques, over rare prime rib."

"Of course not."

"So," Brass said, picking it back up, "you got your
husband to knock off work early."

"Yes—we were going to go out for an early dinner
and then a movie. We get so little time away for ourselves. Between Dustin's business and my career, we
eat up a lot of hours. The rest of the time we try to
spend with our children."

"Your career?" Brass asked.

"I'm a vice president at InterOcean Bank. I work at
the branch office in Henderson."

"You spoke of your children—where are they now?"

"My sister's. Patti sits for the kids—she's a stay-at-home mom—and can handle David and Diana when both Dustin and I have to work late."

"Like today?"

"Like today. I'm doing some work at home."

"Okay," Brass said. "Dustin left work early that Saturday."

"Yes. Kathy walked over just before five. Dustin and I left for dinner."

"At?"

"The Lux Café at the Venetian. It's always been a favorite of ours. We finished dinner just before seven and went to a seven-thirty movie."

"What did you see?"

"Some violent reprehensible action movie that I let Dustin talk me into. It made me ill. Physically ill."

"So, you came home," Brass said. "And then?"

Shifting slightly on the couch, Mrs. Black brushed her pant leg as if scolding it for being rude enough to wrinkle. "The kids were asleep on the couch. I put them to bed and went to bed myself. I was asleep almost immediately. . . . So that's really all I know about that evening."

"Just a couple more questions, please. What time did you get home from the movie?"

"Just after ten."

Grissom frowned. Something was not adding up—literally.

Brass asked, "And what time did you go to bed?"

"Right after. I put the kids down, went to bed, oh . . . before eleven?"

"You were asleep when Mr. Black got home?"

"Yes, but that didn't matter, anyway—Dustin didn't come straight home."

Brass sat forward. "He didn't?"

"No, he said he knew I was ill—that foul movie really did turn my stomach—and he wanted to let me get to sleep. I have trouble sleeping and sometimes, though he doesn't mean to, Dustin keeps me awake. Don't quote me, but . . . he snores."

Brass nodded. "So . . . what did he do, so you could get to sleep?"

"He went by the mortuary to catch up on some paperwork. He got home just after midnight."

Grissom glanced at Brass, then asked, "If you were asleep when he got home, Mrs. Black . . . how do you know it was just after midnight?"

She smiled. "Because he told me, Mr. Grissom—the next morning. I was asleep the whole night. . . . Now, I really have things to do, gentlemen. Can I show you out?"

She did, and at the car Brass said, " 'Don't quote me, but he snores' . . . I'll try to keep that out of the papers, but no promises! . . . What do you make of her, Gil?"

"She's a strong, smart woman. But something's wrong."

"What?"

"I'll get back to you."

Soon, in the car, when Brass was turning onto Serene Avenue, Grissom finally figured out what bothered him.

"Pull over," he said. "Let's talk."

Brass pulled over and parked in front of the Dean home.

The CSI said, "The Deans and the Blacks agree that Dustin Black drove Kathy home."

"Right."

"And the Deans and Dustin also agree that Black dropped Kathy off around midnight."

"Yeah—Mrs. Dean was still up when her daughter got home. They talked."

"Yes," Grissom said. His eyes locked onto Brass's. "So . . . if Mrs. Dean's correct about the time, and Mrs. Black isn't lying about the time she and her husband got home from the movie . . ."

"Why *would* she?"

Grissom shrugged. "For the sake of argument, we'll assume for a moment that she's being truthful. Mrs. Black said they got home just after ten and Dustin drove Kathy home at that time."

Brass was getting it. "But the girl didn't get home until *midnight*."

"Right. Which means it took Dustin Black two hours . . . to drive two blocks."

Brass's eyes were bright. "I'm surprised at how anxious I am for a return trip to that funeral home."

"Without me, this time," Grissom said. "I need to get back to the lab and find out what Sara and Nick've learned. This may be starting to come together, and I want to make sure we have the evidence processed and ready."

When Grissom got to his office, he found Nick waiting for him just outside the door.

"Progress, Nick?"

"Yeah—got some fibers off Kathy Dean's jeans."

"Good. Do we know their origin?"

Nick grinned. "If 'we' didn't, I wouldn't be here."

Sometimes Nick's attitude could get under Grissom's skin. Though Nick had a deep talent for forensics, the young CSI also had a tendency toward cockiness. Or maybe it was just that the supervisor had the unsettling suspicion that Nick reminded him of himself, once upon a time. . . .

"The fibers," Nick said, "came from a Cadillac Escalade."

Grissom considered that. Not long ago, Dustin Black had been climbing out of an Escalade at Desert Haven. On the other hand, the Deans had an SUV, too; he just hadn't caught the make or model. "Do the Deans own an Escalade?"

"I checked with DMV—they drive a Toyota Land Cruiser. Different carpeting, different fibers."

"But Dustin Black does own an Escalade," Grissom said. "Saw him getting out of it today . . . and he drove it to take Kathy Dean home the night she disappeared."

Nick nodded. "The fibers came from the knees of her jeans . . . both knees . . . and, besides praying, I can only think of one reason why she might be kneeling inside that SUV."

It went a long way toward explaining why it had taken Black two hours to drive two blocks to take the babysitter home. "You have anything else, Nick?"

"Always, Gris. Ecklie's people say underwear found in a hamper at the Dean home showed Kathy had sex the night she disappeared."

After a tryst with Black, had she gone home to change her clothes, then sneaked out to meet someone? If so, that someone was very likely the person who had killed her.

Of course, if Black had actually gone home when he told his wife he had, then he wasn't a suspect in Kathy's murder. If he'd *lied* to Cassie, though . . .

Well, from what Nick had told him, that wouldn't be the first time. Brass would be getting back to Desert Haven about now, and this was information the detective could use. He got his cell phone out and hit the speed dial.

A moment later, he heard, *"Brass."*

"Grissom. Developments."

He laid out the story for Brass, explaining the evidence that could be used to make Black finally tell the truth.

"Oh, you did good," Brass said. *"You did fine."*

"Thank Nick—I'm sending him over. Nick'll ask Black for a DNA sample, and if our mortician balks, tell him you'll have a court order in less than an hour."

"On it."

He clicked off and turned to Nick. "Get over to Desert Haven and get a buccal swab from Mr. Black. . . . Oh, and take Sara!"

"Sara's not here."

This case was coming together, and Grissom didn't need Sara off somewhere. "Where is she?"

Nick grinned. "Having dinner . . . with clues on the side."

8

CATHERINE WILLOWS HAD MET her Des Moines contact, William Woodward, at the International Association for Identification convention in Vegas in 2002. They had served on a panel together and she had found the rangy, rugged, fortyish Woodward (like her, a veteran of the divorce wars) to be smart, funny, and, truth to tell, not hard to look at. They had shared drinks and promised to stay in touch—a promise they had kept over the last two years, including getting together again for dinner at a regional IAI conference in Des Moines when he'd brought her in to lecture on blood spatter, her specialty.

He picked up on the first ring. *"Bill Woodward."*

"Lieutenant Woodward," she said, putting a smile in her voice.

"Catherine Willows," he said immediately, and he was obviously pleased to hear from her (just as she was that he'd at once recognized her voice). *"Enjoying that vacation wonderland of yours?"*

"So you've heard about our heat wave."

"Notice I had the good taste not to ask if it was 'hot

*enough for you' . . . in our business, it's always hot, and
temperature is only one measurement."*

She enjoyed Woodward's easygoing baritone. He
was a notorious kidder, possibly because he got kidded
so much himself about "hick Iowa" from other CSIs
who might well have been jealous of his facility's
standing. Woodward's ranked in the top five CSI labs
after L.A., Vegas, Miami, and New York.

"Yeah, well, Bill, you know what they say around
this town—it's a dry heat."

*"Pushing 120 degrees, last three days, CNN says. At that
temperature, humidity be damned—it's just plain damn
hot."*

"Hey, last time I was in your part of the world, it
was so humid I thought I was inhaling water."

He laughed a little, then said, *"I'd love to think this
was a social call, Catherine—but I'm not that confident
about my masculine appeal. What can I do for you?"*

She explained about D.S. Ward Worldwide, Vivian
Elliot's will, and the PO box attorney Pauline Dearden
would be sending a fat check to.

"Dead drop, sounds like," he said.

"Sure does. I got the box number; got a pencil?"

"I'm ready. Read it to me."

She did.

He grunted a laugh. *"Gonna be one of those Mister
Mailboxes. I'll see if I can find out the renter. Anything
else?"*

"Nope. I'll just owe you one."

*"Actually, Catherine, we'll be even. That teen runaway
you helped me with, couple months back?"*

"Yeah—how'd that come out?"

"*Kid's in rehab, doing fine. Hey, even if we are even, I'll buy you dinner, next time you come to Des Moines.*"

"You know, Bill, there *are* a few places to eat, and things to do, here in Las Vegas. You could hop a plane, give yourself a break . . ."

He chuckled. "*We'll complete this negotiation when I get you your info.*"

They clicked off, and Catherine went to Warrick's office to tell him what she'd found.

"You're doing better than I am, Cath," he said, seated at his computer. "Background checks are goin' way slower than I'd like."

She drew up a chair. "How far did you get?"

"Whiting is clean . . . other than this potential lawsuit with Vivian, anyway . . . and the other doctors, Barclay and Dayton, also look clean. Still have some work to do on Miller, but so far he's checking out, too."

"How about the nurses?"

"Well, nothing more on Kenisha Jones. She seems fine."

"Oh, she seems 'fine' to you, does she?"

He smiled. "This is your third warning, Cath. . . ."

"Okay, okay," she laughed. "What else?"

"Well, of course, Meredith Scott had that misdemeanor theft charge. But that's not much to build on."

Nodding, Catherine said, "That still leaves Rene Fairmont."

"Right, and that's who I'm working on now. So far about all I know is, she was married to Derek Fairmont."

"Was?"

"He passed away suddenly about eleven months ago. He was that theater guy at the University of

Western Nevada—you probably read about him or
went to some of the plays he produced. Local celeb."

"Right, right, head of the drama department—fairly
young, wasn't he?"

"Younger than a Sunny Day resident—why?"

"Nothing. Just . . . never mind."

Warrick half-smiled. "What is it, Cath? A hunch? A
feeling? Gris isn't around—feel free to share."

She ignored that and asked, "What was the cause of
Fairmont's death?"

"Heart attack. Presumably."

"Presumably?"

"There was no autopsy."

"Cremated, by any chance?"

"Yeah, he was. But a lot of people have heart attacks,
Cath; and cremation's kinda common, too, y'know."

Catherine nodded. "What else on Nurse Fairmont?"

"Not much of a history I can find, before she married Fairmont. The name on the marriage license was
Rene Gondorff."

"Gondorff?"

"Yeah, isn't that a *Lord of the Rings* mouthful."

Catherine grunted, "Huh," then asked, "Do we
know what her nursing background is?"

"Still checking, but she was working as a caregiver
before she married Fairmont, anyway."

"Where? Who?"

"Doctor's office. Dermatologist named LeBlanc.
Practice on Charleston near the University Medical
Center. She was there about three months before she
married Fairmont."

"And before that?"

Warrick shrugged. "That's as far as I've got."

"Well, hell! We need more."

"Right—that's why Vega's going out to her place to talk to her. Has an appointment in just under an hour, in fact. . . . We can tag along, Vega said. Want to?"

Eyes wide, nodding, Catherine said, *"Ooooh* yeah . . ."

The Fairmont home nestled in Spanish Hills out Tropicana Avenue. A wide, low ranch-style on Rustic Ridge Drive, the house had the obligatory tile roof and a two-car garage, a late-model red Pontiac Grand Prix parked out front. The lawn didn't appear to have met water since spring and—other than a droopy fruit tree—the only other decorative touch was the red, white, and blue FOR SALE sign of a local Realtor.

Vega led the way as the three walked up a narrow sidewalk that led to an inset front door.

The detective rang the bell and, a moment later, the heavy Spanish door was swung open by a lithe blonde, perhaps five-foot-eight, an extremely well-preserved forty-something. She wore the white pants and floral smock of the Sunny Day nurses.

"Detective Vega," Vega said, showing her his badge. "You're Rene Fairmont?"

"Yes," the woman said, her voice husky.

"We spoke on the phone earlier. Afraid we're a few minutes late."

"Traffic in this town," she said, with a shrug. "But I do have to get to work . . . so can we make this brief?"

"We'll do our best. These are Catherine Willows and Warrick Brown from the crime lab."

With a friendly smile, she shook all of their hands, then gestured and stepped aside for them to enter. "But remember, I've only got a few minutes."

"We won't be long," Vega assured her.

To the left of the front entry was a spacious, formal living room, not at all lived-in looking; the interior was brick here and wood there, with a stark geometric feel, including the overhang mantel of a built-in rough-stone fireplace.

Why, Catherine wondered, *did people in Vegas, where the temperature was seldom below sixty, so often insist upon having fireplaces?*

A giant picture window overlooked the brown front lawn, and the furniture—two sofas, three chairs, and numerous tables—were fifties modern, either copies or well-preserved originals . . . *like Rene Fairmont,* Catherine thought. Several geometric modern-art paintings dotted the brick walls and a few abstract sculptures had been carefully placed around the room. The woman's late husband had been a drama professor, after all, and a whiff of the artistic permeated.

A nice home of its era, in fine shape; but something about the lack of yardwork outside, and the dominance of the late husband's taste, gave Catherine the feeling that the Fairmont woman was somehow just . . . passing through. And of course that FOR SALE sign was the best evidence backing up that theory.

Rene Fairmont waved for them to take a seat and she perched on the edge of a sofa; between them was a kidney-shaped coffee table cut from wood and heavily laminated. *A very pretty woman,* Catherine thought, noting the high cheekbones and heart-shaped face, shoulder-length hair, flawless complexion, big dark blue eyes with long lashes, and a smile that seemed both shy and endearing.

Catherine noticed something else, however: a high-gloss hardness, not unlike that shiny coffee table. This might be a product of the sudden death of her husband; she'd seen the quality in recent widows before. And those big blue eyes, for all their smile crinkles, seemed detached from the woman's pleasant expression. She was studying them, the way . . .

. . . the way a cop studies a potential suspect.

Their hostess took the lead. "On the phone you said you wanted to talk to me about Vivian Elliot. I don't have much to share, but please—ask me whatever you like."

"Let's start with your reaction," Vega said, "to hearing she'd died."

"Well, of course I was sorry to hear Vivian had passed. She was a dear sweet lady, very friendly. But she had spine. She couldn't be pushed around or manipulated."

"When did you learn of her death?"

"In the most routine manner—every day we get an update at the beginning of shift."

"Is it commonly known at Sunny Day that Vivian was murdered?"

If Vega had intended this hardball to jar the woman, the effect was nil.

"Of course," Rene Fairmont said. "We do have our little Gossip Club, if nothing else."

"How long had Vivian Elliot been under your care?"

"Well, since she got to Sunny Day. . . . I'm the second shift nurse in that wing, so all those patients are mine—from the time they come in until . . . until they leave us."

Catherine said, "Seems like a lot of patients have been 'leaving' lately. Had you noticed anything unusual about that?"

Shrugging, Rene said, "I've worked in continuing care off and on for nearly fifteen years. You have these little runs of bad luck. It happens. But, by the same token, I must admit it's a little unusual for the streak to go on this long."

"You noticed the 'streak' when?"

"Oh . . . two or three months ago."

"Who did you tell?"

"Tell? I didn't 'tell' anyone. We all knew it. It was a topic of conversation amongst the staff, at least the nurses and orderlies. Of course we talked about it, but, like I said, sometimes these things just happen."

Vega said, "None of you thought it was worth calling the authorities over?"

Her radiant smile seemed wrong as an immediate response to such a question. "Why? It's an *old folks'* home . . . people come there to die. . . . Oh, I'm sure that sounds callous, but when you work in continuing care, you get used to the idea that more of your patients are going to die than live. In that way, I suppose it's much like working in a cancer ward. . . . I would imagine if the average people knew how you *detectives* talk about cases and victims, *you'd* seem callous."

Warrick said, "That's true. But didn't you have a responsibility to say something about this string of deaths?"

"I'm a nurse, Mr. Brown. That would seem the

place, the responsibility, the purview of the doctors. And your coroner's people came out, in every instance, of course. . . . Really, how much more of this is there? I don't want to be late. I have *living* patients who're depending on me."

Catherine ignored that, saying, "You said you've worked in continuing care for most of the last fifteen years."

She sighed; settled. "That's right—until I got married three years ago."

"We understand your husband passed away, not long ago. We're very sorry."

Rene Fairmont glanced toward the fireplace and gestured to a silver urn on the mantel. "We were very close, Derek and I; it comforts me that he's still . . . looking over my shoulder."

"I lost my husband not long ago," Catherine said.

Warrick flicked Catherine the barest sideways glance. Eddie had been Catherine's *ex*-husband, of course, and his schemer's lifestyle had got him killed. But Catherine was trying to make a connection behind the hard smooth surface of another widow—was the woman protecting herself behind a coffee-table veneer? Or did that veneer conceal flaws, or even . . . emptiness?

"Well, then, Ms. Willows—you know what my life is like. You know that it's been hard. Derek was a funny, bright, vital man. He was everything to me."

"You quit your job when you married?"

"His idea, really. I was working for a dermatologist, Dr. LeBlanc—that's actually where I met Derek. He came in to have a biopsy on a mole. We started talking and, you know, just hit it off."

Catherine asked, "You weren't working in continuing care at the time?"

"No, I'd only been in Vegas a short while. I bounced around a lot when I was younger. Late seventies, early eighties are kind of a blur, frankly." Her laugh was attractive if brittle. "We're about the same age, Ms. Willows. You might understand."

"I might."

"Anyway, Vegas is the first place I've really put down any serious roots."

Maybe so, Catherine thought, *but the roots in your front yard are dying. . . .*

The woman was saying, "I tried to find nursing-home work when I came to town, but Dr. LeBlanc was the first nibble I got and I needed a job, so I went to work for him. A lot easier than continuing care, frankly."

Vega asked, "Can you tell us a little more about your late husband?"

She glanced at her watch; when she looked up, her smile was glowing but apologetic. "I'm really sorry, it's getting late and I do have to go. . . . If you're looking into Vivian's death, why are we spending time on Derek?"

The detective shrugged elaborately. "Forgive me. He was well-known around town. I was just curious."

She fidgeted, but said, "Well, I can understand that. He was a wonderful man; I miss him every day. He was a generous, shirt-off-his-back kind of guy. . . . Anything else?"

Warrick smiled, his body language casual, hands folded and loosely draped between his long legs. "He was at UWN for almost two decades, I understand. Everybody loved him."

"Yes, he was legendary in the drama department. Taught acting, directed the two plays every year— drama in the fall, musical in the spring. And, as always, he'll be in *Hamlet* this fall."

"Pardon?" Vega said.

Warrick said, "He plays Yorick." He held his hand out as if cupping an imaginary skull. "As in, 'Alas, poor Yorick'?"

Catherine said, "His skull plays the part. It was in all the papers."

The actor's widow smiled bravely and said, "He wanted to stay active in the theater," a quiver in her voice.

But no tears in her eyes, Catherine noted.

The widow went on "As I say, he was a generous man. Though he was cremated, he'd arranged to donate certain organs to the University Medical Center . . . in addition to his skull to the UWN drama department."

Though she knew the answer, Catherine asked, "Sorry to ask, but . . . how did Derek die?"

Rene glanced at her watch again and rose. "He had a heart attack. . . . I'm sorry, I really have to get to work."

The others rose as well and followed her to the door. As she held it open for them, Warrick asked, "Why no autopsy?"

"Pardon?"

"It's just unusual when a relatively young, healthy man passes."

"Derek was young-*ish,* but he was a chainsmoker and, frankly, a drinker. He led a very full life."

"Where did he end it?"

An edge of irritation tightened the lovely mouth as

she stood holding the door very wide for them to leave.

But Rene Fairmont did take the time to answer Warrick's question: "We were vacationing in Mexico when Derek died. His body was brought back here, where his skull was removed per his wishes."

Warrick asked, "You said he was an organ donor . . . ?"

"Yes—the hospital in Mexico harvested them and handled their transfer to the University Medical Center. Otherwise, my husband's remains were cremated here at home, which had also been his wish."

"Thanks," Warrick said, and they stepped outside, the Fairmont woman, too.

"If you'll excuse me," their reluctant hostess said, as she pulled the door shut and checked the lock.

Then she slipped quickly past them and trotted off to her car. She had backed out of the driveway and disappeared up the street before Vega, Catherine, and Warrick had even gotten to the Taurus.

As they watched her go around a corner and out of sight, Warrick said, "Alas, poor Derek."

Catherine smirked humorlessly. "Something smells in the state of Denmark."

Vega said, "What does Denmark have to do with it?"

"Nothing," Catherine said. "But that's one cold woman, and I think she may be a better actor than her late husband."

"What reason," Warrick said, "do we have to suspect her?"

"She's just on the radar," Catherine said. "But she's really, really bleeping. . . ."

Vega said, "I have a legitimate suspect to talk to . . . Vivian Elliot's neighbor, Mabel Hinton. Wanna come?"

Mabel Hinton was not home, but she wasn't difficult to find. The petite, plump white-haired woman in a white kitty-cat top and pink pastel pants was at Vivian Elliot's home, watering plants.

They sat at Vivian's kitchen table and talked to the woman. She had brown eyes that would have been lovely had they not been magnified and distorted by the thick lenses of tri-focals. She had insisted on their sharing the coffee she'd made for herself, as she tended her duties for Vivian around the house.

"Until an attorney or someone official tells me to stop," the woman said, her voice rather high-pitched, almost child-like, "I'm going to keep helping Vivian. I promised her I would."

Catherine took in what had to be the unlikeliest murder suspect she'd ever encountered. This was a sweet old lady—and if it wasn't, the gal had acting skills that neither Derek nor Rene Fairmont could match.

"We need to clear something up, Mrs. Hinton," Vega said, doggedly staying at his note-taking despite her fussing over getting him coffee, creamer, and sugar.

"Anything I can do to help Vivian's cause. Anything!"

"You told me yesterday that you hadn't visited Vivian the morning she passed away."

"That's right."

"Is there any possibility you might be mistaken?"

"I don't believe so."

Catherine said, "When did you last see Vivian?"

"The day before she passed," Mabel said, unhesitatingly.

"Are you sure? Why, I can think it's Tuesday when it's really—"

"Young lady! I am not prone to senility. I was a schoolteacher and I have an orderly mind and an orderly way about me. I did *not* go to visit Vivian."

Vega said, "Someone signed your name who did visit her."

"Do you have it?"

"Excuse me?"

"This signature of mine. That's *supposed* to be mine."

"Actually, I haven't picked it up yet," Vega said, embarrassed. "It's with the guard at Sunny Day—"

"Well I suggest I give you a sample. And you can compare the two signatures and see if you, or your expert people, really think I signed my name. . . . Maybe that guard got confused. Which one is it? Fred? . . . He's such a ditz."

Catherine smiled and sipped her coffee. She had never seen the competent Vega look so flummoxed.

Warrick said, "What were you doing yesterday morning?"

She smiled sweetly at him. "Do you mean, do I have an alibi?"

"Uh . . ." Warrick shook his head, laughed. "Yeah, Mrs. Hinton. Do you have an alibi?"

"What time would that have been?"

Vega told her.

"Well, I know right where I was: home."

"You live alone?"

"Yes, but I wasn't alone. I was getting my reflexology."

Catherine said, "Excuse me?"

"I take reflexology once a week. It's not just for your feet, you know—it's the science of nerve endings that keeps a person's whole body healthy. Why, if Vivian had listened to me . . . she could be stubborn, you know . . . she might well be with us today. My reflexologist would have gladly gone to Sunny Day and given her the treatments! They're only ten dollars."

Warrick, frowning as he tried to grasp this, said, "Is that a kind of . . . foot massage?"

"Young man, it's a scientific application of pressure. My reflexologist uses a machine and a rubber-tipped hammer pounds my little tootsies ever so efficiently. And look at me! I don't look a day over sixty-eight."

"Indeed you don't," Warrick said, eyes wide.

"I'll tell you what I'll do," the little woman said, getting up and removing their empty coffee cups. "I will write down my reflexologist's name and address and phone number . . . I have the e-mail address, too, if you need that . . . and I will give you an exemplar of my signature. And then you will go off and be detectives, and I will finish my duties here for Vivian."

Minutes later, outside the Elliot home, Vega stood looking shell-shocked. "She's not our killer," he said.

"You think?" Warrick said.

"I hope she isn't," Catherine said.

Warrick half-grinned. "Why's that?"

"Because she would probably outsmart us."

They rode back to HQ and split up. Vega headed out to Sunny Day to talk to Whiting again and finally pick up that check-in page, with a signature that might not be Mabel Hinton's after all. Warrick returned to background checking Rene Fairmont, and Catherine made the reflexologist call (a woman in Henderson) and confirmed Mabel Hinton's story. Then she started poring over the files of patients in the last eight months who had checked into Sunny Day and never checked out.

All the bodies were gone, all the evidence, too—the only thing that the twenty-two people who had died in the last eight months at Sunny Day had in common was that fourteen of them had no families.

Of the other eight, two had been cremated when no one from the families claimed the bodies. Of the six remaining, four had been given autopsies ruling death by natural causes. The last two, whose families had claimed them, had not been autopsied, shredding Catherine's last hope of finding evidence of a serial killer and/or conspiracy of estate fraud; both had died slow agonizing deaths, one from terminal cancer, the other from dementia. Fourteen estates remained that she could look into. She wondered how many had left their property to D.S. Ward Worldwide.

That would take some digging.

Sitting at her desk, her head in her hands, exhaustion nagging at her, Catherine considered whether or not there might be an easier way to catch Vivian Elliot's killer. If Whiting didn't do it—and no one had seen him anywhere around Vivian's room before she coded—Vivian had been killed by someone else in that building . . . and the list of suspects was long.

Truly, anyone could have done it—they had no evidence to speak of and yet they still had a killer to find. There was nothing to do but keep poking around until she knocked something loose. For the next three hours, she never left her office, just plodded forward, record after record, lead after dead-end lead.

Finally, Vega walked in, sat on the edge of her desk. "Whiting's in the clear."

"How so?"

"The good doc was in a room with a patient and another Sunny Day administrator when Vivian coded. Rock-solid alibi."

"As is Mabel Hinton's—I spoke to her reflexologist, who confirmed Mabel was indeed getting her feet pummeled when Vivian was visited by somebody pretending to be her."

"On that subject, I picked up that check-in sheet. It's with the handwriting analyst now, along with the exemplar Mabel provided."

"What's your layman's opinion?"

"Actually, the signatures do look similar. Either the reflexologist is lying to back up Mabel, or somebody took the time to actually do a forgery."

"Interesting. So maybe Mabel *isn't* in the clear. . . ."

"Well, Whiting definitely is."

Catherine's eyebrows went up. "Maybe so, but he didn't mention Vivian was going to sue him—did he have an explanation for that little omission?"

Vega smiled humorlessly and said, "He just didn't see how that particular tidbit was relevant."

Catherine could hardly believe it. *"That's* his excuse?"

"Doctor Whiting said that as far as he was concerned, he and Mrs. Elliot had worked out their differences, and no longer had any problems."

"Vivian just hadn't got round to telling her *attorney* as much."

Vega shrugged. "All I know is, Whiting was under the impression the Elliot woman was no longer contemplating that lawsuit."

"And do you really buy that, Sam?"

"Does it matter, with the alibi the doc's got? And we have no real evidence against him. . . ."

"Or anybody else," Catherine muttered, "for that matter."

"How about you, Catherine? Found anything?"

She sighed. "Well . . . I've started working on the other people who died at Sunny Day. Fourteen had no family and, of those, four died intestate. That leaves ten . . . and here's where it gets interesting, perhaps even sinister. . . ."

"Go on."

She leaned forward. "Every single one of those that I've studied so far . . . they *all* left part or all of their estate to some charity."

"D.S. Ward Worldwide?"

"Not that easy, Sam—fact, none of them are D.S. Ward Worldwide. And there's not a single repetition of a charity either."

"Somebody's being careful, you think?"

Catherine shrugged. "All I know is, no two charities repeat . . . and *none* of the charities check out."

"Check out in what way?"

She threw her hands up. "*Any* way—they're not registered anywhere, they're not on the Internet, no one at the Better Business Bureau has heard of one of 'em. In short, I can find nothing indicating that any of these charities actually exist."

Vega pulled up a chair. "Cath—that money had to go *somewhere*. . . ."

"Well, we know a check went to a drop box in Des Moines; my CSI contact, Woodward, is looking into that. Personally I've started tracking down and talking to the lawyers who handled the estates. The addresses of these possibly-fake charities aren't the same. And the only clue I've got is a lawyer named Gary Masters—he did six of the wills."

"Interesting," Vega said.

"Him I haven't talked to—been getting his machine."

Warrick leaned into the office. "Hey. How are you two coming along?"

They filled him in, individually, then Catherine asked, "Anything on the Fairmont woman?"

In a chair next to Vega now, Warrick shook his head. "Her employee application, and the letters of reference, from her file at Sunny Day? . . . A child's garden of dead-ends."

"Falsified, you mean?"

"Can't say that, Cath—the seven nursing homes, over a fifteen-year period, where Rene Fairmont claimed to have worked . . . all existed."

"Existed—as in, no longer exist?"

"Right. They're defunct. All lucky seven."

Catherine's eyes tightened. "Pretty convenient. And the letters of reference?"

Warrick shrugged. "From doctors at those facilities on letterhead from those facilities, dated back when the nursing homes were still functioning. And no luck yet tracking these guys. I've already talked to the AMA and should have something in about a week."

Vega asked, "Did you tell 'em it was a homicide investigation?"

"Yeah—that's why it's not taking a month."

Catherine asked, "What about nursing school records?"

"Nothing as Gondorff or Fairmont. I've looked everywhere—city directory, every computer database I could think of, including VICAP. I even Googled her with no luck."

Vega looked from Warrick to Catherine. "Are we thinking Rene Fairmont might be our angel of mercy?"

"Not enough to make her much of a suspect yet," Warrick said. "We don't have any evidence indicating she killed anyone at Sunny Day, and she sure wasn't the only person there with opportunity."

Thoughtful, Catherine said, "Maybe we're looking at the wrong case."

"What do you mean?" Warrick asked.

"Where were our instincts leading us," Catherine asked, "in that interview with Rene Fairmont?"

"To her husband," Warrick said.

"Right. Our gut took us straight to Derek Fairmont, all three of us . . . and what *about* Derek Fairmont?"

Vega said, "More dead-ends. There was no autopsy."

Warrick nodded unhappily. "And *he* was cremated, too."

Catherine's smile was sly. "Ah, but not all of him. He donated organs, and his skull is still playing *Hamlet.*"

"Whoa, Cath," Warrick said. "What would you be looking for?"

"How about poison? Any number of toxins create fatalities resembling heart attack—and Derek

Fairmont died of a heart attack in a foreign country."

"Let's say she poisoned him," Warrick said. "It seems to me thin as hell, but . . . let's say she did. Alas, poor Yorick—skulls don't talk."

"Don't they?"

Warrick gave her an "afraid so" nod. "DNA from the skull doesn't do us any good—we already know it's Derek. And if she poisoned him with enough of anything that it got into the bone, it would have been immediately obvious when he died."

Catherine pressed: "Teeth are more porous than bone. It's worth a look. And what about the University Medical Center?"

"The organs he donated?" Warrick shook his head, smirked without humor. "Cath, they'd be long gone."

She nodded. "Maybe—but wouldn't there be tissue samples on file?"

"Hold on," Vega said. "What judge is going to give us the go-ahead to collect this evidence? It's not even the case we're working."

"It's not even a case," Warrick said.

Catherine sighed. "Maybe I'm so tired I'm punchy. . . . What's left?"

"I don't care whether he's answering his phone or not," Vega said. "I'm going to talk to that lawyer—Masters? Who represented six of our dead charity givers?"

"I could stand to get some fresh air," Catherine said. "Even the 120-degree variety."

"Me too," Warrick said. "Take the Tahoe?"

* * *

The office of attorney Gary Masters was in a strip mall on Jones, just off Charleston. Curtains covered the window and blinds were drawn over the glass door, which Vega tried and found unlocked. . . .

With Vega holding open the door, Catherine walked in first and fought the urge to step back outside immediately. The room was dungeon-dark and smelled like fast food that had been left in a hot car too long with a bouquet of cheap wine for good measure.

While Pauline Dearden had taken a small, plain office and managed to turn it into something that seemed spacious and bright, Masters's office had undergone no such transformation.

As Catherine's eyes adjusted to the darkness, she made out a man seated behind, and slumped over, a desk opposite her. The man lay sprawled there, head on his arms on top of a cluttered desk.

"We may have a crime scene, guys," she said over her shoulder, and when the man at the desk . . . the body? . . . did not react to her words, it seemed to confirm them.

She would proceed forward to check for a pulse. If she found one, they would do what they could to save the man. If she didn't, no point contaminating the crime scene any further. . . .

Catherine pulled her Mini Maglite and her pistol. The man at the desk appeared to be the only other person in the shabby room, but in this darkness, she couldn't be sure. She edged forward, gun and light extended before her.

The flashlight exposed a ratty sofa, a thrift-shop coffee table covered with last year's magazines, and dirt-colored carpeting leading to two cheap client chairs in front of the equally cheap metal desk whose clutter included a flashing answering machine, and two wine bottles—one squat and empty on its side, another taller and unopened. The wall behind the desk was crammed with law books; so was another to the left.

No one crouching behind the desk, and nowhere else for anyone to hide.

Catherine holstered her weapon, allowed herself a deep breath, then went to the man and felt for his pulse, shining the flashlight on his face as she touched his neck.

He sat bolt upright and blurted, "What the hell?"

Catherine drew in a sharp breath, and it was even money which of them was more frightened.

The "dead" man brought up a hand to block the light as Catherine took a quick step back. One terrible thought flashed through her mind: If she'd still had her gun out, would she have shot him when he jumped?

Catherine had killed twice on the job. She hoped never to be put in that position again. . . .

"Mr. Masters?" she asked, her voice sounding remarkably calm, considering how her heart was pounding.

"What the hell?" he yelped. "What the hell are you doing?" His breath was sickly sweet—wine redolent. A water glass on its side on the desk held traces of reddish liquid.

She held up a palm. "Mr. Masters, please—calm down. I'm with the Crime Lab. We thought there might be a problem."

He swallowed thickly, rolled his eyes. "I'm not dead. Dead drunk, maybe. . . ."

The fluorescent lights blinked on—Warrick had found the switch, he and Vega inside the office now—and the man at the desk covered his eyes with an arm and moaned to himself.

"Are you Gary Masters?" Vega asked, holding out his badge to the attorney, who was now peeking over the top of his arm like Dracula behind his cape.

"Yeah. Didn't I say that already? You're crime lab? What's that about?"

"I'm Detective Vega, LVPD. This is Warrick Brown from criminalistics and you've already met Catherine Willows. She's also a CSI."

"What am I under arrest for?" Masters asked, rubbing his forehead.

Vega rarely smiled, but he did now—a dark grin. "You aren't. Should you be?"

"No!" Masters said. "No, of course not. . . ."

He finally got his hands and arms away from his head and Catherine got a good look at the attorney, as he stood to straighten himself out a little, and search for some dignity, unsuccessfully. Short, balding with wisps of brown hair on top, and a thick wreath of hair around his ears, the lawyer had an easy smile full of teeth that looked capped. His tan shirt appeared sweaty and wrinkled, his striped tie loose around his neck, his pants slept-in.

"Are you sober?" Vega asked.

"Why . . . is it illegal now, driving a desk under the influence?"

"You'll have time to make up all kinds of witty remarks," Vega said, "if you spend the next twenty-four hours in the drunk tank."

Masters held up his hands in surrender. "I'm sober, I'm sober! Little hungover, maybe, but sober. As a judge."

Catherine asked, "Up to answering some questions?"

"What about?"

"A series of homicides."

His eyes, bleary though they were, widened. "Homicides?"

"As an officer of the court, I'm sure you'll want to help out. Have a seat. Let's talk."

Masters did as he was told. "So, talk already."

Catherine withdrew a list from her pocket and handed it to the lawyer. He studied it briefly, then looked up at her expectantly.

"Know those names?" she asked.

He nodded. "Clients of mine. Where did you get it?"

"We're investigating their deaths. You know anything about that?"

Masters shrugged. "Just that they're dead. Not homicides, though. They all cleared the system."

Catherine smiled. "Well, the system's having another look—did you ever notice that they all died in the same place?"

"Yeah, it's a nursing home." He shrugged, made a face. "People die there. All the time."

"You ever been out to Sunny Day?"

"Yeah, some." He looked from Catherine to Vega, to Warrick. "I haven't been ambulance-chasing or anything—I just go out to see my clients . . . when they have papers to sign, stuff like that."

Catherine asked, "When was the last time you were there?"

Another shrug. "Couple of months ago, I guess."

"Never since?" Vega asked, an edge in his voice.

Masters shook his head. "Don't have any clients there right now. Why?"

Catherine asked, "How did you come to have so many clients at Sunny Day?"

"Hey, they called me. One satisfied customer leads to another."

"Referrals from other clients?"

"Pretty much."

"Anyone on staff who might have been . . . helping you out, finding clients?"

"Is that illegal?"

"We're not with the Bar Association, Mr. Masters. Do you know a Rene Fairmont?"

". . . She's a nurse out there, isn't she?"

Warrick said, "Was she shilling for you, Mr. Masters?"

"I resent that. They called me, these clients. I took them on. End of story."

Catherine said, "Each of these Sunny Day residents came to you separately?"

"Yeah. What of it?"

"Did you take time to investigate any of the charities that your clients were leaving their estates to?"

"Why would I?"

Vega leaned forward and smiled a truly ghastly smile. "Because they're all fake, Mr. Masters."

"Fake?"

The usually controlled Vega's rage was showing. "And as far as I'm concerned, you're behind them all—ripping off your clients, bilking them out of their money! Maybe killing them!"

"Take it easy!" Masters said. "I am an attorney, and you're on very shaky legal ground, Detective. Anyway . . . I didn't steal a damn thing. Look around! Do I look like I've been plundering my clients? Must be how I live in the lap of luxury like this!"

"You invited us to look around," Catherine said, standing up, "and that's exactly what we're going to do."

Masters shrugged. "Go ahead—knock yourself out! I'll cooperate. I got nothing to hide. . . ."

"Thank you," Vega said tightly.

"But shake a leg. Getting late in the day for me— I'm going to knock off when you people are done. . . . Mind if I relax?"

The attorney was gesturing to the unopened wine bottle on his desk.

"Be our guest," Warrick said, rolling his eyes.

Masters uncorked the bottle of Beaujolais and asked the detectives if they'd like to have a glass. He had nothing to offer but Styrofoam cups, but . . .

"No offense, Mr. Masters," Warrick said, "only don't you usually drink the kind of wine with a screw-top cap?"

"Usually," he said, smiling as the burgundy glug-glugged into the water glass, "but this is a gift from a grateful client. . . . Go on, look around to your heart's content!"

For the next half hour, while their host drank himself further into a stupor, that's exactly what they did, Warrick and Catherine going over Masters's office from top to bottom. When they were done, they still had nothing.

They were about to go when the lawyer stood. At first

Catherine thought it was a gesture of farewell, but then the man's obvious distress signaled something very different—his eyes were huge; his face a ghastly white. . . .

"Can't . . . can't breathe!" he gasped. He was clawing his chest when he went down, hard, taking some items with him, on the floor behind the desk. "Oh Lord . . . can't . . . can't . . ."

And he lay still, eyes wide, mouth agape.

Warrick went quickly to the fallen attorney, crouched over him. "I don't think he's breathing!"

Warrick used CPR to no avail, then was about to give the fallen attorney mouth-to-mouth when Catherine, nearby at the desk, leaning over the lawyer's latest . . . indeed last . . . glass of wine, said, *"I wouldn't—* he might transfer some of this poison."

Warrick reared back with a startled expression, then rose and joined Catherine, who was calling 911. When she'd finished, she looked from Warrick to Vega, and grimly said, "I was right the first time—this *is* a crime scene."

Warrick's expression was incredulous. *"Poisoned?"*

She nodded toward the wine bottle. "Unless that's bitter-almond–flavored Beaujolais." Catherine was already getting into her latex gloves. "But look on the brighter side, Warrick—we may be able to have a look at those tissue samples at the University Medical Center after all."

"Not to mention the UWN drama department," Warrick said, eyes flicking wide.

"Yeah. Derek Fairmont would be pleased."

"He would?"

"Not every actor gets a command performance."

9

A SQUAT HACIENDA AFFAIR across from Sunset Station, Habinero's drew business from both a mall and casino/hotel nearby.

When Sara approached the hostess's station, the attractive if frazzled woman in a low-cut white peasant blouse and full black skirt reported a twenty-minute wait for a seat in non-smoking. The smoking section—a glassed-in area with blaring baseball on big screen TVs, an endless circular bar, and assorted tables and booths—had a tobacco haze that could have concealed Jack the Ripper. What was a twenty-minute wait, Sara decided, in the grand scheme of things?

Anyway, a little time seated in the waiting area would give the CSI a chance to observe the operation of the place, and maybe even get lucky and, checking waitress and waiter nametags, spot the mysterious "A" who signed the *Lady Chatterley's Lover* note Sara had found. That is, of course, if "A" was an employee and not a customer, or if the note didn't turn out to be two years old with "A" quitting or getting fired in the meantime. . . .

Before leaving the lab, Sara had dropped the note off with handwriting analysis, although it would probably be tomorrow before any results were in. The twenty-minute wait turned into almost thirty, but she didn't really mind: Sara was trolling for nametags starting with the letter "A." By the time she was seated at a booth in a large dining room, to the accompaniment of mariachi Muzak, she had eliminated numerous Habinero's employees and even the frazzled nametag-less hostess (whom one of the waitresses had called "Sherry").

Of course, "A" could be an Internet handle or a nickname. As near as Sara could tell, four waiters and six waitresses were working tonight; already she had dismissed Tony, Kady, Sharon, Brandy, Maria, Barry, and Juan. That left one waiter and three waitresses whose nametags Sara hadn't yet glimpsed.

Eventually she would go to the manager to get a complete employee list; but a girl had to eat, didn't she? And she liked sizing up the restaurant and its help, without making her official presence known.

When a waiter named Nick brought Sara her water with a twist (kinda nice having a Nick wait on her), one of the remaining three waitresses, Dani, squeezed past and continued up the aisle to stop at a table.

Sara ordered a vegetarian tostada with rice and re-fried beans, and the order came quickly. She was halfway through her meal when something in the next row of tables caught her eye. The waitress, whose nametag remained elusive, was using a pink pen to take an order. . . .

As she partook of several more bites of tostada, Sara watched as the waitress crossed to the bar, brought drinks to the table she'd been waiting on, then went to another table where a couple had just been seated. Tall, thin, Hispanic, the waitress had long black hair in a ponytail, and was pretty but with a hardness in the eyes. Like the other wait staff, she wore a white shirt, black slacks, and two-pocket apron.

The waitress headed toward the kitchen, giving Sara a look at her nametag—Shawna. *Damn*, Sara thought, but then the hostess stopped the waitress.

"Those people at 12-C," the hostess said, "are getting antsy for their drink order. See if it's ready."

"I got an order up, Sherry."

"Do this first, Abeja. Now."

Sara had finally found an "A"—and something about the pretty, hard waitress made her think this just might be the "A" she'd been looking for. . . .

Dropping a twenty on the table for her abandoned meal, Sara stood as the waitress delivered a food order, then the CSI intercepted the waitress whose nametag said Shawna, but who had answered to the name Abeja. . . .

"I need a minute," Sara asked, and discreetly showed the young woman her ID.

The hard dark eyes didn't betray anything except perhaps mild irritation. "I'm busy right now. I'm off in two hours. How's that sound?"

"I already waited twenty minutes for a table," Sara said. "We'll talk now, 'Abeja.' "

"How'd you know my nickname?"

"I don't miss all that much," Sara said cheerfully.

"Let's go somewhere private . . . unless you prefer to talk about Kathy Dean out in the open."

That got a flash of reaction in the dark eyes. "Is that what you wanna talk about? How'd you know Kathy Dean and me were friends?"

"I didn't. But I do now."

The waitress said, "I got a drink order to take to that table over there, okay? Then we can talk."

When the young woman came back, she nodded toward the front door. They walked together past the hostess, to whom Shawna/Abeja tossed a few words: "Need five for a smoke, Sher."

The hostess didn't receive this news warmly, but Shawna paid no heed to the woman's glare, and led Sara out into the darkening evening.

The temperature was still over ninety, but at least a breeze had wound its way down out of the mountains. Withdrawing a pack of cigarettes from an apron pocket, the waitress lighted up, then offered the pack toward Sara, who declined.

"So," Sara said, "you did know Kathy Dean?"

They were standing next to Sara's Tahoe and the waitress leaned against it and drew on her cigarette. She released a wraith of smoke as she answered: "All the kids do . . . did."

"Really?"

"Everybody knows she's gone." She swallowed, and was having to work at maintaining her hardness, now. "Hell, it was on TV."

The media had only reported the discovery of the Dean girl's body in the cemetery; the circumstances of the coffin body-switch remained under wraps.

"So I could have asked anybody," Sara said, "and they'd've said they knew Kathy?"

"Yeah. And?"

"And . . . why do I think I still picked out the right one to talk to, Abeja?"

The waitress laughed. "You *don't* miss much, do you? Yeah, we were tight, Kathy and me. What can I say? Lots of bitches around these days—maybe you noticed that, too? But, Kathy? She was really sweet."

"Maybe you can help me, then," Sara said. "I'm looking for someone who knew Kathy, a friend."

"I told you! *We* were friends."

"I'm looking for a specific friend." Sara took her photocopy of the note from a pocket and held it out to the young woman. "Did you write this note, with your pink pen, Abeja?"

The young woman took one last hit off the ciga-rette, stubbed it out under the toe of her shoe, then took the note from Sara and looked at it. A tear made a glistening trail down the waitress's cheek, the note trembling in her grasp.

Hanging her head and crying for real now, Abeja covered her face with a hand and wept.

Sara gave the girl a tissue.

Abeja dried her face, smearing her eye makeup, and got control of herself. "I wrote it, okay? I wrote it."

" 'A' for 'Abeja.' Isn't that Spanish for bee?"

"It's just a stupid nickname. Everybody here calls me Abeja. Owner of the place, Pablo, gave it to me. I do things at my own pace, I mean things get done, but you don't rush me—so it was a jokey nickname, 'busy bee'; plus I don't take no crap, so I can sting you, ya know . . . when you get on my bad side?"

"Nicknames common around Habinero's?"

"Oh, yeah, everybody's got 'em. Kathy was Azucar, sugar, you know? Because she was always so damn sweet to everyone. . . ." Abeja broke down again. "Sorry . . . sorry. I just heard about Kathy on the TV, before I came to work today. Sorry . . ."

Sara contributed another tissue, waited for the girl to get herself together, then asked the key question: "Shawna . . . Abeja . . . who is 'FB'?"

The young woman shook her head and shrugged. "Who?

"FB."

"Got no idea. Don't mean crap to me, honest."

"But you wrote the note. . . ."

Abeja gestured with two open hands. "I did, but I still don't know."

Sara frowned. "You better start explaining."

Lighting another cigarette, the waitress took a deep drag, then sighed smoke. "Kathy's social life was . . . uh . . . complicated."

"Complicated in what way?"

"Well, mostly. . . . You ever meet her parents?"

"Yes."

"Then maybe you get it. They're like . . . way beyond not cool. They're not mean or anything, they just . . . I dunno, they're like parents out of a TV commercial. Commercial from hell."

"They struck me as strict," Sara said with a nod. "Little old-fashioned."

"Oh, did they? You *are* a detective! Man, her parents were mad strict with her. I mean, God, she was *nineteen*. . . . They didn't let her start school till she was six, y'know, she was one sheltered *chica*. Even at nineteen, they still didn't want her to have a boyfriend . . . and they wanted to know where she was every second. They practically stalked her!"

"Why did she put up with it?"

"*I* wouldn't have! But sometimes, when you're raised a weird way like that, particularly when you ain't shook loose of the parental handcuffs, and got your own place and all? Well, you get used to, like, a lifestyle."

"What kind of lifestyle?"

"Well, having to sort of sneak around to have a social life. She . . . uh . . . liked guys."

"Don't we all?" Sara said with a grin.

"Yeah, but you weren't thirteen, doin' your history teacher, was you?"

"Uh . . . no."

"I told her, she needs more respect for herself. She says . . . you'll love this . . . she was two-thirds a virgin till not too long ago."

Sara frowned. "What did that mean?"

"Well, I think it meant, she went down, and she let guys in the back door, but she was saving her virginity for Mr. Right."

". . . I don't think she found him."

The waitress smirked. "Why, lady—you think he's out there to be found?"

"If he is," Sara said, with a weary little smile, "he doesn't want to be."

"Didn't stop Kathy from looking. I mean, she was

always dating more than one guy at a time. But it wasn't about sex."

"It was about attention."

The waitress laughed, once. "Hey, you aren't dumb, are you?"

Sara laughed herself. "Not very."

"I mean, it ain't like Kathy was Queen Slut or anything. . . . It's just, when you got parent issues like that, when you're not under their thumb, away from the house? You kinda tend to cut loose. And did Kathy ever cut loose. . . ."

"Funny. To hear her parents tell it, she spent all her time at her job, the blood bank, and school."

"They don't know shit, do they? She was a good student—and at track? She was amazing. But she only volunteered at the blood bank about, oh . . . two hours a week? But she had her parents thinking she was there three or four hours, three nights a week."

"Did she exaggerate her Habinero's hours to her folks?"

The waitress shook her head. "No, she probably would've, but she couldn't, really. Mommy and Daddy, they came in here at least once a week—but always different days. They said they liked the food, but what they were doing was, they were checking up on her. You know, I haven't seen them *once* at this place, since she disappeared. So much for the food."

"Tell me more about her 'complicated' social life, Abeja."

"Well . . . sometimes her friends had to help her set up dates. Her folks really were freaks about her using the phone or meeting guys. She didn't even bother having a phone in her room—used a cell, but even there they limited her hours. And Kathy told me they monitored her e-mail."

"Her friends helped her how?"

The young woman shrugged. "They would talk to the guys for Kathy, set up times and places, then get the info to Kathy in a sort of code . . . and she would find a way to meet them."

"A *lot* of guys?"

"Well, like I said, she would see two or three at the same time. Always some older dude for sure—daddy issues. You know, before she turned eighteen? The list of guys who coulda got in a statutory jam over Kathy . . . you don't even wanna think about it."

"You know the name of the latest older dude?"

"No—but she had this new guy she was really having fun with."

"Old or young?"

"I don't think she ever said."

"You know his name?"

"Just FB—like in the note."

Sara frowned in frustration. "Anybody you can think of, guy here at the restaurant maybe, with initials like that?"

"Wouldn't matter, 'cause she never used their real names. You don't know the James Bond life she led, 'cause of those sick parents of hers. . . . Kathy and whatever friend set up the date always had a secret name for whoever the guy was."

Sara sighed. "Abeja, I don't mean to give you a hard time . . . but I can't understand how you could come to write a note about a person you *don't* even *know.*"

The young woman shrugged elaborately, and gestured with the photocopy of the note. "Hey, this was from the day she disappeared! Well, technically, I guess, day before. But I wrote this on Saturday and she wasn't, like, really missing until Sunday."

"Got it," Sara said. "So what happened Saturday?"

"Janie . . . she's a friend of Kathy's? And I kind of know her and stuff, well, she came in and was looking for Kathy, only Kathy was just working the lunch rush, 'cause she had a babysitting gig that night. Anyway, Janie came in early, like right after we opened at eleven. She had set up a date for Kathy after babysitting—that's the 0100 in the note, one A.M.? The reference to 'your place' wasn't Kathy's house, but where they picked out they were going to meet."

"Was that always the same?"

"No, Kathy liked to move it around, you know, just in case her parents were on to her somehow—they'd never be able to stake out just one place."

Sara asked, "But *did* she have a favorite spot?"

Abeja nodded. "There was this convenience store out in Pahrump she liked? And I know she met the dudes there, sometimes. She could park her car there, and know it would be safe if they went somewhere in the guy's car."

Sara was nodding. "All right. So this Janie came in Saturday, early. Does she have a last name?"

"Glover. Janie Glover. Doesn't work here at Habinero's, just knew she could find Kathy here."

"I see."

"Yeah, anyway, Janie stops by and Kathy isn't here yet. Janie has to go, I don't remember why, and she just gives me the message and I write it down on my order pad to give to Kathy when she comes in."

"Which you did?"

"Which I did."

A tall, well-built Hispanic man strode out into the parking lot, looking around, then spotted Sara and the waitress.

"Oh, hell," the young woman said, stubbing out the second cigarette. "That's Pablo—my boss! He's probably coming to tear me a new one." She stuffed the note back into Sara's hand.

Pablo—in a white open-neck shirt and black slacks with black sports jacket, to distinguish himself from the waiters—looked displeased. His straight black hair was swept back and he had a full, black mustache; he was maybe forty.

"Shawna," he said, noticeably not using the affectionate nickname, "this is an unscheduled break, and Sherry says it's already longer than any *scheduled* break! If you and your friend—"

Sara stepped up and displayed her ID. "Las Vegas Crime Lab. Talking to Shawna about the disappearance of your employee, Kathy Dean."

Pablo stopped cold and his surly expression dissolved into a somber one. He crossed himself. "Kathy—such a nice girl. If there's anything we can do to help. . . ."

"I'm just curious," Sara said. "What kind of employee was Kathy?"

Taking this opportunity to make a different kind of break, Shawna scurried back inside the restaurant.

Pablo seemed on the verge of tears himself. "The *best* employee. Smart, hardworking, pleasant . . ."

Sara immediately wondered if she might be talking to one of the succession of "older dudes" with whom Kathy had worked out her "daddy issues". . . .

"Kathy and that one," Pablo was saying, pointing toward where Shawna/Abeja had disappeared, "they're my two best girls. Detective Sidle . . . ?"

"CSI Sidle. Yes?"

"Will you find the animal that did this thing?"

Sara nodded. "We'll find him. And cage him."

"Good," Pablo said, his voice icy. "So many bad people live long lives. For Azucar to die so young? There's no justice."

"Actually, sometimes there is," Sara said, and asked the manager if they could talk in his office.

Brass waited while the young greeter, Jimmy Doyle, knocked at his boss's closed office door.

"Yes?" came a voice from within.

"Mr. Black," the assistant said, edging the door open, "that detective is here to see you again—"

Brass pushed past Doyle, saying, "Thanks son," and then closed the door on the boy's wide-eyed expression.

The mortician rose behind the big uncluttered desk. His face was dark red with rage. "Captain Brass—this is outright harassment!"

Helping himself to a client chair, a mildly smiling Brass crossed a leg and said, "Might be considered harassment . . . *if* you'd ever bothered to tell us the truth at any point during this investigation."

The mortician leaned his hands on the desk. His angry expression remained, but his shaky voice conveyed fear. "What could I possibly have to lie to you people about?"

"Apparently . . . everything."

"I have done my level best to cooperate with you, every step of the way. Give me one example where I did otherwise, and—"

"Well for instance," Brass said pleasantly, "the two hours it took you to drive Kathy Dean home the night she disappeared?"

Black slumped back into his chair, the red draining from his face. "What makes you think I lied?"

"Your wife."

Alarm flared in his eyes. "Cassie? What did she tell you?"

"That you and she got home from the movie just after ten and you immediately left to take Kathy home."

Black grunted dismissively. "Cassie wasn't feeling well that night—she probably got the time wrong. It was more like midnight."

"I don't think so."

Shrugging, Black said, "What you think doesn't matter. I'm sure Cassie will tell you herself that she was so sick that she may have been confused about the time, when she first spoke to you."

"Must be nice to have such a devoted wife."

A touch of smugness came into the mortician's expression; his voice, too. "Actually it is."

Brass beamed at the man. "You think she'll still be that devoted to you, Mr. Black, when she finds out it was your habit to take your teenage babysitter home the *really* long way?"

"What you're implying is—"

"What would you say fibers from your Escalade on the knees of Kathy's jeans imply?"

The mortician's face lost its redness; in fact, it became very white.

Brass continued: "Now of course there may be some innocent way in which that transfer of fibers from your car's carpet to her knees occured. But we're looking right now at her clothing from that evening—other evidence may have been transferred. Remember Bill and Monica? We have the girl's underwear as well. And then there's a sad piece of evidence—the unborn fetus Kathy Dean was carrying. Three little letters, Mr. Black—DNA."

The mortician's gaze fell to his lap.

Which made sense to Brass, because that's where the man's guilt began.

Brass said, "DNA evidence will likely show that not only were you having an affair with Kathy, but you got her pregnant . . . and that gives you a motive, Mr. Black. To go with opportunity."

Black looked up, shaking his head, his eyes pleading. "I didn't do this—you have to believe me."

"Actually, I don't . . . especially since you've done nothing from the start but lie to us."

A knock on the door made Black jump; but Brass had been expecting it.

"Come in," the detective said.

Nick entered, crime scene kit in hand.

"This is Nick Stokes from the crime lab, Mr. Black," Brass said, gesturing for Nick to join them. "Nick, meet Dustin Black."

Eyeing the silver case suspiciously, Black asked Brass, "What's he *doing* here?"

"Nick is going to take a DNA sample from you."

The mortician swallowed and straightened in his chair. "What if I refuse to cooperate? What if I say I want to talk to my attorney?"

Brass shrugged again. "You certainly have that right. I'd suggest there are two ways for you to play this—one, you become indignant, call your lawyer, who will tell you to demand a court order, which we'll obtain, and then we'll take the DNA sample anyway, and while you gain yourself a tiny bit of time—for what purpose I can't imagine—you get on our bad side, and we'll think you're avoiding cooperation be-cause you've got something to hide."

Black swallowed thickly, as if Brass's words had been a big brackish spoonful of medicine. "This DNA evidence—if it proves this affair you allege, even in-cluding a . . . a baby—that doesn't mean I killed the poor girl."

"It doesn't, you're right. And if you *really* didn't, if you'd like to demonstrate your innocence, that brings us to your other option: Accept the inevitable and vol-untarily submit to the buccal swab."

Nick withdrew from his kit the plastic tube that protected the actual swab, and said, "Mr. Black, it won't hurt at all."

His glance going from Brass to Nick, then back to Brass, Black considered these options for only a few seconds before saying, "What do I need to do?"

Nick smiled, in a not unfriendly manner. "Just open your mouth, sir. You don't even need to say 'ah.' "

The CSI took only a second to wipe the swab on the inside of the mortician's mouth.

"Thanks," Nick said to the mortician, his smile so easygoing even Brass couldn't detect any sarcasm.

And the CSI was gone.

Running a trembling hand over his bald head, Black asked, "Does Cassie have to know about this, Captain Brass?"

"Unless you lie to her," Brass said, "she's going to know tonight, most probably."

Alarm flared in the eyes again. "Why? Are you going to tell her?"

"Unless you're a stupid man, Mr. Black, and I don't take you for one . . . you're going to tell her yourself."

"I am?"

Brass nodded. "When she comes here to pick you up—unless, of course, you want to ride a hearse home."

"What?"

Brass got out his cell phone. "You see, I'm about to call a tow truck to impound your Caddy. . . ."

The detective did so, then continued to the mortified mortician: "Now you could make up a story, about your vehicle going in for service or whatever. But Mr. Black—and I say this whether you are guilty or innocent . . ."

"Innocent!"

". . . the time has come to start telling the truth. You can't cover up this affair with the babysitter any longer—and any effort to do so will only look like you're covering up the girl's murder."

Black blanched. "But I haven't *done* anything!"

Brass grunted. "Really? You were having an affair

with a teenager who may have been pregnant with your child when she was murdered. I wouldn't sweat keeping that information from your wife temporarily, when you should be worrying about other little things . . . like possibly facing lethal injection."

"Oh my God . . ."

"Mr. Black—*can* you account, I mean accurately account, for your time the night Kathy Dean disappeared?"

The mortician sat frozen, as stiff as the corpses that passed through his portals.

"I didn't think so," Brass said.

"What should I do?" the mortician asked, leaning forward with sudden animation. The helpless expression was unusual for such a highly successful businessman, particulary one whose specialty was offering controlled consolation.

The detective felt a wave of something for the suspect so much like pity that it surprised him. Maybe it was this room, where so many of the bereaved had received sympathy while making arrangements that would make Dustin Black wealthy.

"Mr. Black," Brass heard himself saying, "you really should call your lawyer."

While they waited for Dustin Black's DNA results, Nick got to work on the Escalade in the CSI garage. He glanced at his watch and hoped Sara would be back soon. Either he or she could run the gas chromatograph and mass spectrometer on samples of the Escalade's carpeting while the other searched the vehicle itself for more evidence.

He started in the back, the most likely place for Kathy and Black to have trysted. The carpeting was navy blue, which would make it harder to pick out hairs and other kinds of fibers. Still, Nick was diligent and that usually won out in cases like this. With a suspect like Dustin Black, who'd been so prone to lying since jump street, Grissom's dictum about trusting what can't lie—the evidence—seemed particularly apt.

Nick began at the rear bumper and worked his way slowly forward. The two rows of seats left the back half of the vehicle empty. Most families would use that for storage, while Black had made it his own personal playroom for himself and young Kathy Dean. Here, Nick found several reddish hairs the same color and length as Kathy's. In a storage compartment, he found a blanket that he thought Black might have used for his inside-the-car picnics. The ALS (Alternative Light Source) revealed a number of apparent body-fluid deposits on the blanket; but none of them were blood, so Nick set the blanket aside to take its many samples later.

He was just finishing the front seat when Brass, Grissom, and Sara came in.

"Progress?" Grissom asked.

"Our most important product," Nick said with a smile, and told his boss about the findings thus far, including more hairs in the passenger seat and its headrest, some of which seemed to belong to the husband, wife, and kids.

"We'll have to wait for the lab to know for sure," Nick said. "But it looks like Kathy Dean spent a lot of time in the back of the Blacks's SUV."

"Good job," Grissom said. "There's more for you to hear."

They sat down at a worktable at one side of the garage.

Sara explained about the *Lady Chatterley* note and what she had found out from Shawna/Abeja the waitress.

"You know, that D. H. Lawrence book," Nick said, "that might be another link to Black."

Sara frowned. "How so?"

But Grissom understood immediately: "Might be the kind of book an older man would share with a young lover."

Sara gave Grissom an odd look, then said, "Well, her tastes otherwise did seem to run to Stephen King. . . . As for that convenience store in Pahrump, where Kathy liked to leave her car? I went straight out there, from Habinero's. Guy recycles his security tapes every three weeks."

"Kathy Dean's been gone three *months*," Nick said.

"Yeah, but I brought all the tapes in, anyway. Gonna have Archie go over the beginnings and endings of the tapes."

Sara meant Archie Johnson, CSI's resident computer/video whiz.

Nick nodded. "Worth a shot—if we get lucky, Kathy and her mystery date may've survived the constant erasing."

Sara's eyebrows lifted. "I've been trying to find this Janie Glover, who was supposed to have known the identity of 'FB'. No luck so far. But I'm just getting started."

"What's next?" Nick asked.

Grissom held up a sheaf of papers. "Search warrant. While the lab works on all the trace and video evidence, we're going to the Black home, and then the mortuary."

Nick said, with a forced smile, "Doesn't *that* sound like a good time. . . ."

The nightshift crew had caught up with themselves: It was approaching midnight when their Tahoe drew up in front of Black's brick fortress. Only one light shone in the living room, and the whole neighborhood was as quiet as Desert Palm Memorial Cemetery. Grissom and Nick followed Brass to the door, where the captain used the oversized brass knocker.

A few moments later, a strained-looking Dustin Black opened the door and Brass handed him the warrant. The mortician now wore a green polo shirt and faded denim shorts and sandals with no socks.

"A search warrant?" the mortician asked. "For my home?"

"And your business," Brass said.

"You people haven't done *enough* to ruin my life today?"

Grissom said blandly, "Homicide investigations move quickly."

Brass asked, "Are your wife and children here, Mr. Black?"

"Why no," Black said with heavy sarcasm. "Thank you for asking! Cassie took the kids and went to a hotel. I followed your advice and told her everything, got it all off my chest, completely honest . . . and she walked out on me. Happy?"

Ignoring that, Brass said, "I need you to step outside, please, while the investigators perform the search."

"Any way I can be of help," Black said mockingly, and obeyed, while gesturing as if a gracious host for them to enter. "Oh . . . and by the way? . . . When this is over, I intend to sue your asses for ruining my life. Assuming you're ever able to catch Kathy Dean's real murderer, that is."

Brass turned to the mortician, face a cold polite mask. "Mr. Black, it isn't our business to ruin anyone's life, though sometimes in the pursuit of justice that does happen. But I might suggest that you had a hand in your own 'ruination.' "

"Is that right?"

"We weren't the ones having an affair with a teenage girl. We weren't the ones who got her pregnant, and we're sure as hell not the ones wasting the department's time by lying about all of that from the beginning."

The mortician lapsed into brooding silence.

Grissom, halfway in the door, turned and smiled at the two men and raised a finger, like a precocious student correcting a teacher. "*Might* have got her pregnant. We don't have the DNA back yet. . . . Excuse me."

Inside, while Sara and Nick covered the rest of the house—Nick starting in back, Sara in front—Grissom headed upstairs where he began in the bathroom of the Blacks' master suite.

The bathroom was a modern affair with mirrors and glass and a massive glass-enclosed multiheaded shower that looked like a weapon in a science-fiction film. Grissom spent nearly an hour checking drawers, drains, the inside of the toilet tank, anywhere he might hope for evidence . . . finding nothing. He hadn't expected to discover much in the bathroom, however, and he'd been right—a thought that gave him no comfort as he moved into the equally opulent bedroom.

The light green room was dominated by a wall-mounted plasma television and a bed about the size of Grissom's first apartment. Modern art tastefully punctuated the walls over a long dresser and a narrow dressing table. The TV took one wall above an entertainment center whose bookshelves were home to a scattering of framed family photos. The final wall consisted of massive his-and-hers walk-in closets; these were larger than Grissom's *second* apartment. . . .

The CSI supervisor spent nearly another hour going through the bedroom, the two closets interesting him the most. He went through the pockets of all of Black's suits and jackets, the drawers that held his underwear and socks, and shoe boxes of both husband and wife. He found nothing.

Grissom went on to do the rooms of the children, to no worthwhile end.

Nick and Sara were just finishing up downstairs when Grissom joined them.

"Anything?" he asked them.

Sara said with a shrug, "Some of Kathy's hairs in the living room . . . but that's all I found."

"No gun in this house that I could find," Nick said. "And we've looked everywhere."

"You ready to move on?" Grissom asked.

"You mean, to the mortuary?" Nick grinned.

"Ready but not anxious . . . oh, and we should do the wife's car."

Grissom nodded. "It's undoubtedly at the hotel with her and the kids. So let's tackle Desert Haven next."

Outside, where Brass leaned against the brick and Dustin Black sat dejectedly on his front stoop, Grissom gave the captain a curt shake of his head as the CSIs marched past.

"Didn't find the gun, did you?" Black taunted. "Know why? . . . Because it's not there! I told you, I didn't kill that girl."

Brass asked, "Would you care to accompany us to the mortuary, Mr. Black?"

"Do I have a choice?"

"Yes. You have keys for us, or shall we break the lock?"

Scowling, the mortician got to his feet. "I'm coming, I'm coming. . . ." Then he sighed heavily. "I, uh . . . - don't have a car. You impounded it, remember?"

"We'd be delighted to have you ride with us."

"I just bet you would."

They all piled into the Tahoe, Nick driving, Black in the passenger seat, Brass and Grissom flanking Sara in the back. As they drove toward the mortuary, Grissom tried to smooth the waters some with the mortician. It was clear the man had gotten under Brass's skin and the tension between the two threatened to get in the way.

"I know you're unhappy with us, Mr. Black," Grissom said, "but you can understand why, at this point, you're a suspect we have to seriously consider. If you're innocent, your cooperation now will help clear you."

Black said nothing for a while. Then he sighed and nodded slowly. "I . . . I apologize for my behavior. Please understand . . . I've worked long and hard to keep Cassie happy, and to allow her to live in the manner she believes befits her. But the truth is, I haven't loved my wife for years. And I'm not sure she ever loved me."

The others stayed quiet. The darkness of the vehicle had turned it into a kind of confessional.

"That realization's been as hard to deal with as getting caught cheating," the mortician admitted. "Harder, really. I guess on some level I wanted Cassie to find out about the affair. But not like this, *never* like this. . . . Kathy was a wonderful girl. I had deep feelings for her, and she was an extremely affectionate young woman who felt trapped by her parents."

"Do you mind my asking," Grissom said, "whether she told you about this pregnancy?"

"She did. She wanted me to leave my wife and marry her."

This frank, unhesitating admission of motive shook even the unflappable Gil Grissom.

"What," Grissom asked, "were you going to do?"

"I . . . I hadn't made up my mind. I was honest with Kathy. I said I'd take care of her, of . . . the child . . . for sure. However she wanted to handle it. And the word 'abortion' was never uttered by either of us."

"I see," Grissom said.

"But I needed to do some soul-searching before I could decide whether the ramifications would . . . I have a standing in the community, after all . . . she was just a child. . . . Well, I was trying to think it through, work it through."

Eyes tight with thought, Grissom asked, "Is that why it took you two hours to take Kathy home that night, Mr. Black?"

"Yes . . . yes. We did make love. I won't deny it. In fact the memory of it is something I'll treasure to my dying day. But we also talked. I wish . . . I wish . . ."

"What did you wish, Mr. Black?"

"I wish I'd told the girl I would leave Cassie and marry her, like she wanted me to. I don't know why, but I . . . I have this feeling that if I had . . . she might be alive right now."

"Why do you feel that way?"

"Doctor Grissom, it's a feeling. 'Why' doesn't come into it."

Grissom wondered if he was sitting in the company of an innocent man or sharing a ride with a killer who was also a brilliant actor. In his extensive career he had seen both, and right now he wouldn't lay odds either way. Dustin Black was, after all, in the business of trying to make people feel comfortable at the most uncomfortable time of their lives, telling them what they needed to hear in a difficult time.

Were Grissom and the others in that same category right now?

If Black was guilty, though, the man was going to be great on the witness stand. . . .

They arrived at the mortuary and piled out. After Black unlocked the door, the little group moved into the darkened lobby. They waited as the mortician got the alarm shut off and the lights turned on. Once this had been done, Black and Brass went back outside to wait in the parking lot. The tension between the two men had lessened considerably.

Grissom outlined the plan to Nick and Sara. "We're going to take our time—we'll start at the back, then move forward. We'll do one room at a time, beginning with the garage."

Once there, Nick used his Maglite to find the light switch, revealing a garage three doors wide, the first bay open, a workbench against the near wall. The limo sat in the middle bay, the hearse in the far bay.

Nick said, "Here's something I thought I'd never hear myself say . . ."

Grissom took the bait. "What, Nick?"

". . . I'll take the hearse."

Grissom smiled. "And I'll take the bench and work area. Sara, that leaves you the limo."

"Got it."

The toolbench was an afterthought constructed of plywood and two-by-fours, with several cardboard boxes stacked on one end. Overlooking the area was a pegboard with the typical screwdrivers, pliers, hammers, and other hand tools, and a shelf below held a locked steel toolbox.

Grissom decided to start there.

He hit the power button on the overhead door and walked around the building, instead of back through. He found Brass and Black at the front corner of the building, the mortician puffing nervously on a cigarette.

Grissom gestured with a thumb. "There's a toolbox under your workbench. Could you unlock it for us?"

Black said, "That's for Jimmy—he works on the cars. Keeps the good tools in there, locked up."

"Do you have a key?"

"No."

"I'm going to open that toolbox, then."

"Do what you have to," the mortician said non-committally.

Grissom returned to the Tahoe, got his bolt cutters out of the back, and in the garage, popped the lock on the toolbox, finding exactly what Dustin Black had said he would—tools, good tools.

Then Grissom went through the cardboard boxes on the workbench, three rows, three boxes each. Some contained clothes, others had chemicals, and the very middle box, the center square in the tic-tac-toe of cardboard, held several eight-ounce boxes of mortician's wax and, on the bottom, something else. . . .

"Gun!" Grissom called over his shoulder.

In seconds, the other two were at his side.

Nick snapped pictures and Sara opened an evidence bag as Grissom carefully picked up the .22 Smith & Wesson automatic handgun and dropped it in.

"Shall we keep searching?" Nick asked.

"Not right now," Grissom said. "We'll be back, but . . . not now."

They packed up their gear, closed and locked the garage doors, then met Brass and Black out front.

"Mr. Black," Grissom said, "you need to lock up. And you may need to make arrangements—you're not going to be back for a while."

The mortician dropped his cigarette, his expression tinged with panic. "What? You didn't find anything. You couldn't find anything! There was nothing to—"

Grissom held up the evidence bag and Nick shone

his flashlight on the pistol inside. The light glinted off the metal, winking at Black.

After Brass read Dustin Black his Miranda rights, the CSIs hung in the background as the captain accompanied Dustin Black to lock up the mortuary. The man was crying as Brass cuffed him and led him to the Tahoe.

"I didn't do this," he kept saying. "That's not my gun—I've never seen that thing before!"

"Not the first time I've heard that song," Brass said, and loaded him into the backseat.

Nick was studying his boss. "Gris—you don't believe him, do you?"

"I don't believe anybody, Nick. I believe evidence—and I've always been greedy."

"What do you mean?"

"To paraphrase Oliver Twist—I'd like some more."

And the three CSIs joined the detective and the suspect in the Tahoe.

10

THE SMALLEST OF THE CSI WORK AREAS, the Questioned Documents Lab was about twelve by fifteen feet, dominated by a long plastic-covered, backlit table. Sweeping around this workstation on a wheeled desk chair, Jenny Northam—formerly an independent contractor, now full time with the department—rolled away from a job she was doing for Sara Sidle to come around to where materials for the Vivian Elliot case awaited.

Catherine Willows stepped farther into the room, not comforted at all by being directly in Jenny's path.

"Vega said they look like a match," Catherine said.

"That's why they pay me the medium-size bucks, Cath," Jenny said. "No frickin' way."

Jenny had tamed her notorious longshoreman's vocabulary after coming onto the city's payroll; but hints remained. She held up Mabel Hinton's exemplar in one hand and the Sunny Day sign-in sheet in the other for Catherine to form her own opinion.

The CSI shook her head. "To me, they're dead on."

"A wax grape and a real grape look alike, too,

y'know. . . . Somebody *tried* to copy Mabel's signature, but while it may look hunky-dory at first glance, a close look . . . reveals the sign-in sheet as an obvious forgery. . . . Go on, Cath, take a closer look."

Catherine studied them for a few moments. "Is it the loops?"

"What about the loops?"

"Too small?"

Jenny smiled. "Good, Cath. . . . Anything else?"

"Something . . . something about the slant?"

"Bingo," the handwriting expert said. "On the sign-in sheet, the slant is forced—you can tell the writer's *natural* slant is in the opposite direction. Pressure points are in the wrong places."

Catherine nodded. "So—there's no way the same person wrote both of these?"

"No way in heck."

Catherine laughed. "You have cleaned up your language."

"Frickin' A," Jenny said.

Again Catherine's eyes affixed themselves to that sign-in sheet. *If Vivian's friend Mabel Hinton hadn't signed it, then who had?* Catherine's gaze traveled to the column to the right of the forged signature, where in a box had been scrawled what appeared to be a car license number.

"Jen—did Vega say anything about this?"

Frowning at the number Catherine pointed to, Jenny said, "No . . . no, just the signature. . . . What are you smiling about?"

"Leads have been a little scarce in this case. Always nice to find one. . . . Thanks, Jen."

"Any time, Cath."

Back in her office, Catherine ran the number through DMV to quick result. She grabbed the print-out, headed for the door, and—in less than ten minutes—pulled the Tahoe to a stop in front of the rundown, one-story concrete bunker housing Valley Taxi Company. Inside, she approached the dispatcher, a bald man in his sixties with Coke-bottle glasses, a dangling half-smoked cigarette, and a short-sleeve plaid shirt with evidence of breakfast on it.

"Need a cab, young lady?" he asked.

Flashing a smile, and her ID, she said, "Yes, but a specific one."

When she'd explained the situation—and given the license number of the cab that had taken "Mabel Hinton" to Sunny Day on the morning of Vivian Elliot's murder—the dispatcher got on the radio.

Catherine knew by all rights she should have rounded up a detective for this; but things were moving quickly now, and Brass's people were spread just as thin as the CSIs. So she'd taken the initiative. . . .

And in under two minutes, the dispatcher had given her the address of a café on Boulder Highway, where driver Gus Clein was taking a break, and would wait for her.

Soon Catherine was in a fifties-style diner, sitting in a booth across from a pudgy middle-aged man with graying hair, lumpy features, and a mouthful of burger. The cabbie wore a Wayne Newton T-shirt that might have been purchased at the entertainer's first Vegas engagement.

"Any chance you remember the fare I'm talking about?" Catherine asked.

Clein nodded and kept chewing; the burger he was working on was smaller than a hubcap—just. "Yeah, I do remember, 'cause that's the only fare I had out to that rest home in . . . forever."

"But the fare herself—do you remember *her?*"

He swallowed, nodded, taking a drink from a Lake Mead–size Coke and said, "Sure. Little old lady. I been doin' this a long time, and I'm one of them chatty cabbies . . . only way I keep sane. And usually, the older ones? They love the attention, they stick right with me . . . but her? She was so quiet I thought she passed away. I mean, I kept tryin' to talk to her, but she didn't show much interest."

"Where did you pick her up?"

He took another bite of the monster burger, chewed as he thought about it, then washed it down with more soda before answering. "In Spanish Hills somewhere."

Catherine felt a spike of excitement. "Where, precisely?"

Clein wiped his hands, picked up his clipboard from the seat next to him and paged through. Finally he said, "Here it is—Rustic Ridge Drive."

Catherine's notebook was in hand. "Got a house number?"

"Sure," he said, and gave it to her.

Hel-lo! Rene Fairmont's address.

Catherine smiled, said, "Thanks, Mr. Clein," and got out her cell phone.

"Hey, it's my pleasure. Are all the CSIs as cute as you?"

She gave him a wry grin. "You may not like me as much as you think you do, Mr. Clein."

"Why's that, cutie?"

"I'm impounding your cab . . . cutie."

"Aw, hell. . . ."

"Sorry, but it's evidence in a murder investigation now."

"Damn it!"

"I really am sorry. You were a big help. Here . . ." She put two quarters on the tabletop. "You'll want to check in with your dispatcher and have somebody pick you up."

"I don't need your charity, lady! I got a radio in the cab."

"You would, if you still had a cab."

"Damn!" Clein said again. Then he heaved a sigh, accepted the coins, adjusted to his new lot in life, and returned his attention to the burger.

Catherine went outside to call for a tow truck, but when she clicked the phone, the battery was deader than most leads in this case. She changed batteries and called the LVPD garage. Her second call was for a uniform to sit on the cab until the tow truck arrived. Her next call was to Warrick.

"What corner of the earth did you drop off?" Warrick asked, mildly irritated.

"Sorry—didn't know my cell had gone dead." She told him where she was and what she'd been doing. "What's up on your end?"

"Well," Warrick said, *"Greg served the court orders for the skull and the tissue samples."*

She laughed. "Greg'll do anything to get out in the field."

Warrick said, *"Well, I couldn't go—I was working the*

evidence from the Masters crime scene; then I couldn't find you, and Greg was free. With our budget, manpower is manpower."

"When it isn't woman power," she said. "Meet you at the DNA lab in fifteen."

"It's a date," he said and clicked off.

Vega and Warrick were walking down the hall, on their way to DNA, when she got back. Catherine fell in between them.

"The taxi will be here soon," she told them, "and we can go over that. With all the fares in between the false 'Mabel Hinton' and now, I don't know what we can hope to find."

Vega half-smirked. "It's been a grasping-at-straws kind of case."

"Mind handling that solo?" Warrick asked Catherine, meaning processing the impounded cab. "I'll still be processing the Masters evidence."

"Fair enough," Catherine said. "But let's see what Greg's been up to."

They entered the lab and found Greg bent over several reports. On the counter next to the spiky-haired lab tech was a human skull, grinning in welcome.

Hearing them enter, Greg turned and bestowed one of his silliest smiles and gestured to the skull in tah-*dah* fashion. "If I may, I'd like to present the head of the UWN drama department."

"Stop the presses," Warrick said. "Greg Sanders gets head."

"Spare me the puns, children," Catherine said, bending down to look Derek Fairmont in what had once been his face. "These *are* human remains."

"Question is," Warrick said, "is this a murder victim?"

Greg raised a hand. "Let's not get ahead of ourselves. . . . Sorry. That one was accidental."

Catherine, hands on hips, asked, "What luck have you had with the skull, Greg?"

"Well, you were both right—Warrick saying that it was unlikely any poison could be absorbed into bone before madness set in. But I am looking at the teeth, Catherine, which are indeed more porous than bone."

Catherine's eyes tightened. "Do they show traces of—"

"Haven't got that far yet."

"How far *have* you gotten, Greg?"

He gave a smug pixie smile. "Oh—just enough to say that Derek Fairmont was, in fact, poisoned."

The two CSIs and the detectives traded expectant expressions, allowing the lab tech to savor his dramatic pause.

"I tested the tissue samples from the University Medical Center," Greg said, "and found traces of prussic acid."

Warrick grunted. "Cyanide."

Vega asked, "If these organs were donated, wouldn't that have turned up before now?"

"No," Greg said. "These are traces. Wouldn'ta got on the medical radar. And the organs that have been transplanted—which is all of 'em—would function just fine."

Catherine was frowning. "With just traces, could that be written off as an . . . accident of some kind? Some innocent exposure to prussic acid?"

"If Fairmont had been a cow, Catherine—yes. I might in that case think these traces were accidental.

Prussic acid poisoning is a problem with grazing animals, since it occurs in the epidermal cells of sorghums, and other related species those animals eat. Since Fairmont was a human, I'm gonna go waaay out on the edge and say . . . this is poisoning."

"Probably," Catherine said wryly, "nobody forced sorghum on him."

"Not likely. My educated guess? Rat poison."

Warrick winced in thought. "Plain old-fashioned commercial rat poison?"

"Yes—not that hard to get, and several major brands still use prussic acid as their active ingredient. It inhibits oxygen utilization by the body's cells. For all intents and purposes . . ."

Greg gestured to the skull, and his expression was somber now; nothing funny about this.

". . . Derek Fairmont suffocated. What's more, it's the same poison that killed Gary Masters."

"Good!" Catherine said, then realized her response sounded odd. She explained, saying to Greg, "I was hoping you'd run that right away."

"I anticipated that, and what I found was, the toxic stuff is all over the wine bottle . . . *and* the glass he was drinking from." He held up the autopsy report. "And my associate, Doctor Albert Robbins, concurs: death by poisoning. Actually, not that common a murder technique, these days."

"Making it easier to miss," Warrick said almost to himself, "than you'd think."

Vega said, "We've got her using the same poison for two victims."

Catherine said, "Don't break out the champagne

just yet—the same poison doesn't an MO make. The husband was killed over a long period of time, in small doses . . . hence the traces of poison in his remains."

Greg said, "She's right."

Warrick, smirking humorlessly, said, "Well, we do know Rene Fairmont's poison of choice, at least. All we need now is a way to prove our nasty nurse did these murders."

Greg scratched the side of his head. "Didn't you guys mention that Derek died in Mexico?"

Warrick nodded.

Catherine said, "Yeah."

Greg cocked his head. "Did you come up with a Mexican death certificate?"

Catherine wondered where Greg was going with this. "Yeah, we did, it was faxed to us—says heart attack."

Greg's smile was almost as charming as one of Grissom's. "Tell me—was there a consular mortuary certificate?"

Catherine winced. "A what?"

"If the Mexican death certificate said heart attack, my guess is someone was bribed," Greg said. "I mean, the poison was right there for anyone to see . . . and if there's no consular mortuary certificate, and Derek here really did die in Mexico . . . then his wife brought him back illegally. Which is against the law. I mean, that's a federal law she's broken."

Catherine looked at Greg with a newfound respect. "How did you know all that?"

"It's 22 U.S.C. 4196; 22 CFR 72.1."

"Huh?"

"That's the part of the federal code that deals with

the death of U.S. citizens abroad." Greg smiled. He showed the cheat sheet in his hand. "Hey, where would science be without Google?"

Vega had a grimly satisfied expression. "We need to report that to the feds."

"I'll do it," Catherine said.

"And in the meantime," the detective said, "I'm going out to Sunny Day and have another chat with Rene Fairmont."

"We may not have enough to arrest her yet," Warrick said. "But this is a hell of a series of coincidences—seems like everyone she knows turns up murdered."

"Why don't you come with me, Warrick," Vega said, then turned to Catherine. "How about you, Cath?"

"No, Sam—I'll make that federal call . . . doing my best not to have to talk to agent Rick Culpepper . . . and then I'm going to see if I can run down those presumably bogus charities of hers. Keep Rene talking, and maybe between Uncle Sam and my own Google-ing, you can put the collar on her."

"We have enough to bring her back here for questioning," Vega said.

When Vega and Warrick were gone, Catherine turned back to Greg. "Thanks, Greg."

"No problem."

"Don't lose your focus, now—heads up."

"Oh yeah," Greg said, and he reached for the skull.

Warrick took the Tahoe and drove, Vega riding, and when they drew up at the Sunny Day guard shack, the CSI found the silver-haired guard, Fred, on duty.

Fred approached the vehicle and asked, "Hello again, fellas. What can I do for ya?"

"Hi Fred," Warrick said. "Rene Fairmont on duty this afternoon?"

The guard said, "Well, she was, but then she left about half an hour ago. Funny deal."

"Funny how?"

"She was only in for, oh I'd say . . . five minutes? Then she took off. Drove outta here, faster'n a bat out of hell. Next time I see her, I'm gonna talk to her about that. That's reckless behavior, for an employee."

Warrick looked at Vega and said, "Flight risk?"

"Oh yeah," the detective said with a curt nod. "Go!"

"Fred, stand clear," Warrick said, and jammed the Tahoe into reverse to peel out the driveway. He braked, tossed the gearshift into drive, and floored it, tires squealing as Vega got the dashboard light flashing and pulled the cell phone from his pocket.

"Who're you calling?" Warrick asked.

"Dr. Whiting—just watch the road!"

Warrick did as he was told, thanking the powers-that-be that Lake Mead Drive would eventually turn into Interstate 215. Trying to drive clear across this busy city, through snarled street traffic, would have cost them precious time, even with a flasher going.

Rene Fairmont had the same knowledge, of course, *and* a half hour head start. The siren's whine kept Warrick from hearing much of Vega's brief conversation with Dr. Whiting. When the detective hung up, they had to shout to be heard over the shrill siren scream.

"What did Whiting *say?*" Warrick yelled.

"That Rene said she had an emergency and just

split! He tried to ask what was wrong, but she just grabbed her things and said she had to leave."

"I don't think Fred's ever going to get a chance to have his talk with Rene about recklessness."

"Me neither," Vega said. "But maybe *we* can. . . ."

Warrick kept the pressure on the accelerator. The angel of mercy had the sense to know they were getting onto her, it seemed; maybe she wouldn't know how close they were . . . maybe they would reach this angel in time, before she flew off into her next identity. . . .

Catherine had returned to looking into the various bogus charities, seeking some commonality between the entities themselves or at least their dead-drop mailboxes: ten different charities, not counting D.S. Ward Worldwide and its Des Moines drop, with ten different drop box sites.

Although three of the mailboxes were local, the other seven were out of state. She would check, in person, the three locals, scattered around the city; already she'd memorized their locations.

Out of state would be trickier: Jonathan Hooker Ministries in Salt Lake City; Father Lonnegan's Children's Fund, Laramie, Wyoming; Shaw Ministries, Grand Island, Nebraska; Pastor Henry Newman Charities in Joliet, Illinois; and three more even farther east.

If Rene Fairmont was behind all these scams, how exactly was she picking up the money? In-person pickup was required. Could the woman have an accomplice in every one of these cities? That didn't seem likely—this was a loner's game. . . .

The CSI decided to turn the computer loose on the

problem. Into a search, she typed all the keywords from the charity names. While that ran, she pulled up a map of the United States and highlighted all the cities with Rene's drops.

In less than a minute, Catherine felt her mouth drop and her eyes pop.

All of the cities lined up.

From Vegas, I-15 north to Salt Lake City, then east on I-80 through Laramie, Grand Island, Des Moines, Joliet and so on. It wasn't just a network of scams, and certainly not an indication of accomplices hither and yon: *This was an escape route.*

The plan opened like a blossoming flower to Catherine, in all its sick beauty. With this route waiting, Rene Fairmont could pick up, leave town, and melt into the sunset. Well, sunrise actually, since she'd be traveling eastward.

Depending on how much money waited at each drop, their venal angel of mercy could come and go from each city, whenever she wanted. As far as Rene knew, no one figured out her route or her plan.

A chill prickled the back of Catherine's neck: She knew—and it was well beyond a hunch, even Grissom couldn't question this—that Rene was getting ready to run. The sleazoid local lawyer used in several of the estate scams the woman had tied off like the loose end that he'd become—perhaps right after Catherine and Vega had spoken to her at the Fairmont home—and probably right about now Warrick and Vega were discovering that Nurse Fairmont had departed Sunny Day as well.

Catherine was reaching for her cell phone when the results of her computer search came up.

The charity names all had something in common, too—they represented a colossal, arrogant thumbing-of-her-nose by Rene to anyone who sought to catch up with her.

The names had led Catherine to IMDb.com, the Internet Movie Database. And every one of the names of the fake charities came from a single source—*The Sting*, the 1973 film about clever con artists taking down a big score. D.S. Ward Worldwide was a reference to the picture's writer, David S. Ward; Jonathan Hooker, Johnny Hooker, Robert Redford's character; Pastor Henry Newman, taken from the first name of Henry Gondorff and the last name of the actor who'd played that role, Paul Newman . . . they all had some resonance within the famous movie. Robert Shaw had portrayed the villain, Lonnegan, his name and the character's showing up in a pair of the charities.

In a matter of seconds, she'd taken this in, and—hopping mad—she hit speed-dial for Warrick.

Surprisingly, she got Vega instead, as well as the distinctive sound of a wailing siren.

"Warrick's busy driving," Vega said, signal crackling and breaking up. *"We think Rene Fairmont's making a run for it."*

"I'm sure she is," Catherine said. "That's what I called to tell you—she's got an escape route set up, conducive to picking up her stashes at the mailbox drops."

Vega said something that got eaten up in static— one of the downsides of working in Las Vegas was the cell phone signal sometimes just plain sucked.

"What?" she yelled into the phone.

Vega's voice came back, clearer now. *"Warrick and I are headed for her house."*

"I'll check the local drops," she said, clicked off, and ran out.

No red Grand Prix awaited in the driveway when Warrick pulled up to the ranch-style house on Rustic Ridge Drive with its browning lawn and FOR SALE sign. The CSI and the detective came out of the Tahoe, guns drawn. Warrick grabbed the ram out of the back—the Fairmont woman's flight gave them probable cause—and Vega led the way toward the house. Howling sirens in the distance told Warrick backup was on its way.

While Vega covered him, Warrick holstered his weapon long enough to swing the battering ram into the front door—the lock exploded inward, the door yawned open, and Warrick dropped the ram to pull his pistol again.

With Vega in the lead, the duo went through room by room. When the house was established as clear, the CSI holstered his gun and shook his head in frustration.

No doubt about it: Rene Fairmont was already gone.

The master bedroom, more than anything, told the story, the closet door thrown open, rejected clothes on the floor, the bed, and still hanging in the closet. The woman had clearly packed quickly and bailed.

"What next?" asked an exasperated Vega.

"Next," Warrick said, "we go through this damn house and see what we can find."

Not long after Warrick and Vega had hit the door, the uniforms had shown up, and they now had the neighborhood cordoned off.

Vega said, "Guess I better canvass the neighbors, and break up the siege outside. I don't suppose she's coming back. . . ."

"Sure she is. Right after M.C. Hammer."

The detective sighed, and ambled out, saying, "Better put out an APB on her car, too."

After a cursory look around, Warrick retrieved his crime scene kit from the Tahoe and began work in earnest.

In the bedroom, little useful presented itself, at first. The CSI did find a cream-colored dress with red roses on it, on the floor, which he bagged. Then he rooted around in the closet, coming across something really worth finding: a plastic grocery bag on the floor containing several wigs, one of which was gray. A pair of glasses that looked like tri-focals but were clear glass was stuffed in the bag as well.

When Vega came back from his canvass of the neighbors, Warrick held up the wig in one evidence bag and the glasses in another.

The CSI said, "Meet the *other* Mabel Hinton."

"Hello Mabel," Vega said dryly.

"What about the neighbors?"

The detective shrugged. "Nobody's seen much. They say Rene Fairmont isn't a friendly neighbor. Keeps to herself. Woman next door says Rene left right before we got here. Says Rene loaded her car with suitcases before peeling away."

"You got the APB out, right?" Warrick asked.

"Yeah," Vega said. "But it's a big city and 'red Grand Prix' may not narrow it much. . . . Should we contact the airport and train station?"

"If you want, but Catherine says there's an escape route via car and interstate."

"Better cover our bases," Vega said, and got on his cell.

Warrick kept looking.

In the bathroom adjacent to the bedroom, he found a drawer filled with elaborate theatrical makeup. Later, in the kitchen wastebasket, amid coffee grounds and other trash, he discovered forensics treasure: a square envelope in Mabel Hinton's handwriting addressed to Vivian Elliot and three typing-paper sheets of practice attempts (presumably by Rene Fairmont) to duplicate the signature that was part of Mabel's handwritten return address.

After bagging and tagging, Warrick shared this gold with Vega, who was pleased, or as pleased as the man could be with their angel of mercy on the run.

Warrick got on the cell and updated Catherine.

"Not just the wig and dress," he said, "but the greasepaint and the works—never mind *Derek* Fairmont . . . Rene could have run the UWN drama department from Rustic Ridge Drive."

"*So,*" Catherine's voice crackled over the cell, "*Rene went into Sunny Day in disguise, killed her victim, then just melted out of sight in all the distraction of the code blue.*"

"Looks like it," Warrick said. "That way she never drew attention to herself. Didn't want all the victims to die on her shift. . . . And she seems to have swiped an envelope from a get-well card sent to Vivian at Sunny Day. I got three pages of forger practice sheets, Cath."

"Sweet. . . . Look, Warrick, I'm going to the Rent-A-Box on Warm Springs. Why don't you and Sam meet up with me there?"

"How come?"

"If Rene's really splitting, maybe she'll stop to pick up some traveling money. One of the charities she used has a drop at the Rent-A-Box. I've been to two others with no luck."

"Maybe she hadn't been there yet."

"I called to post uniforms at both. Listen, I can't believe she won't stop at one of 'em, before she books it."

"On our way. Where on Warm Springs?"

"Strip mall near Green Valley Parkway."

"I know it," Warrick said. "See you there."

A block away from the Rent-A-Box, Catherine turned off the flashers (she wasn't using the siren, not wanting to warn Rene Fairmont), slowed down slightly, then passed through the last intersection and wheeled the Tahoe into the parking lot.

Along with the mailboxes location, half a dozen or so other businesses made up the modest strip mall, with maybe fifteen cars in the parking lot. She quickly scanned the vehicles for Rene's Grand Prix, didn't see it, but then caught a glimpse of bright red beyond a big navy blue SUV. . . .

Pulling forward, to see past the SUV, Catherine's flicker of red identified itself as a red Pontiac Grand Prix all right. The CSI was about to pull forward, to block the car's path, when the Pontiac suddenly backed out of its parking place, nearly hitting the Tahoe, and zoomed out of the parking lot to turn west onto Warm Springs Road.

Catherine, having slammed on the brakes when the Pontiac backed up, needed a few seconds to get moving forward again. By that time, the light at the exit had changed and she watched helplessly as several cars slowly eased past her while, up the road, the red Pontiac threatened to disappear.

Using her ear bud, Catherine could talk to Warrick on the phone and keep her hands free to drive. That was, of course, if the damned line of cars ever got out of her way. . . .

Catherine was about to say the hell with it and hit the siren when she found a spot to get in. She could turn on the siren, and catch up to the Pontiac quickly; but she was in no big hurry to take down a murderer without backup.

She got through to Warrick as she began weaving through traffic. "Where are you?"

"*On the beltway,*" Warrick said. "*We're headed your way.*"

"Better find another route," Catherine said. "She's turning north on Eastern."

"*Roger that,*" Warrick said. "*We're getting off on Paradise.*"

Paradise would allow Warrick and Vega to run parallel with Rene and Catherine. If Rene turned left, the suspect would be turning right into their path. Catherine was getting nearer, and having an easier time keeping the Pontiac in sight. She wanted to pull the woman over—Warrick was closer now—but did she dare do so in the middle of all this traffic?

Though Rene was driving fast, the woman wasn't speeding any more than most of the drivers on the road—which was good, because it might mean the suspect didn't know Catherine was back here on her tail.

Maybe Catherine could afford to wait until Warrick was even closer, when they might get a chance to bust this woman without doing it in the middle of a traffic jam. Serving and protecting citizens was a concept at odds with putting them in the middle of a shoot-out or a high-speed chase. . . .

Then Rene swung left on Sunset.

Catherine followed, three cars between them, and suddenly she had the feeling that everything was going to work out.

"Warrick," she said. "We're eastbound on Sunset, headed your way."

"I'll be waiting," his voice replied.

But Catherine's confidence took a dive as she saw the Pontiac lunge right, cross two lanes of traffic, and disappear into a parking lot. The CSI stomped the brakes, heard tires squeal behind her, then jumped the two lanes of traffic herself . . . only she missed the access drive!

She didn't want to hop the sidewalk, and—realizing she was in front of a branch of the First Monument Bank—caught the next drive into the bank, going in the one-way wrong. She kept her foot on the brake, pausing there, facing the one-way drive-thru (which was customerless at the moment), as if contemplating a right turn into the parking lot in front of the bank.

The red Pontiac was nowhere in sight and Catherine figured Rene had driven behind the bank building, to come back this way and around through the drive-thru.

"Warrick," she said crisply, "we're at the First

Monument Bank on Sunset. Suspect seems about to use the drive-thru. Her driving may indicate she spotted me; or this could be a cash stop. In any event, we need to bust her before she leaves the bank."

"We're onto Sunset," Warrick's voice assured her.

Catherine saw the other Tahoe in her rearview mirror. "I see you! Sight for sore eyes . . ."

"We'll go in the entrance, go around, and come up behind her."

"Ten-four," Catherine said, as Rene's Pontiac drew around the corner of the building.

Rene's hand came out the driver's side window, dropped something into the slide drawer, then disappeared back into the car.

Where was Warrick? He should've been coming around the building by now . . . and then, finally, there was Warrick and Vega in their own beautiful SUV, easing up behind Rene.

The drive-thru drawer opened again, and Rene withdrew an envelope. Her hand disappeared back inside the car and the Pontiac didn't move for endless seconds.

Catherine started creeping forward, hoping Rene wouldn't notice the Tahoe closing the distance between itself and the Grand Prix, and not turning into the parking lot. She needed to nail Rene just after the woman pulled away from the drive-thru window, before she got back on the road.

The glass of the drive-thru window would be bulletproof, but Catherine saw no reason to take any chances at all. Warrick was in line immediately behind Rene, and they would soon have her boxed in. The only thing left was to close the trap.

The car started toward her and Catherine hit the gas to cut her off.

Rene hit the brakes, stopped the Pontiac and came barreling out of the car, on the driver's side, a large canvas bag of a purse slung over a shoulder.

The suspect had made them!

And now Rene, blonde hair flouncing, in a white blouse, dark slacks, and heels, was trying to make her escape on foot.

Catherine slammed on the brakes, threw the Tahoe in park, and leapt from the vehicle, yanking her pistol from its hip holster. She didn't point the weapon at Rene, since—right behind her—Warrick and Vega were coming out of their vehicle and were in Catherine's line of fire. If she shot and missed Rene—a distinct possibility, with the range changing every second—she could easily hit one of her own team.

Conversely, if they should fire and miss, she'd be on the target line.

Catherine resisted the urge to raise the weapon, even as Rene came rushing toward her. Then, at the last second, Rene veered away from Catherine, toward the bank.

Wheeling, the pistol finally up and ready to take aim, Catherine could see why Rene had cut to one side—an older woman . . . gray and frail and not so different from the Sunny Day victims of the angel of mercy . . . stood on the sidewalk in front of the bank. The older woman had just come out of the building and held her purse in both hands, probably waiting to be picked up.

The old gal didn't have long to wait: Rene swung

around behind her, making a shield of the woman, who squawked in surprise as her assailant's left arm looped around her neck, the other hand fishing in that big purse.

Catherine kept the gun trained on the pair as a syringe rose up in Rene's right hand, stopping just short of the older woman's creped throat.

"I always wanted to say this to a cop," Rene snarled. *"Freeze!"*

Warrick and Vega came up alongside Catherine, and made with her a three-person line facing Rene and her hostage—the two CSIs and the detective each with a handgun poised to shoot.

"What's in the syringe, Rene?" Catherine said. "Prussic acid?"

"How'd you *guess,* bitch?"

Traffic had slowed, and bystanders were peering from windows of nearby buildings, and Catherine hoped 911 had been called by now—backup would be nice. Sweat trickled down Rene's face, like the tears the killer was probably incapable of shedding, and the hostage's eyes were wide, pitifully so, brimming with terror.

"Well," Catherine said, "it's what you used on your lawyer friend, isn't it? And what you gave to your husband."

Catherine had a fine line to walk, between scaring the hostage further, and keeping the attention of a serial killer.

Rene's eyes were wide now, a weird echo of her hostage's frightened countenance. "How the hell could you know about Derek?"

"He told us—his generosity did, anyway, leaving his

skull to the college and his organs to the medical center. . . . Rene, it's over. You need to let that woman go."

"Think so? I'll need a new lawyer, won't I?"

Without a word being spoken, the trio from LVPD slowly started fanning out—Vega was at left, Warrick in the middle, Catherine on the right, nearest the street.

"You got cocky, Rene—and then sloppy. We know about *all* of them—not just Derek and the lawyer and Vivian Elliot, but the other victims at Sunny Day."

Rene was a beautiful woman; still, her smile over her hostage's shoulder was hideous. "Oh, you think that's *all* of them?"

Catherine and Vega each eased yet another step away from Warrick. . . .

And this time, Rene spotted it. "I said freeze, damn it! All of you!" The syringe drew closer to the old woman's neck. Rene looked toward Vega. "You—! Drop the gun."

The detective took a long moment, glancing at Warrick and Catherine for support they couldn't offer; then finally complied.

"Now you," she said to Warrick.

Warrick knelt, carefully placed his pistol on the concrete in front of him, and slowly stood.

Rene turned slightly, the hostage moving with her now, and faced Catherine, looking over the old woman's shoulder. "Now you, Nancy Drew. Drop it!"

Catherine knew her only advantage right now was having the late afternoon sun at her back. She must be a silhouette to Rene, little more. . . .

"Make me ask *again*, bitch—and see what happens!"

Catherine held up her left hand in a "slow down" fashion, then began to bend to lay down her weapon, though she had no intention of doing so. It was well within Rene Fairmont's character to grab one of their weapons from the cement and shoot all three of them.

The CSI would have to shoot . . .

. . . though with precious little of Rene showing to aim at, and no margin at all for error. Catherine kept crouching lower, the shot ever more precarious.

Vega said, "Give it up, lady—you got no way outta here."

"I think I do," Rene said, and shook her hostage, who cried out in fear. "I have a *senior* travel *discount.* . . ."

Catherine was hunkered down now, the gun barely inches off the pavement. "Say you *do* make it out of here," the CSI said, "by car or plane or magic carpet. You're still washed up."

"Shut up and put the gun *down.* . . ."

"Y'see, we know where all your drop boxes are—all your fake charities. So much work, so much death—and you're never going to see a penny of it."

Something feral went off inside Rene.

The angel of mercy pulled the syringe back, incrementally, to gain momentum to drive the needle into the old woman's neck . . .

. . . but in the momentary window that provided, Catherine rolled to her left, nearly sweeping Warrick's feet out from under him, and on her stomach, with a better angle, she fired up, the sound of it like a whip crack as the shot shook Rene's shoulder, sending the syringe spinning through the air where it bounced onto the parking lot with a plastic clatter.

The other two rescuers snatched up their weapons

even as Rene—with an animal cry of pain and rage—fell backward, taking the old woman with her. The hostage landed on top of Rene, then rolled off and scurried away with surprising spryness, leaving the killer prone on the ground with a wounded arm, the wind—and her future—knocked out of her.

Vega went to the hostage and swept her into his arms, getting her away, as Warrick stood over their suspect with his handgun aimed at Rene's face.

"Just try something, Nurse Fairmont," Warrick said, "and it'll be time for *your* shot."

Catherine felt bile rising within her and fought the urge to purge.

She wasn't upset about the shooting. It was righteous enough. But she would lose sleep over possibly endangering that suspect with such Annie Oakley nonsense. Still, she'd had less than a second to make her decision and knew she'd made the right one.

Oddly, she was relieved she hadn't had to kill the angel of mercy, much as the monster might deserve it. Catherine Willows already had two kills to live with, and that seemed sufficient to her.

Suddenly Warrick was at her side. "You okay, Cath?"

"Yeah. Yeah. Peachy. I was just thinking . . ."

"Yeah?"

"Wasn't Sunny Day supposed to be a *normal* call?"

11

Gil Grissom sat in his darkened office at a desk piled left and right with paperwork, which he was ignoring in favor of staring into his thoughts.

Jim Brass poked his head in and said, "Brooding? Meditating? Saving the city on the electric bill?"

Grissom waved Brass in. The detective took the liberty of hitting the light switch, which caused the CSI supervisor to grimace.

Brass dropped himself into the chair opposite. "We have a good suspect, finally. Why are you troubled?"

"I'm not troubled," Grissom said. "I'm just not convinced."

"The evidence—"

"Not enough yet. And there are anomalies."

Brass winced. "I hate it when you use that word. . . ."

"Such as . . . whoever murdered Kathy Dean also disposed of Rita Bennett's body. Where are those remains?"

"Who knows? But who better than a guy like Black to stage the disappearing act? Getting rid of corpses is his racket."

"Why, then—in a house of corpses—would our presumed guilty party, mortician Dustin Black, choose a high-profile local celebrity like the Bennett woman for the switch?"

"I have no idea," Brass admitted. "She must have been . . . handy."

"Handy? The choice of Rita is further compounded by the used-car queen having been a *friend* of our mortician."

Brass shrugged. "I have to tell you? People do wacked-out things"

"Granted." Grissom sat forward. "But doesn't it strike you as odd that Black, running a mortuary where dozens of bodies move through in a week, didn't pick a stranger for his shuffle?"

Brass ticked off on his fingers. "Motive points to Black. Opportunity points to Black . . . means to dispose of the body, possession of the murder weapon. Somebody told me once that the evidence doesn't lie."

"No. But you have to ask it the right questions."

Amusement twitched at Brass's lips. "You know what, Gil? I think you're a man with a hunch. Hey, happens to the best of us. Even atheists pray in foxholes."

Grissom arched an eyebrow. "Well, right now I'm praying for more evidence. At the moment, I'm waiting for lab results. Anything on your end?"

"Also waiting. Patrolmen are bringing in Grunick and Doyle from the Desert Haven staff—assistant morticians who helped with Rita Bennett's funeral."

"Makes sense," Grissom said, nodding. "If Black did switch the bodies, one of them may have seen something. Meaning no criticism, Jim—we should have interviewed them sooner."

Brass sighed. "Yeah, I know, and we *would* have, if Black hadn't kept us hopping, chasing down his lies."

"Let me know when the junior morticians arrive. I'd like to watch the interviews."

"Will do."

First to be led by a patrolman into HQ was Mark Grunick, in a conservative suit the color of a storm-bearing sky, his short dark hair fading north of his forehead, ears sticking out slightly.

In the observation booth adjacent to the interview room, through the one-way glass, Grissom watched and listened.

Seated at the table with its two chairs, a portable cassette recorder nearby, Grunick had a passive manner that may have reflected the fatalism of his chosen profession. If being interviewed by a police detective created any anxiety in this subject, Grissom would hate to see the assistant mortician bored.

Brass, seated across from Grunick, hit the RECORD button. "State your name, please."

"Mark Patrick Grunick." The young man looked at Brass with an unblinking expression that was not quite sullen. "I'd like to know why I was brought in."

Brass outlined the situation in very general terms, which were nonetheless startling, though you wouldn't know it by the assistant mortician's shrug.

"I don't think so," Grunick said.

"What don't you think?"

"That any kind of switch was made. Mix-up maybe—that's a long shot. But a switch? It's not a horror movie; it's a funeral home."

Brass cocked his head. "Mr. Grunick, I was there

when the casket was exhumed. That wasn't Rita Bennett in the coffin. It was a young woman named Kathy Dean."

"Fine, if you say so—but I don't know how that could've happened. Before the service, Jimmy and I closed the coffin ourselves."

Brass smiled with what might have been patience but wasn't. "Why don't you think carefully and give this to me in more detail? A lot more."

Grunick sighed, which was the first indication the young man was capable of an emotional response; he looked skyward, as if referring to notes in the air.

Finally he said, "We sat through the service, took the casket out, loaded it in the hearse, went to the cemetery, had the committal service there, and the casket was interred. The end. Literally."

Brass's eyes narrowed. "You were with the coffin for every second?"

"*Yes*—that is why it's *impossible*. . . ."

Brass tossed a picture of Kathy Dean in the coffin onto the table in front of the interview subject. "Not impossible. It happened . . . and I'm asking you again. Think hard. Were . . . you . . . with . . . the . . . coffin . . . *every* . . . second?"

His brow knit as he indeed thought about it. Then the color drained from Grunick's face.

"Wait," he said. "Wait a minute . . . I'm sorry. I *am* sorry."

"About . . . ?"

Energy came into the young man's manner and his expression. "I *do* see how it happened. . . . Understand, in most cases these days, the pallbearers are ceremonial.

We're the ones that do the work, and it's always the same: After Mr. Black backs the hearse up to the door, Jimmy and I do the lifting. That one funeral, Rita Bennett, though—it didn't go down that way, not exactly."

"What did happen 'exactly,' Mark?"

"Well, Mr. Black and Jimmy were talking about something. I was leading the way, and the two of them were pushing the cart with the coffin down the hall . . . toward the side door? Anyway, they were blabbing and I couldn't hear about what, nor did I care . . . but suddenly Jimmy peeled off and went back into the chapel. And when we got to the door, Mr. Black told me *he'd* watch the body while I got the car."

"So Black was alone with the coffin."

"Sure, which means he was alone with the body. And I'll bet *that's* when the switch went down!"

Brass nodded now, playing along as the guy got more into it. "What happened, Mark, when you came back with the hearse?"

"Well, we loaded the coffin in the hearse."

"Who did?"

"Jimmy and me."

"Where was Mr. Black?"

Mark Grunick shrugged. "I'm not really sure. Maybe in the limo, already . . . didn't think about it then. Jimmy was there, and him and me loaded the body. Things were, you know, back to normal."

"When do you remember seeing Black again?"

"Oh, well, by the time the procession was ready to leave, Mr. Black was behind the wheel of the limo. Jimmy and me, we were in the hearse."

In the observation booth, Grissom heard the door

behind him open and he looked back at a grave Nick, in the doorway. The younger CSI gestured for Grissom to join him out in the hall.

"Something, Nick?"

"Something, all right. I fingerprinted Black."

"Good."

"Then I compared his prints to the ones we had from the coffin? His prints are on the casket Kathy Dean was in."

"Also good. If to be expected."

"Well, maybe that is. But I lifted prints off the gun—"

"Really? You got prints off the gun? Unusual."

Nick shrugged. "Being packed away in that box, all those smaller boxes on top of it, kept the gun cool and safe from the weather. Desert Haven's garage being air-conditioned didn't hurt, either."

"So," Grissom said, "is that the unexpected development?"

"Not really." Nick's expression was apologetic. "I printed Black, and his prints don't match the ones on the gun. Indicates Black is not the shooter."

"Well."

"And the hairs found in the casket with Kathy? Not the undertaker's either. Sorry."

Grissom shook his head, then said, "Never apologize for the evidence, Nick. We listen to it, it doesn't listen to us."

Nick said, "Well if it did, it'd hear me saying, 'Huh?' "

"Is the weapon with the firearms examiner?"

"Yeah, I dropped it off. We haven't confirmed it as the murder weapon yet, though the caliber is right."

"One step at a time," Grissom said. "Now, here's what I want you to do next. . . ."

He laid out a plan and Nick nodded, and went off to carry it out. Grissom was about to head back in to the observation booth for the rest of the Grunick interview when his cell phone chirped.

"Grissom."

"It's Sara. Got the results of the DNA tests—Dustin Black is the father of Kathy Dean's baby."

"Not really a surprise."

"And I finally tracked down Janie Glover. Off to interview her now."

"Janie Glover? Remind me."

"Kathy Dean's friend . . . who told our Habinero's waitress about 'FB'?"

"Ah. Good."

"Is Black looking more guilty, or less?"

"Too early."

They rang off.

As he turned back toward the booth, the interview-room door opened and Mark Grunick filed out, followed by Brass. A free man, the slightly shell-shocked-looking Grunick kept going, while Brass fell in alongside Grissom.

"Well," Brass said cheerfully, "young Mr. Grunick seems to like his boss for the body switch. And so do I."

"Don't get ahead of yourself, Jim."

Exasperated, Brass invited the CSI supervisor into the observation booth so their discussion wouldn't be in front of the whole world.

Forcefully, the detective pointed out, "The murder weapon was found in Black's place of business."

"We haven't confirmed that it's the murder weapon."

"It's the right caliber, it's been fired. . . ."

"Probably is the murder weapon. Probably isn't enough. We'll know soon."

"For the sake of argument, then. Say it's the murder weapon."

"All right," Grissom said. "Let's say it is."

"Now we're getting somewhere. . . ."

"Black's fingerprints weren't on it."

Brass's eyes popped. "What . . . ? Well, then Black wore gloves, or wiped it clean."

"Someone else's prints are on the gun."

"Who in hell's?"

Grissom shrugged. "We don't know yet. May I make a suggestion?"

"Please!"

"Get the prints from the other mortician's assistant—Doyle."

Brass's eyes narrowed. "What about the other assistant—Grunick?"

"I posted Nick up around the corner—waiting to bump into Mr. Grunick, as he exits. My guess is when they separate, Nick will have some helpful fingerprints."

Finally Brass seemed to like something Grissom had said. "Sneaky," he said with admiration.

"And if Black is innocent," Grissom said, "these two are our next most likely suspects. They're the only other ones who had access to Rita Bennett's casket."

"Makes sense."

"And Kathy Dean was seeing a younger man, in addition to Black—the assistants are in that age range."

"Now you're talking. . . ."

"If one of them's the killer, Jim, we can't put too much stock in what they individually have to say in interview. We can't expect either one to be cooperative or honest, when it comes to helping us catch him."

"One should be telling the truth. . . ."

"Right. Not to tell a skilled interrogator what to be looking for, but inconsistencies between Grunick's interview and young Doyle's could be . . . helpful."

Brass's cell phone rang. "Brass . . . Yeah, all right, interview room one." He hung up. "Doyle's here," he said.

As if those words were the starting gun, Grissom dashed off, leaving Brass wondering what the hell that was about. In the breakroom, the CSI got a can of soda out of the fridge; he wiped it down with a towel and held it gingerly by the top edges and took it to the interrogation room, where Brass was waiting for Doyle to come in.

"For me?" Brass said, looking at the soda can. "I didn't think you cared."

"I do care," Grissom said. "About this case . . ." He placed the can on the table, touching only the sides of the top. "Offer it to Doyle, a few minutes in."

Brass, smiling knowingly, nodded.

Then Grissom exited to assume his position in the observation booth. Moments later a uniformed officer escorted Jimmy Doyle into Interview, depositing him at the table.

Unlike fellow mortician-in-the-making Grunick, Doyle's attire was unfunereal—navy blue Dockers, a lavender dress shirt, open at the throat, loafers with no socks. His black hair was slicked back. The anonymous funeral home helper suddenly struck Grissom as a young man who might have looked attractive to affection-hungry Kathy Dean.

Brass hit RECORD again and filled in Doyle about the body switch and the discovery of Kathy Dean's body. He put the dead girl's photo before the interview subject—the same in-the-coffin shot.

Doyle glanced at the photo of the deceased Kathy Dean. "Never saw her before—good-looking girl, though."

Brass twitched a smile. "Considering she was dead for several months when this was taken, you mean."

The young man shrugged. "I work in a funeral home. I can see past that."

"Ah . . . Tell me what happened with the Rita Bennett service."

Doyle lacked Grunick's sullenness; he seemed fine with helping the police.

"Mark and I closed the casket, right before the service. Afterward, Mark rolled the coffin back, Mr. Black and me pushed it, as we went from the chapel . . . to the side door where we load, y'know?"

"I'm familiar," Brass said.

"Mr. Black said that the flowers from the top of the casket were missing, which they were. I said I was sorry, that I thought he'd put 'em back on after we closed the coffin. He said no, and sent me back, toot sweet, to the chapel."

"For the flowers?"

"For the flowers." Doyle shrugged. "It was just a small spray, and no one noticed it during the service, but a good mortician pays attention to details, and Mr. Black's a good mortician. Anyway . . . I catch up, and the coffin's sitting alone in the corridor. And there's no sign of Mr. Black."

"That's unusual?"

"Real unusual! So Mark pulls up with the hearse, then him and me load the coffin. Just as we're wondering where the hell Mr. Black is, he comes out and jumps in the limo. To me, he looked sweaty, and . . . well, this is an opinion. Is that all right to express?"

"Sure, son."

"Well, he looked like something was really bothering him. Freaked out, kinda."

Brass leaned in. "Any idea what was the matter?"

Doyle shook his head. "No, sir. Not a clue."

"You okay, Jimmy?" Brass gestured to the soda can. "Help yourself, if you're thirsty."

Shaking his head again, Doyle said, "Never touch that junk—too much sugar."

On his side of the mirror, Grissom frowned. But then, to his amazement and pleasure, the CSI saw Doyle pick up the soda can and move it next to the tape recorder, closer to Brass. *"But you can have it if you want, Captain Brass—won't bother me."*

Brass smiled again. *"Thanks, Jimmy. Maybe later."*

The interview continued, but the explosive aspects had all passed; everything else was mundane material about Doyle's work at Desert Haven. Soon the talk was over, and James Doyle was allowed to leave.

Grissom slipped into the interview room and carefully took charge of the soda can and transported it down to the lab for fingerprinting.

If the boy was telling the truth, the CSI could easily see how Dustin Black could have committed the crime.

Kathy Dean—shot to death the night before—is packed away in a matching coffin. The mortician knows his business, after all, and keeps his inventory, so only he will know that the two coffins are both gone.

Black sends Jimmy Doyle back into the chapel, for the conveniently missing flowers, and Mark Grunick out to fetch the hearse. This allows the mortician a minute, maybe even two, to make the well-planned switch. Storage rooms of various sorts are off the corridors of Desert Haven, each one under lock and key—locks and keys controlled by Black.

The mortician Black unlocks a door, rolls out a waiting cart with Kathy in the matching casket. He leaves that in the hall, and pushes Rita's casket somewhere, and hides it for later disposal, at his leisure. . . .

No one would've found anything unusual about seeing the mortician rolling a casket cart along. Business as usual. But a nagging question remained— if Black's prints weren't on the murder weapon, then . . . whose were? And what about the hairs in Kathy's coffin that were not hers?

Grissom had dropped the soda can off and was heading back to his office when a voice from a doorway called out to him.

Archie Johnson—the slender Asian video tech— waved to him from a lab door, a self-satisfied grin playing on his lips.

"Got a second to look at something, Doctor Grissom?"

"As long as it's not another episode of *Happy Tree Friends*, Archie."

Archie grinned. "Almost as good . . ."

Grissom followed the young tech into the video lab where a black-and-white image was frozen on a monitor. Grissom moved closer and realized he was viewing the inside of a convenience store, from a security camera aimed at the door. Most of the front windows could be seen, the front counter and register as well. The picture quality was far superior to what Grissom might have expected from a convenience store security cam.

"How much have you made this image dance, Archie?"

"It's been to ballet class, all right," Archie said. "But nothing that'll preclude admissibility in court."

"This image is that important?"

"You tell me. . . . The convenience store has decent equipment, but the tapes are crap and they've been erased and recorded over and over."

"What am I looking at, Archie?"

"This is the Pahrump stop-and-shop where Sara picked up the tapes, and where she thought Kathy Dean might have rendezvoused with her lover."

The phrase "Pahrump paramour" came unbidden into Grissom's mind.

"Anyway," the tech said, "I've been looking at these tapes, beginnings and the ends, that is."

Grissom nodded. "Places where it was possible they might not've been taped over."

"Right. Still, it was a slim chance . . . but I *think* maybe I found something."

"Sometimes haystacks do give up needles."

Archie nodded. "This may be one of 'em. . . . I know this was three months ago, and it's only about five seconds of tape that might not even be the right day . . . but it could be."

"Show me," Grissom said, concentrating on the screen.

Archie hit PLAY and Grissom saw a male come in, and walk off camera; then the frame cut briefly to an obese woman in a flowered dress at the register, and then to an empty store—later recordings.

Archie was frowning at the screen. "Did you *see* it?"

Grissom shook his head. "See what?"

"I'll cue it up and freeze it this time."

Archie did. The tape ran about a second and froze. Grissom saw the entryway of the store, a man in T-shirt and jeans walking in, his face down, a ball cap covering his hair.

"What am I supposed to see?" Grissom asked. "If it's the guy, I'm not getting much. . . ."

"No," Archie said patiently. "Look in the window."

Grissom adjusted and followed the tech's instruction. At first he saw nothing; but when he stopped trying, the image revealed itself. . . .

There, in the window, was a reflection of someone slightly out of camera range: a young woman with auburn hair and a Las Vegas Stars T-shirt . . .

. . . Kathy Dean.

So clearly could he see her that he could make out the dangling cords of the iPod earbuds.

"I see her, Archie—does she come on camera?"

"Barely—I think they both know the camera's there, and they're careful to avoid it. I don't know why. It's not like they're robbing the place. . . ."

"Still, they're not taking any chances," Grissom

said. "The girl is paranoid about her over-protective parents . . . and whoever's under that ball cap may well know he's about to commit murder."

Archie grunted. "Date night in Vegas."

"Nice catch, Archie. Play it all the way through, will you?"

The lab tech did.

Eyes on the window, Grissom watched Kathy and her baseball cap date embrace, then turn and go.

Frustrated, Grissom asked, "We never see his face at all?"

"There's one second worth a close look," Archie said. He cued up the tape, ran it to the point just before the guy pushed open the door to leave, his arm around Kathy, both of them with their backs to the camera. "Check out the glass door."

At first Grissom couldn't make out anything but shadows. Then Archie did a frame-by-frame advance, walking Grissom through, and suddenly the face appeared in the window.

Even though the hat covered the man's hair and the guy did his best to keep his face lowered, for a second frozen in time, Grissom could see the face clearly.

This, at last, was the evidence he needed.

"How did I do, Grissom?"

"Archie—A-plus-plus."

The lab tech grinned just as Grissom's cell phone trilled.

"Grissom."

"It's me," Sara said. "Talked to Janie Glover. She says FB means Funeral Boy. You'll never guess who that is!"

"Jimmy Doyle?"

"Damn it, Grissom!" Sara's exasperation leapt from the phone. "A hundred years ago, they'd've burned you as a witch!"

Grissom smiled. "Thank you."

If Grissom had a problem with Black as a suspect, then Jim Brass had a problem, too. He had faith in the CSI supervisor's instincts, even if Grissom himself claimed such things as hunches and assumptions weren't in his makeup. The detective decided that the best thing for now was to re-interview the mortician.

In interview room one, Black—now garbed in the standard prisoner orange jumpsuit—was marched in by a uniformed officer, who (at Brass's behest) removed the mortician's handcuffs.

Once Black was seated, Brass hit RECORD and asked Black to state his name.

Black did.

Brass said, "You indicated you were going to call your attorney. Can we proceed without him?"

"I did call my attorney only to discover that my wife has secured his services in a divorce action. He gave me a referral number to a criminal lawyer, who I have a call into."

"You are, however, willing to speak to me?"

"I'll answer any questions that I think may help you unravel this affair. I am innocent, Captain Brass. Some of what I told you . . . in the van the other night, before you read my rights to me? . . . I was in an emotional state. I won't go into those matters again until I've discussed them with my criminal representation."

"Fair enough."

That meant that the mortician's affair with Kathy, the loveless marriage to Cassie, and details about the night of Kathy's disappearance remained off-the-record. Still, Brass decided to press on, guiding Black to the day of Rita Bennett's funeral.

"What happened after the service?" Brass asked.

Black said, "We got the congregation out, then the three of us—Mark, Jimmy, and I—moved the coffin."

"Do you remember how?"

"On a cart, of course."

"No—what I mean is . . . in what order? Who pushed, who pulled?"

"Oh." He thought about it. "Mark was in front . . . Jimmy and I pushed the casket."

"And then?"

"Jimmy realized he'd left a floral spray behind in the chapel. I told him to go back and get it. Then . . . when we got to the door . . . I sent Mark after the hearse."

"And you were alone with the body."

"Yes. Yes, yes, yes! But I didn't—"

"Settle down, Mr. Black. Think back—is there any possibility you were away from the casket, for even a few moments?"

"No, I . . . well." He frowned, and then his eyes widened. "Actually, there was . . . but only for a little while . . . a minute at the most."

"Tell me."

The mortician was staring into his memory as it came back to him. "I was with the casket, but Marie . . . one of our part-timers . . . came and said I had a phone call, someone wanted to talk to me right away. Marie followed me back, and I rushed to my office to tell whoever it was I'd call them later . . . only by the time I got to the phone, the line was dead. When I returned to the rear area, Jimmy and Mark had Rita's . . . or what I *thought* was Rita's casket . . . loaded. I got into the limo and drove the family to the cemetery."

"All three of you were together after that, through the graveside service? The casket was never out of your sight?"

"No, just when I briefly went to get the phone."

"Why didn't you mention this before?"

"I'm sorry. . . . I'd completely forgotten, because when I got there, there was no one on the line. Captain Brass . . . do you think somehow that's when the bodies were switched? But there wouldn't be time, would there?"

"Thanks, Mr. Black. I appreciate your help."

"You almost sound like . . . like you . . . *believe* me, Captain."

"I believe you enough," Brass said, "to go check the phone records. . . . Stay put. This shouldn't take long."

Sara was seated across from Grissom in the latter's office when Nick, looking very pleased with himself, leaned in.

"You will never guess," Nick said, "whose finger-prints were on that gun. . . ."

"Jimmy Doyle," Sara and Grissom said simultaneously.

Nick's astonishment was matched only by his disappointment. He fell into a chair with a dazed look.

"How," he managed, "could you have guessed *that?*"

"I didn't guess, Nick," Grissom said. "Sara got

videotape from the security camera at that convenience store in Pahrump. Archie helped us spot
Jimmy Doyle, picking up Kathy Dean on what ap-
pears to be the night she disappeared."

Sara said, "And one of Kathy's friends told me that
FB . . . you know, the initials from the *Lady Chatterley*
note? Was 'Funeral Boy,' Jimmy Doyle's user ID. . . .
Don't feel bad, Nick. When I called Grissom to share this
scoop, he already knew about Doyle." She gave her boss a
look. "From the videotape I provided, I might point out."

"Hey," Grissom said. "Credit where credit is due."

Nick said, "My money says the black hairs in the
coffin with Kathy Dean are also Jimmy Doyle's."

Brass stuck his head in the door. "Thought you CSIs
would like to know that occasionally somebody else
cracks a case around here. . . ."

"Really?" Grissom said.

Brass stepped in, his expression smug. "Black says
he got called away to the telephone . . . at the moment when he was alone with that casket. I just
tracked the number that called, and guess whose cell
phone it belongs to?"

"Jimmy Doyle," the three CSIs said in perfect unison.

For a moment Brass just stood there, looking like
he'd been doused with a bucket of water.

Then, without even asking Grissom and company
for an explanation, Brass said, "Why don't we go nail
his ass?"

When uniformed officers had no luck finding Doyle
at his home, Grissom obtained Dustin Black's keys,
and Brass got the security code from the mortician.

Soon Grissom, Brass, Nick, and Sara were racing toward the mortuary, the first two in the Taurus, the latter pair in a Tahoe. Heading to Desert Haven had been Nick's suggestion.

"Besides his house, it's the only place we know of where we may find the kid . . . and if Doyle thinks after being interviewed we could be zeroing in on him, then he'd want to get rid of any evidence that might still be at the mortuary."

Sara had wondered, "You don't think Rita Bennett's body could still be there?"

"It's possible."

Grissom pointed out that even if Doyle didn't think he was a suspect, the boy had hidden the probable murder weapon in the mortuary . . . and had no knowledge that the CSIs had already found it.

"If Doyle knows his prints might be on the gun," Nick said, in the Tahoe, "he'll want to retrieve it."

"Or maybe wipe it clean and use it to frame Black," Sara suggested.

Both vehicles arrived at the mortuary just as darkness was settling over the place. Nick and Sara took the back, Brass and Grissom the front.

Nick's voice crackled over Brass's radio. "Got a car back here—empty. Looks like Doyle's already inside."

"Well, you and Sara stay outside," Brass said. "Call for backup, and make sure Doyle doesn't come out that way. We'll go in the front door."

Brass had his gun drawn as Grissom unlocked the entrance.

"Gun out, Gil—you may need it."

Much as Grissom disliked guns, he did as he was told. He had no desire to let himself, or any of his people, become martyrs in the field.

Brass moved to the alarm box, but the light was already green—Doyle turned it off upon entering, apparently. Brass took the lead, as the detective and CSI went down the hall, edging slowly toward the back, Brass's gun outstretched in both hands, Grissom hugging the wall, gun barrel up.

They didn't see so much as a light under a door until they were approaching the rear of the building. At right—from under the outward-opening double door to a room neither man had been in—a long slice of light beckoned. . . .

Using hand signals, Brass bid Grissom to open one of the double doors so the detective could rush in, the CSI supervisor following.

Grissom nodded.

They got into position. Then Grissom jerked the door open, and Brass entered with gun extended. . . .

Barely had Brass stepped inside the darkness when something shoved through, thrusting open the other door, slamming into the detective, pinning Brass against the corridor wall with a sickening crunch!

Grissom watched in shock as he realized a massive concrete vault on a cart had been shoved into Brass . . .

. . . and poised in that open double-doorway was Jimmy Doyle, in his spiffy lavender shirt, the wild-eyed wielder of the cart.

Brass winced in pain; his gun had slipped from his hand. Grissom's first thought was for his friend, and he was grappling with the square slab of concrete as Jimmy

296 Max Allan Collins

Doyle slipped around the other end of the thing and went running down the corridor toward the garage.

Grissom somehow shoved the vault-on-the-cart out of the way, freeing Brass, who crumpled to the floor.

"Never mind me," Brass sputtered. "G-get the bastard!"

Grissom didn't argue—he sprinted down the hall after Doyle, while from behind him he heard Brass talking into his radio: "Doyle's in the garage, Nick—careful!"

Under the door to the garage was another slice of light. The CSI supervisor did not think of himself as a hero; he didn't even consider himself a cop. Situations like this were beyond his purview.

But he took a deep breath, expelled it, jerked the door open, and came into the garage low, fanning his vision—and the gun-in-hand—around the room. At left a frantic Jimmy Doyle was at the workbench, going through boxes like a hyperactive kid on Christmas morning . . . looking for the gun that was no longer there.

"It's gone, Jimmy," Grissom said, voice echoing. "We already found it."

The boy grabbed a wrench off the wall and whirled with eyes flaring and teeth bared, attack-dog fashion; he brought his arm back to pitch, but it froze as another voice called out to him.

"Jimmy," Nick said from his doorway at the far end of the garage, "there are two guns on you. You might want to put that down. . . ."

The boy's face morphed from savagery to pitiful surrender, and the wrench clunked to the workbench as Doyle's hands went tremblingly up, and locked behind his neck. He stood complacently, waiting for the cuffs that Nick quickly brought to him.

When Grissom turned to go check on Brass, the detective was already leaning in the doorway, his suit rumpled, blood trickling from his bottom lip, and one arm pressed against what were likely broken ribs.

"I'll call nine-one-one," Grissom said.

"Beat you to it," Brass said.

"You don't look so good."

"They come prettier than you, too, Gil."

They exchanged tiny grins.

Sara entered the garage, a plastic evidence bag in hand.

"What do you have there?" Grissom called over.

Holding the bag up like the prize catch it was, Sara said, "Most likely, Kathy Dean's iPod! I just got it out of Jimmy's car."

"That's mine," Doyle protested meekly.

Sara came over to where Doyle, wrists cuffed behind him, stood slump-shouldered next to Nick. "Digital songs are computer files—they can be tracked."

Doyle swallowed thickly.

Sara gave him the sweet smile she reserved for the worst people. "After our computer expert is done with it . . . ? We'll know for sure, whether it's yours or Kathy's."

Tears filled the young man's eyes, but hung there stubbornly, as if not wanting to admit a defeat that was already complete.

"You know, Jimmy," Nick said with a devilish grin, "if you've been downloading tunes without paying for them . . . you could be in a lot of trouble."

12

While Catherine Willows felt no remorse about shooting Rene Fairmont, she did regret having to frighten the elderly hostage. But the reality was, Rene's hostage had already been checked out and sent home, shaken but uninjured, while Catherine was still here, hostage to her job.

The angel of mercy lay on a small hospital bed in the emergency room, a curtain pulled around the tiny cubicle for a semblance of privacy, as her white blouse had been unbuttoned and then scissored away to give the young East Indian ER physician access to her wound. Accordingly, Detective Vega waited on the other side of the curtain.

The suspect's left hand was handcuffed to the bed, and she lay so still that the cuff never rattled against the metal of the rail. The doctor, working from a tray, hovered over the woman's right shoulder; soon he had nearly finished suturing the wound, a process the killer seemed not even to notice in her sullen, self-imposed catatonia.

While Warrick had stayed behind to work the crime scene outside the bank, Catherine had accompanied the woman on the ambulance ride, and observed the prisoner's treatment in the hospital, too. In all that time, Rene hadn't uttered a word, not a single syllable (including "Ouch"), as the doctor cleaned the wound and began sewing it up.

"Before long, Nurse Fairmont," Catherine said pleasantly, "you'll be taking your own brand of medicine."

A tiny frown indicated for the first time that the woman was listening . . . also, that she didn't understand this remark.

So Catherine clarified: "I mean, you're a master of lethal injection yourself . . . right?"

The cold eyes registered something—not much, just a tightening—and what happened next was so fast, Catherine's memory could only report back a blur. . . .

The prisoner raised the hand of her wounded arm and snatched the scissors from the doctor's tray, looped her arm around his neck, and brought his head down against her chest, the closed points of the scissors resting against his throat, the metal gleaming and winking against the dark flesh, dimpling it, drawing a pearl of glistening blood. The young physician looked more startled than scared at first.

Rene Fairmont's eyes were hard, feral, glittering things in a face whose prettiness was lost in an animal snarl, as she held the doctor to her breast as if he were some oversized helpless child.

To Catherine she snapped, "Handcuff keys, bitch—*now!*"

The CSI looked at the fearless prisoner and the frightened doctor, and she drew the nine millimeter from her hip and placed the nose of its barrel against the forehead of the prisoner, whose reaction seemed more indignant than shocked.

Wearing the coldest expression she could muster, Catherine said, "Ask the doctor—when I fire this gun your motor responses will stop and he will be in *no* danger. . . ."

"You think I'm *kidding?*"

"You think I am? Drop the scissors . . . *bitch.*"

The suspect did so.

The doctor, relief not yet washing away his alarm, backed away. Vega, hearing the commotion, swam through the curtains and now stood with his own weapon trained on the again catatonic Rene Fairmont.

"Take over for a moment, Sam," Catherine said. "This just became a crime scene—and I need to take a couple pictures and bag those scissors."

Vega, usually unflappable, seemed very much flapped at the moment; but he said, "No problem, Catherine."

Catherine slipped on latex gloves and collected the scissors, then walked the shell-shocked doctor outside the cubicle.

She spoke reassuringly to the physician—with her own best bedside manner—explaining they'd need a statement from him. In moments, he seemed all right, and they were able to discuss the transfer of the prisoner to the high-security ward of the Clark County jail—a move the doctor would be all too happy to help facilitate.

Half an hour later, Catherine left the hospital thinking about the over-a-dozen people (at least) who had died at this pretty monster's hands; but the hell of it was, despite two hostage takings, Catherine still didn't know if she had enough evidence to prosecute Rene Fairmont for even one of the murders.

Oh, they could keep the angel of mercy off the streets, and out of the nursing-home wards, all right; but a lot of people, alive and dead, deserved to see Rene Fairmont's spree of murder resolved, every evil act cleared up.

Catherine would go back to HQ and start sifting through everything again. What had already been a very long shift promised to get much, much longer. Still—stopping a serial killer would make being tired at the end of a long day really, really worth it. . . .

Nick Stokes was not anywhere he would ever have hoped to find himself.

Grissom and Brass had returned to HQ with Jimmy Doyle; Sara was back in the lab working with Tomas Nunez, matching the iPod files to Kathy Dean's computer; and Nick had been left to deal with the evidence at Desert Haven.

So here Nick was, alone in a mortuary in the middle of the night. . . .

In the garage, he photographed the boxes Jimmy Doyle had been rummaging through. The photos, and Doyle's fingerprints, would provide a compelling circumstantial case that the young man had expected to find the .22 automatic he'd stowed away.

Then, in the hallway, Nick fingerprinted the concrete vault Doyle had used as an improvised weapon to attack Captain Brass. This, too, Nick photographed, then wheeled back inside the workroom, which was essentially a warehouse for coffins and vaults.

About the size of the garage at CSI, the chamber had metal shelving, five high, lining three of its four walls—the bottom two devoted to the large concrete and metal vaults, the top three home to numerous coffins of varied styles in metal or wood, the metal ones running to gray, blue, and even the occasional pink, the wood ones mostly oak.

In the center of the room, looming above and attached to metal rails, hung a crane very similar to the one in the CSI garage. A tall, wheeled staircase stood to one side of the crane, to help workers attach the device to the needed coffin. On the floor, in the middle of the room, was a row of three tables, each about the size of a human being.

Staging area, Nick thought.

An embalmed body would be put on the table while a particular casket was readied; then the body would be placed inside the coffin, the details arranged, after which the coffin would be wheeled to the appropriate viewing room for the service.

At Desert Haven, death was an assembly-line business—so much so, bodies moving in and out with such matter-of-fact haste, that two bodies . . . actually *coffins* . . . had been switched, one disappearing completely, and no one even noticed.

Nick glanced back at the concrete vault he'd pushed into the room—the only one in the chamber on a wheeled cart; he wondered if this vault had already been out for some particular purpose of the funeral home . . . or could Doyle have been doing something with it, when the good guys interrupted?

After all, the kid wouldn't have had time to go get the vault, load it up, and roll it out to serve as a battering ram—the assistant mortician had been surprised by Brass's entrance, and simply responded with what was handy.

Nick's curiosity got the best of him, and he went to the trouble of attaching the crane on either side of the lip of the vault lid. When he pushed the button, the crane lifted not just the lid . . . but the entire vault!

Meaning: The vault was sealed.

This struck Nick as peculiar, and he got on his cell to Sara.

"It's me," he told her. "Are Grissom and Brass in interviewing Doyle?"

"Not yet. Doyle's in holding; Brass is still getting his ribs taped, and probably trying to talk the doctors into letting him go back to work. . . . Having fun by yourself at the mortuary in the middle of the night?"

"Oh it's swell. If anybody comes up behind me and says 'boo,' I'll just shoot them is all. . . . Listen, Sara— I've run into what Grissom likes to call an anomaly."

"Which is?"

He told her about the sealed vault.

Sara said, *"I don't know enough about the funeral-home business to say whether that's unusual or not. Why don't you ask Dustin Black?"*

"Good idea. He still there?"

"No—Grissom shook him loose an hour ago. Guy looked whipped when he left."

"That's no surprise. You got his home phone number?"

"I can get it for you," she said, and did.

Nick broke the connection and made another call.

The machine came on, and a cheerful Cassie Black's greeting—from a day or so (or a lifetime) ago—was followed by the familiar beep.

"Mr. Black—it's Nick Stokes, from the crime lab. If you're still awake, please pick up—we need your help."

A weary-sounding Black came on the line and said, *"I really don't know why I don't just ignore you people, at this stage."*

"Possibly because the future of your business hinges on us cleaning this matter up," Nick said, "and clearing you."

"Good point. What do you want?"

"I really am sorry to disturb you, but I was wondering . . . why would there be a sealed vault at your mortuary?"

"There wouldn't be."

"That's what I thought. Wouldn't a sealed vault have gone directly to the cemetery?"

"Yes—are you sure it's sealed?"

"I have had *some* experience with sealed vaults before—for instance, I was one of the team that opened Rita Bennett's coffin and found Kathy Dean instead."

An uncomfortable silence followed. Then: *"We have no sealed vaults in storage. That would be pointless."*

"Well, could the lid be stuck on so tight that the entire vault could be craned up, without dislodging it?"

"That's doubtful."

"Sir, right now your place of business is a crime scene. If you'd like to help make it just a *business* again—"

"*I'm on my way.*"

The line clicked dead.

Appropriately enough.

Just as Catherine had expected—had hoped—the evidence quickly began piling up against Rene Fairmont.

Handwriting expert Jenny Northam matched the forgery practice sheet from Rene's wastebasket to the signature on the Sunny Day sign-in sheet. Catherine had already confirmed that a cab had gone from Rene's house to pick up "Mabel" and take her to Sunny Day; hair from the backseat of the taxi matched a wig Warrick had taken into custody.

Though the modus operandi was different in the poisonings of Derek Fairmont and Gary Masters, the poison itself had been the same. And prussic acid had turned up a third time when Rene held that syringe to the throat of the woman in the bank parking lot—the recurrence of the poison making circumstantial but compelling evidence. If Catherine could match the batches of prussic acid from Masters and the syringe she'd confiscated at Rene's arrest, the case would be practically airtight.

A canvassing of the other businesses at the strip mall where Masters kept his office had, thanks to Sergeant O'Riley, turned up three photo identifications of Rene Fairmont; in-person ID's would likely follow. The only dead-end had been computer expert Tomas Nunez's failure to tie Rene to any of the e-mails on Vivian's PC.

But with the prisoner's fingerprints, Catherine was able to make a match through AFIS, and the results were as satisfying as they were unsurprising and, frankly, tragic: Under various names, in several states, Rene Fairmont was wanted for murder. Her fifteen-year career in continuing care had been a ruse to help her bilk money out of the patients she was hired to help; once she had an estate earmarked for one of her "charities," she killed the victim.

A study of those cases revealed a very clear line of bogus charities and dead-drops stretching from Florida to Vegas. Rene had been planning to leave here and make her way back east. Though a sociopath, the angel of mercy had the ability to portray a compassionate, caring person who entered the lives of a succession of older, lonely, needy people; for fifteen years, she had fooled not only her victims, but law enforcement agencies and nursing homes and God only knew who else . . .

. . . and the arrest Catherine, Warrick, and Vega had made appeared to be the only time Rene had ever come close to getting caught.

Her fingerprints had ended up in AFIS only because she had been printed at several of the care centers she had worked in. Only after she had disappeared from a town, and what she'd been up to had been perceived after the fact, were her prints posted. And despite the short but impressive list of jurisdictions looking for Rene, Catherine could only wonder how many other victims had gone unrecognized as such.

To Rene's credit, she'd never gone for the big score. She had kept her cons relatively small, flying just under the radar of the authorities, making every murder look like a plausible death. At the first sign that she'd drawn any attention to herself, Rene would make tracks (but not leave any).

Catherine and Warrick compared notes and consolidated their evidence. Convinced that all the ducks were in a row, Catherine returned to the ER, where the transfer to the jail hospital was pending.

Rene Fairmont had a small private room in the ER now, with two uniforms on the outside and another inside, sharing space with Vega and Rene herself, who was in a hospital smock with both hands handcuffed to the bed rails.

Catherine entered, and Rene's blank stare gave no indication she had even noticed.

Vega met Catherine and they confabbed at the foot of the bed and spoke as if the angel of mercy weren't present.

"She's been a good girl," Vega said. "Hasn't taken anybody hostage since you left . . . and hasn't said a word, either."

"Maybe that's because you're calling her by the wrong name, Sam. You're using Rene Fairmont." Catherine turned toward the prisoner and gestured. "Meet Rene Delillo."

Rene's eyes tightened. Though the woman's face remained otherwise blank, the animal behind the mask somehow made its presence known to Catherine.

"Rene Delillo, huh?" Vega said matter of factly.

"That's the name she's wanted under in Las Cruces, New Mexico, anyway."

The prisoner stared at Catherine and her lips parted

slightly in an expression that was at once a smile and a sneer.

"Or," Catherine said, "you could call her Judith Rene—the name she's wanted under in Baton Rouge; and there's two or three more. Unless she tells us, we may never know her *real* name, or how she got started in this interesting line of work."

Rene continued to fix her gaze on the CSI, but petulance had crept into her defiant glare.

"That is," Catherine went on, "if she even *remembers* her name anymore."

That one must have struck a nerve, but the only reward for Catherine was a single trickle of tear down Rene's cheek.

Catherine moved alongside the bed. She looked at the prisoner but spoke to Vega. "You know, Sam, I really didn't think Rene here was capable of feeling anything for anybody—a bad seed, born without compassion. But I was wrong."

Rene's lip was trembling now; another tear rolled down a lovely cheek.

"She does feel something," Catherine said, ". . . for herself."

In the interview room at CSI HQ, tears were streaming down another killer's face.

Jimmy Doyle—seated across from Brass and Grissom, with Sara Sidle hovering in the background—hadn't been nearly as hard to crack as the detective's ribs. Once they got Doyle in the interview room, he'd started bawling like a kid who wanted his mommy.

"I . . . I didn't mean to," Doyle said.

He'd been offered the opportunity to call an attorney, but hadn't acted upon it.

Right now Doyle was just a scared kid, but a kid of age, and Brass intended to keep him scared. "Didn't mean to, Jimmy? What, did you *accidentally* shoot her in the back of the head?"

Doyle grasped at the tissues from the box that Sara had provided him; he struggled to gain control. "I mean, I didn't . . . didn't *want* to."

"She asked you to do it, then," Brass said, mocking. "It was a kind of suicide . . . a mercy killing."

"Stop it! Stop it! It wasn't that way at all. . . ."

"What way was it, Jimmy?"

"You didn't know her . . . how she could be . . . how she could wrap a guy around her little finger. If you knew, you'd get it—you'd know this was all *her* fault."

The detective fought the urge to come out of the chair and . . .

Sara asked, quietly, almost gently, "How was it her fault, Jimmy?"

He swallowed snot; his face glistened with tears. "She was going to ruin *everything*. Everything I worked for."

Calm again, Brass asked, "Ruin it how?"

Though his hands were cuffed, Doyle's fingers tapped out a nervous rhythm on the table. "I'm not a rich kid. I didn't have no . . . any silver spoon. But in high school, Mr. Black gave me a job. I lived with my mom, my dad's off in . . . somewhere. Mr. Black, he's been like a father to me."

Brass thought, *He was like a father to Kathy Dean, too.*

The boy was saying: "Not easy to get help at a funeral home. Not just any kid can take it, you know. I had the stomach for it. I had the talent. Mr. Black saw it in me, and I took the work, and he paid my way to school, and I'm his top assistant now. I went around a lot of guys, way older than me, landing that spot. You know how successful Desert Haven is? A few years, and I could be rich . . . respectable."

"How did Kathy get in the way of that?"

"Kathy said she was pregnant. She . . . she wanted to know if I was willing to marry her."

"What did you tell her?"

"I told her yes! Sure! *Of course,* I'd do the right thing."

Sara asked, "Why did you do the wrong thing instead, Jimmy?"

His head hung; tears dripped onto the table, tiny rain. "You don't understand . . . Mr. Black, him and his wife . . . they're very, very straight. Very, very conservative. If they found out I had to get married, that I knocked some girl up . . . Mr. Black, he'd fire me! I'd lose everything! Including . . . including his respect."

The words hung in the room. The two CSIs and the detective exchanged now-I've-heard-everything glances.

"I . . . I couldn't let that selfish little slut ruin everything. I told her to get an abortion. We could still get married and have kids down the road—just not now! *She* ruined her life, not me! She said she was using birth control! She was a liar!"

Grissom said, "She said you were the father of her baby?"

"Yes! Yes, yes . . . of course."

"Why did you believe her?"

"Huh?"

Grissom shrugged. "She was a liar. Why believe her?"

The slick-faced boy looked from face to face; when he landed on Sara, she spoke.

"It wasn't your baby, Jimmy," Sara said.

"What?"

"She was pregnant, but not with your child."

The boy's eyes froze into marbles; the tears had stopped.

Grissom said, "Dustin Black was the father."

"No . . . no, that's impossible. Not Mr. Black! And Kathy wouldn't even've *told* me she was pregnant, unless I was the father and she wanted me to marry her . . . right?"

"You were the backup."

"Huh?"

"If Dustin Black didn't want to leave his wife . . . he was a successful, respectable businessman, remember . . . ? she needed somebody to step in and take responsibility."

Brass said, "Maybe it wasn't admirable, Jimmy— but she was just a kid, after all. Worried about the future. With dreams."

"Maybe," Sara said, "she was just looking for somebody to love her. Somebody to give her consolation, comfort . . . maybe just somebody to talk to her, in a bad time of her life."

The boy swallowed; his expression was pitiful. ". . . You think?"

Grissom shrugged. "We don't know what Kathy was feeling or thinking. Our job is science. DNA tests prove conclusively that you weren't the father of Kathy's baby . . . but you did kill it, when you killed her."

His fingers no longer tapping, Doyle sat there with the empty eyes of a corpse.

The killer was led off to lock-up, and in the hall Sara showed Grissom and Brass a handful of papers. "By the way, that iPod? It's Kathy Dean's, like we suspected. Tomas just finished matching the files in the player to Kathy's computer."

"We probably won't need even half of this evidence," Brass said dryly. "Kid knows he's caught, and he's trying to buy off his conscience by telling us everything he knows."

Grissom asked, "Anybody hear from Nick lately?"

"He found something interesting at the mortuary," Sara said.

"Such as?"

"A sealed concrete vault. He got Black's number from me. Where that went, if anywhere, I have no idea."

Grissom's expression was thoughtful. "I think I know what might be in that vault . . . let's have a look. You and your ribs up to it, Jim?"

"If somebody else drives," Brass said, "I am."

"I'll stay here," Sara said, "and keep at this evidence."

But Grissom and Brass were already on their way.

Together, Nick Stokes and the mortician Dustin Black pried the concrete vault open.

A casket was revealed within; Nick recognized it as identical to the one in which Kathy Dean had been found.

Nick looked across the vault at the mortician, who gazed back with wide eyes.

"Rita," Black said.

Nick said, "Your assistant called you away for a nonexistent phone call, and then he just switched the coffins. . . ." The CSI sighed. "We need to confirm. Let's pop the top. . . . No disrespect meant."

Using the crane, Black hauled the casket out of the vault and rested it on one of the tables in the center of the room. Nick waited for the mortician to climb down the ladder and join him before unlocking the casket. The two exchanged wary glances, and then Nick threw open the lid.

Inside, still perfectly preserved from being in the airtight vault and air-conditioned shelves of the workroom, lay an at-peace Rita Bennett. Beautifully coiffed and dressed, she might have walked off the set of one of her used-car commercials to lie down for a nap. Not even the smell of death was present to disturb the illusion.

"What now?" the mortician asked.

"These remains, and this casket, are evidence in two cases, Mr. Black."

"*Two* cases?"

Nick nodded. "We exhumed Rita . . . or tried to . . . because of suspicion of foul play in her death."

The mortician closed his eyes. "When will this be over?"

As if in response, a voice said, "Soon, you evil son of a bitch. Very, very soon. . . ."

In the workroom doorway, in a polo shirt and jeans

that looked slept-in, stood Kathy Dean's father, Jason. He somehow appeared both bleary-eyed and alert, his regular features touched with several days' growth of beard, his wispy blond hair askew.

Dean held a Glock in his right hand.

Barely six feet from Nick, the broad-shouldered, menacing figure was on the other side of the casket from the CSI, pointing the pistol directly at the undertaker.

Nick had no idea whether or not the distressed father was a decent shot, but at this range he wouldn't have to be. Black would be dead with a squeeze of the trigger; Nick would be dead before his own weapon cleared its holster.

But maybe Dean didn't realize Nick was armed—after all, the casket blocked the man's view of the hip-hugging nine mil. . . .

"Unholster the gun," Dean said, his voice a deadly monotone, "and use only two fingers."

Nick did as he was told.

"Drop it in the casket."

Nick again obeyed, placing the weapon on the late Rita Bennett's midsection.

"Now close the lid."

Nick complied, and said, "Mr. Dean, we are handling this. We have your daughter's killer in custody."

"My daughter's killer is standing right in front of me."

Black said, "No . . . no, I didn't . . ."

Nick said, "It was a boyfriend—named Jimmy Doyle. He worked here for Mr. Black."

"I never heard of him," Dean said, and raised his handgun and trained it on the mortician's chest.

Black said, with resignation in his voice, "My wife called you."

"Yes," Dean said. "Yes. She told me everything. Are you going to deny that you defiled my daughter?"

Black said nothing.

"She was pure. She was a virgin. And you . . . old enough to be . . . you *defiled* her. . . ." The man's voice was trembling, but his gun-in-hand was not.

Nick said, "We have evidence that—"

"Shut up!" Dean swung the gun around so that the barrel now aimed at Nick's face. "Move around to this side. I want you over here with the dead man."

Nick raised his hands slightly and came around to Black's side of the coffin.

The mortician was in full capitulation mode, hands raised high, no sign of fight in his body language, ready to offer himself up to the angry father.

Ready, Nick thought, *to die.*

"I trusted you," Dean said, the gun swivelling back to Black. "You have children! How could you be so goddamn *low* . . . ?"

Black said nothing.

"You . . . you took advantage of her. You . . . you . . ."

"Loved her," Black said quietly. "I loved her."

The wrong thing to say!

Nick watched Dean's face tighten and so did the finger on the trigger and just as Nick was about to leap, Brass's echoing voice stopped all of them.

"*No,* Mr. Dean!"

Though the gun never left its Black-bound trajectory,

Dean's eyes darted from side to side searching for Brass, who was somewhere behind him. Nick saw the detective just inside the doorway, his gun pointed at the middle of Dean's back. Grissom stood next to the detective, no gun in his hand, but with a grave, determined expression.

"You know what he did to my little girl!" Dean said, voice echoing off cement walls. "Why *shouldn't* I kill him?"

"I do know what he did," Brass said. "I've got a daughter, too. I know how you feel . . . I understand your rage, and your contempt."

"Then don't try to stop me."

"If you don't put that gun down, Mr. Dean, I'm going to have to shoot you . . . to stop you." The regret in Brass's voice was as real as the threat. "I can't take any chances—I'll have to take you down."

"You'd kill *me?* Is that *justice?*"

"No it isn't, but it is my job—you're threatening the lives of a citizen and a CSI. And I will take you down."

"It's *worth* it. . . ."

"Is it, Mr. Dean? . . . You're hurting, and so is your wife. Crystal needs you, Mr. Dean. Don't give her another tragedy to have to deal with . . . alone."

Nick was watching Dean's eyes—they were wild, careening, though the gun-in-hand remained steady and poised to shoot.

Suddenly Grissom spoke. "Let him live," the CSI said. "That'll be your best revenge."

"What?"

"He's ruined," Grissom said matter of factly. "You know what a high-profile business he has. His wife's left him, and the reason why'll all come out soon enough. Whole city will know. They call us Sin City, but you know at heart, this is a conservative town— he'll be a pariah."

Dean finally seemed to be faltering. Nick could see the man sliding an inch toward sanity. . . .

"Grissom's right," Brass said. "If you really want Dustin Black to suffer, Mr. Dean—let him live."

Dean considered that for a long time . . .

. . . and then he fell to his knees and began to sob, the gun limp in his fingers when Nick stepped forward to lift it from the man's grasp.

Nick cuffed the distraught father, but when he went to take his own gun from the casket, Grissom said, "Uh uh uh . . . it's evidence now, Nick."

"Oh. Sorry, Gris."

Grissom leaned close to Nick. "Take Mr. Dean out, Nick," the CSI supervisor whispered. "So Jim doesn't have to."

The detective approached the mortician. "You all right?"

Black said, numbly, "You and Doctor Grissom . . . you saved my life."

"You know," Brass said, "if I wasn't a cop? I'm not convinced I wouldn't've just laid back and watched."

Black began to smile, a slow, ghastly thing that had little to do with the usual reasons for smiling.

"Captain Brass," the mortician said, "I'm not sure I don't wish you hadn't done that very thing. . . . Just now? I'm not at all convinced you and Doctor Grissom did me a favor."

*   *   *

The CSI crew was having breakfast at the diner on Boulder Highway (where Catherine had met cabby Gus Clein).

Catherine and Warrick sat on one side of the booth, Sara and Nick on the other, Grissom occupying a chair at the end of the table. They had just finished filling each other in on their respective cases and were now quietly digging into their food.

"Kathy Dean's finally at rest," Sara said.

"More than can be said for Jimmy Doyle and Dustin Black," Grissom said. "Or her parents. . . . What could turn a decent normal kid like Kathy into such a manipulative little schemer?"

"Mom and Dad," Sara said.

Grissom's smile was distant. "Like so many parents, the Deans loved their child not wisely but too well."

"So what about Rita Bennett?" Warrick asked.

Nick shook his head. "No sign of poison. She wasn't murdered. Heart attack all along."

"So investigating a murder that *wasn't* a murder led you to a real one?"

"Yeah. Yeah, that's about right."

Catherine said, "So, then . . . Peter Thompson gets to keep his wife's estate, and his stepdaughter, Rebecca, is left out in the cold?"

"Hey, Cath, it's Vegas in August," Nick said. "It's not that cold. . . . Besides, she's got a job—she's doing fine, at least financially."

"What about Atwater?" Sara asked. "Does our esteemed sheriff still have a hefty contributor, even though he never told Thompson that Rita's body was missing?"

Grissom said, "I wouldn't say 'never.' "

Sara was shocked, in an amused way. "Rory *did* get around to telling Thompson about the body switch?"

"In a manner of speaking. Atwater sent Brass—that's where Jim is now, trying to mend the sheriff's political fences."

"Well," Warrick said, raising a glass of orange juice, "here's to us—in a matter of days, we cracked two of the most complicated cases any CSI anywhere ever saw."

Clinks of juice glasses and coffee cups followed.

Grissom said, "Let's not get too cocky—the first team did fine, but the second team made it happen."

Catherine was nodding. "Gil's right—our assistant coroner, David, had to push us into accepting Vivian Elliot as a murder case; then Jenny Northam's handwriting analysis, and Greg's findings from the remains of Derek Fairmont, gave us our case."

Sara nodded, too. "Greg's DNA findings handed us the father of Kathy Dean's baby, and Tomas linked the vic's iPod to Jimmy Doyle. Here's to our support team—without them, where would we be?"

And again the glasses clinked, and Nick said, "Let's just not tell them," and laughter ensued.

All their beepers squealed at once, causing the other diners to turn their way.

"A call *now?*" Warrick moaned.

Catherine said, "Poor Warrick . . ."

"I knew him well," Grissom finished.

Warrick half-smirked in response, albeit good-naturedly.

As they headed into the parking lot and another

scorcher of a day, Nick shook his head. "Y'know, Gris—we been working so much, I don't know whether this is the end of the shift . . . or the beginning?"

"Some mysteries, Nick," Grissom said, "are beyond science."

A Tip of the Test Tube

My assistant Matthew Clemens helped me develop the plot of *Grave Matters*, and worked up a lengthy story treatment that included all of his considerable forensic research, from which I could work. Matthew—an accomplished true-crime writer who has collaborated with me on numerous published short stories—has taken frequent research trips to Las Vegas, essentially location scouting, and if any sense of the real city is achieved in these pages, he must take much of the credit.

We would once again like to acknowledge criminalist Lieutenant Chris Kauffman CLPE—the Gil Grissom of the Bettendorf, Iowa, Police Department—who provided comments, insights, and information; Chris, thank you for all you do! Thank you also to Lieutenant Paul Van Steenhuyse, Scott County Sheriff's Office, for help with computer forensics; Sergeant Jeff Swanson, Scott County Sheriff's Office for autopsy and crime scene assistance; Stephen M. Thompson, D.O., for help on the Vivian Elliot case; and Marcus Cunnick, Cunnick-Collins Mortuary, for his "behind the scenes" look at the running of a funeral home.

Also, Matt and I spent two days with dozens of real

investigators at the actual CSI headquarters and lab in Las Vegas; in a future book we will list many of these helpful individuals—for now, a big thanks to all of these dedicated law-enforcement professionals.

Books consulted include two works by Vernon J. Gerberth: *Practical Homicide Investigation Checklist and Field Guide* (1997) and *Practical Homicide Investigation: Tactics, Procedures and Forensic Investigation* (1996). Also helpful were *Crime Scene: The Ultimate Guide to Forensic Science*, Richard Platt; and *Scene of the Crime: A Writer's Guide to Crime-Scene Investigations* (1992), Anne Wingate, Ph.D. Any inaccuracies, however, are my own.

Ed Schlesinger at Pocket Books provided gracious and friendly support. The producers of *CSI: Crime Scene Investigation* provided scripts, background material (including show bibles), and episode tapes, without which this novel would have been impossible. In particular, I'd like to thank Corinne Marrinan, with whom it's a genuine pleasure to work.

Anthony E. Zuiker is gratefully acknowledged as the creator of this concept and these characters; and the cast of the show must be applauded for vivid, memorable characterizations that make it easy to write for the theater of the mind. Our thanks, too, to various *CSI* writers for their inventive and well-documented scripts, which we frequently drew upon for inspiration and backstory.

Max Allan Collins . . .

. . . a Mystery Writers of America "Edgar" nominee in both fiction and non-fiction categories, has been hailed as "the Renaissance man of mystery fiction." He has earned an unprecedented twelve Private Eye Writers of America "Shamus" nominations for his historical thrillers, winning twice for his Nathan Heller novels, *True Detective* (1983) and *Stolen Away* (1991). His other credits include film criticism, short fiction, songwriting, trading-card sets, video games, and movie/TV tie-in novels, including the *New York Times*-bestselling *Saving Private Ryan*.

His graphic novel *Road to Perdition* is the basis of the Academy Award–winning DreamWorks 2002 feature film starring Tom Hanks, Paul Newman, and Jude Law, directed by Sam Mendes. His many comics credits include the *Dick Tracy* syndicated strip (1977–1993); his own *Ms. Tree; Batman;* and *CSI: Crime Scene Investigation*, based on the hit TV series for which he also writes a bestselling series of novels.

An independent filmmaker in his native Iowa, he wrote and directed *Mommy*, premiering on Lifetime in 1996, and a 1997 sequel, *Mommy's Day*. The screenwriter of *The Expert*, a 1995 HBO World Premiere, he wrote and directed the award-winning documentary *Mike Hammer's Mickey Spillane* (1999) and the innovative feature, *Real Time: Siege at Lucas Street Market* (2000).

Collins lives in Muscatine, Iowa, with his wife, writer Barbara Collins; their son Nathan is majoring in computer science and Japanese at the University of Iowa.